LAST LULLABY

ALICE WALSH

Vagrant PRESS

Copyright © 2017, Alice Walsh

All rights reserved. No part of this book may be reproduced, stored in a retrieval system or transmitted in any form or by any means without the prior written permission from the publisher, or, in the case of photocopying or other reprographic copying, permission from Access Copyright, 1 Yonge Street, Suite 1900, Toronto, Ontario M5E 1E5.

Vagrant Press is an imprint of Nimbus Publishing Limited
3731 Mackintosh St, Halifax, NS B3K 5A5
(902) 455-4286 nimbus.ca

Printed and bound in Canada
NB1245

This novel is a work of fiction. Names, characters, places, and incidents are either the product of the author's imagination or are used fictitiously.

Library and Archives Canada Cataloguing in Publication

    Walsh, Alice (E. Alice), author
    Last lullaby / Alice Walsh.
    Issued in print and electronic formats.
    ISBN 978-1-77108-508-3 (softcover).—ISBN 978-1-77108-509-0 (HTML)
I. Title.

PS8595.A5847L37 2017   C813'.54   C2017-904100-2
                                                                                       C2017-904099-5

Nimbus Publishing acknowledges the financial support for its publishing activities from the Government of Canada, the Canada Council for the Arts, and from the Province of Nova Scotia. We are pleased to work in partnership with the Province of Nova Scotia to develop and promote our creative industries for the benefit of all Nova Scotians.

For my beautiful niece, Breanna

PROLOGUE

Lauren kept her head down as she cut through the crowd surrounding the courthouse. Although it was only a preliminary hearing, reporters, spectators, cameramen, and photographers had been waiting for hours. By now, most people had heard about the bizarre case and were eager to watch it play out in court. It had been high-profile from the beginning, but once the truth came to light a media circus was unleashed. Lauren was constantly being pursued by hungry reporters. She sometimes caught glimpses of herself on the nightly news where the anchor would refer to her as "one of the key players in the case," or "the lawyer who cracked the case wide open." She'd been invited to appear on Charlie Rose, 20/20, Fox News, *and a long list of other shows. For a while, she had basked in the glory, but now all she wanted was for her life to return to normal.* I'm glad this is finally coming to an end, *she thought as she quickened her pace.*

Journalists had come not only from around the province, but across Canada and the States. As she neared the courthouse, Lauren looked around at the excited faces: a reporter from CNN was interviewing a local couple. Another from CBC stood on the sidewalk talking into a microphone. "The unexpected twist in this case is so incredible you couldn't make it up," she heard him say as she strode past.

Lauren shook her head. Three months ago, most people had never heard of Paddy's Arm, Newfoundland. Now, it was in the news daily, the story splashed across every major newspaper in the country. Zealous reporters in pursuit of details interviewed anyone who would talk to them. They stalked university students, even schoolchildren.

Lauren had almost made it to the courthouse steps when someone shouted: "There's Ms. LaVallee now." As TV cameras swung in her direction, she involuntary took a step backward.

"Ms. LaVallee," a reporter from CBC called, "what do you think about this crime being compared to the Caylee Anthony case?"

Before Lauren had a chance to respond, another reporter thrust a microphone in her face: "What would you like to see happen now?"

"I want justice to prevail," Lauren answered, truthfully. "Two people are dead, one of them an innocent child."

CHAPTER

1

THREE MONTHS EARLIER

Lauren stifled a yawn as Olivia Fillmore read her paper to the class. She snuck a glance at her watch. Twenty more minutes and we can all go home.

"For a felony such as this, the perpetrator would probably benefit from community service," Olivia said, concluding her paper.

"*Indictable* offence," Lauren corrected. Nearly a month into the term and some students still didn't know an indictment from a summary offence. Why had she let herself get talked into teaching another term? She was a lawyer, for heaven's sake, not a professor. Lauren cast a glance around the classroom. "You guys watch too many American cop shows," she continued. "'Felonies' and 'misdemeanours' are American terminology. In Canada we have indictable and summary offences." She looked at Rebecca Taylor, an RCMP officer and one of her brightest students. "Right, Constable Taylor?"

Rebecca pushed dark bangs away from her eyes. Although she was in her late twenties, and married with a child, she looked younger than some of the other students. "Right," she said. "And if this *were* the States, the crime Olivia described would be a misdemeanour *not* a felony."

"Thank you, Constable Taylor, for pointing that out." Lauren reached for a textbook on her desk and turned to her students. "For Monday, read up to chapter 12 in your *Canadian Criminal Justice*."

"The chapter on attorney-client privilege?" asked Devon Saunders.

Lauren stared at him a long moment. Had she heard a sneer in his voice? "Yes, that chapter," she snapped. "And don't just read it, study it." She stood, signalling that class was dismissed.

Am I being paranoid? Lauren wondered as she watched her students file out of the room. Devon's remark was innocent enough. Had she read too much into it? Was it her guilty conscience? *Let it go*, she chided herself. She couldn't let the past hold her back.

Long after her students had left the classroom, Lauren stood by the tall windows that overlooked Paddy's Arm. *Coming here was the right decision*, she told herself as she took in a gigantic iceberg that loomed in the distance. A fishing boat was making its way across the harbour. It had been a mild winter so far, and the sea had not frozen over as it had in past years. Had it been only four years since she arrived here? Four years since she'd fled Quebec in disgrace, her law license suspended, her reputation in tatters? The mere memory of it still made Lauren shrivel in shame. To complicate things further, she had been three months' pregnant.

Moving away from the window, Lauren started down the hallway toward the English department. Emma Buckle, the acting chair, had left two messages on her voice mail and Lauren hadn't had a chance to return them.

The outer office was empty, the secretary away from her desk. Through the partially open door, Lauren saw Emma grading papers. She glanced up when Lauren knocked. "Come on in, girl," she called.

Lauren smiled. Emma often called students and co-workers "girl" or "my son." She had a pronounced Newfoundland accent that she sometimes exaggerated.

"I'm glad I caught you," Lauren said, taking a chair across from Emma's desk.

"A nice surprise, this is," Emma said, "but why the long face?"

Lauren laughed. "Am I *that* obvious?" She shook her head. "I should never have let Frances talk me into staying another term."

Emma raised an eyebrow. "Then why did you?"

"It'll be fun," Lauren said, mimicking Dr. Frances Turple's gravelly voice. "Mature students mostly—RCMP officers, social workers, probation officers—people already settled in careers. It's not like dealing with freshmen straight from high school."

Emma smiled. "I take it that's not how it turned out."

"Not by a long shot." Lauren could count the mature students in her class on one hand: An RCMP officer, a high school teacher who wanted to join the police force, and a couple of middle-aged housewives with aspirations of becoming the next J. B. Fletcher.

"Frances told me the instructor they hired bailed at the last minute," Emma said.

"Yes, he left her in a bind, all right. Frances was in a panic. I felt obligated to step in. I owe her big time."

"Go on, girl," Emma said. "You don't *owe* her anything."

"Well, she did hire me when I was down on my luck. At the time, I was so desperate I would have taken any job." Lauren shook her head. "I don't know how I survived."

"You turned things around, forged a new life for yourself. We're all proud of you, sure."

"Since my law license was reinstated, things have gotten better," Lauren agreed. "I love my job at Beck Hayes. Bailey is happy. Still, I feel indebted to Frances. It was teaching that initially allowed me to stay here."

"Don't be down on yourself," Emma said. "The department was lucky to get you."

"Well, Frances could have had her pick." It was well known that the college got more applicants than it could handle. Lauren gestured toward the window, where long wharves and fish stages jutted into the bay. "The scenery alone is enough to entice most people. And our town is growing," she added.

"True," Emma said. "I saw an article in *Urban News* that listed Paddy's Arm as one of the fastest growing towns in Canada. Imagine now."

Lauren smiled. In the four years she'd been here, she'd watched the population nearly double. Overnight, it seemed, new streets were put in and high-rise apartment buildings went up. Five-star restaurants, fast-food chains, and brand-name clothing stores popped up everywhere. "Must be…what, over seven thousand people now?"

"For sure," said Emma. "It's amazing how the expansion of the college changed things. Sure, when I first started teaching here St. Bridget's offered only a handful of courses. Now look at us."

Although the school was more a college than a university, students who wanted to complete a degree could now do their foundation year at St. Bridget's. They offered certificate programs in everything from criminology to creative writing. However, the drama department was the biggest asset, attracting students nationwide. It offered a four-year degree program and some of the best people in the country taught there.

Emma peered at Lauren. "I take it this will be your last term teaching."

"I'm afraid so. I'm just too busy." She smiled. "But at least now I get to see more of you, Emma. You look great, by the way. What have you done to your hair?"

Emma touched her stylish layers. "Just a cut and a few highlights."

"Looks fabulous," Lauren said, taking it in.

Emma continued to study her. "Anything else bothering you?"

Lauren took a deep breath. Only a few close friends knew about her humiliating past. Even Emma didn't know all the details. Lauren repeated Devon's remark. "Maybe I'm being overly sensitive," she added.

"You need to let that crap go, sure. Don't let it define you."

"I know. I know. Still, I can't help thinking about how my foolishness could have gotten me disbarred."

"It's all in the past now. No need to even go there."

"You're right," Lauren agreed. "I'm sorry I didn't get a chance to return your calls," she said, suddenly remembering the reason for her visit.

"Don't worry about it, girl," Emma said. "Sure, I know how busy you are. I did want to talk to you about one of your students, though: Jade Roberts. Has she been attending classes?"

"Not regularly, no. And she's behind on all her assignments."

Emma frowned. "She'll lose her bursary if she doesn't keep up her grades."

Lauren grimaced. "I don't know how she'll manage if that happens. A single mom with an infant."

"Since her baby's birth, she's become a changed person, that one."

"It happens to all of us."

"Except Jade's become *less* responsible."

Lauren knew that Jade had lost her driver's license due to impaired driving. And she had come to school hungover on a couple of occasions. Still she felt a tug of sympathy, knowing how difficult it was raising a child alone.

"You busy right now?" Emma asked.

Lauren thought of the stack of unmarked papers on her desk. She had a client at two, a court appearance at three. "I have a little free time," she said.

"I thought we could visit Jade, have a chat with her."

"Well...I suppose," Lauren hedged, not sure how involved she should become in her students' lives. They were adults, after all. And this job was only temporary.

"The scholarship committee needs to be informed if students are not fulfilling their commitments," Emma reminded her.

"True," Lauren agreed. Sooner or later, she'd have to confront Jade about her absenteeism and failing grades. "Does she know we're coming?"

"Her phone's disconnected. We'll have to drop by unannounced."

Lauren stood up. "Give me fifteen minutes and I'll meet you in the parking lot."

—

"This is it," Emma said, parking across the street from a three-storey apartment building.

Lauren stared out the car window at the sagging balconies enclosed by rusting wrought iron. A wooden fire escape ran up one side of the building. A sign advertised apartments, ranging in price from five to six hundred dollars monthly.

Emma turned off the engine. "Let's hope Jade's home."

In the foyer, Lauren ran a finger down the list of tenant names posted on the wall, found the apartment number, and rang the doorbell.

"Come in," Jade called over the intercom, buzzing them in without question.

After climbing two flights of steps, they opened a door into a narrow hallway. Television sets and stereos blared behind thin walls as they stepped over toys and footwear. Fried onions and other food odours mingled with the stale cigarette smoke that hovered heavily in the air.

Jade stood outside her apartment door. She'd lost weight, Lauren realized. Shadows dark as bruises rimmed her eyes. She wore torn jeans and a button-down shirt rolled up at the sleeves. She frowned as Lauren and Emma approached. "Professor Buckle...Professor LaVallee?" She looked past them down the dim empty hallway.

She'd been expecting someone else, Lauren realized.

"We tried to call, but your phone's disconnected," Emma said. "What's up, girl?"

Lauren smiled, liking the easy rapport Emma had with her students.

Jade leaned against the door frame, eyeing them warily. "I couldn't pay the bill. Had my service suspended until I can catch up. It's not easy, you know."

"We understand, but we need to talk," Lauren said.

Jade pushed open the door. "Come in," she said, ushering them into a tiny living room with broken-down furniture. A hideous brown carpet covered the floor. Bright butterflies were stuck to walls and furniture, adding colour to the otherwise drab room. Jade's baby was in a portable carrier chewing on a set of plastic keys. A purple butterfly with white silk wings was stuck to the side of the seat.

"Jade, your little girl's adorable," Lauren said, kneeling on the floor beside the infant. "What's her name?"

"That's Cara." Jade shook her head. "She's a handful."

"She has your colouring," Lauren said, taking in the baby's olive skin and dark eyes. "How old is she now?"

"Almost seven months, and just starting to crawl. Soon she'll be into everything."

The baby smiled, showing toothless gums.

"Don't mind the mess." Jade picked up toys and books, making room for them on a battered sofa.

Emma and Lauren sat next to each other. Jade remained standing, arms crossed over her chest. They made small talk about the weather, the price of gas, a play the drama students were putting on. Jade restlessly paced the room, her eye on a cat-shaped clock on the living room wall. "Mind if I smoke?" she asked. Without waiting for an answer, she pulled a package of cigarettes from her pocket.

Lauren looked from Jade to the sleeping baby.

"I'll blow the smoke outside." Jade opened a set of glass doors that led to a small terrace. A number of butterflies were fixed to the glass. She took a cigarette from the package and lit it.

"Jade," Emma began, "you haven't been attending classes, and your grades are slipping."

"What are you, the campus police?" Although Jade smiled, there was no mistaking the hard edge in her voice.

"We're concerned about you," Emma continued. "You need to keep up your grades to hold on to your bursary. Your two papers are long overdue. They should have been in a few weeks ago. But you know that, sure."

"I've been looking for a job." Jade blew a plume of smoke through the patio door. "They fired me at the jail because of all the time I missed." She motioned toward the baby. "Everything's changed since Cara came."

"It's not easy being a single mother," Emma agreed. "My baby was fifteen months old when my husband died. And Professor LaVallee—"

"I never married Bailey's father," Lauren cut in.

Jade puffed on her cigarette. "But you both have good jobs."

"We're better off financially," Lauren agreed, "but you have a chance to better yourself, Jade."

"I'm thinking about putting Cara in foster care."

Lauren flinched. She couldn't imagine choosing to do that.

"It's temporary," Jade said. "Just until I can save some money. Diapers and formula are expensive."

So are cigarettes, Lauren thought, but she said nothing.

"You got family here?" Emma asked.

"My mother lives in St. John's." Jade looked from Emma to Lauren, glaring at each of them in turn. "It's not like I'm abandoning my daughter."

"We're not here to judge you," Lauren said quietly.

Jade took a last drag from the cigarette then threw the butt onto the terrace. She closed the door and turned to face them. "I could've got a lot of money for Cara, you know."

"Money?" Lauren stared at her. Had she heard right? "Someone offered to *buy* your baby?"

"They didn't see it as a sale," Jade said. "I was offered a few thousand, so I guess it amounts to the same thing."

"Was this before Cara was born?" Lauren had once worked for a firm that handled adoption cases. It was not uncommon for clients to pay the mother's expenses while waiting for the baby's arrival. Sometimes in their eagerness, clients offered extravagant fees. The firm had been careful not to let clients cross the line where an adoption became a sale.

"It was a few months back," Jade admitted. "Just think of what I could've done with that kind of money. But I could never part with Cara."

"Who offered you money?" Lauren couldn't resist asking.

"I'd rather not say." Jade eyed the clock. "Look, I don't mean to be rude, but I'm expecting someone. Okay?"

CHAPTER

2

Lauren's favourite part of the day was picking up her daughter at Kiddy Academy. Pulling into the preschool's parking lot, she spotted Bailey in the schoolyard playing soccer with half a dozen other kids. Patrick Shaw and another young teacher were supervising them.

Lauren parked the car and then stood for a few moments, watching.

"Go get it, Tyler!" Patrick cheered. "Great shot, Bailey!"

"Hey, Toots!" Lauren called as she opened the gate.

"Momma!" Bailey ran toward her.

Lauren embraced her in a hug.

"Momma, I scored two goals," Bailey said when Lauren released her.

Patrick came to stand beside them. "She's really a great soccer player," he said, affectionately ruffling Bailey's red curls. "Our girl here puts Beckham to shame."

"Why you come now, Momma?"

"I thought I'd pick you up early." Lauren smiled. It was as if Bailey had a built-in radar. Whenever Lauren was late, she'd find her waiting by the door, knapsack on her back, a worried frown on her elfin face.

Lauren took Bailey's hand and started toward the car. "How was your day?"

"Ryan had to sit in time-out."

"Oh?" Lauren opened the door and lifted Bailey into her car seat. Bailey loved drama, and relished telling on kids who got in trouble.

"Ryan bringed his mom's nail polish to school. He painted David's toenails." Bailey giggled. "Colin spilled it, and Ryan got mad and bited him."

Lauren gave Bailey a smile. Would her daughter always be this carefree? Already, she was asking questions about why she didn't have a daddy like the other kids at school. Was she wrong not to let Daniel know he had a daughter? Was she doing the right thing by keeping him out of Bailey's life?

Thinking of Daniel, Lauren had to blink back tears. They had been seeing each other for three years when she got pregnant. Knowing a baby wasn't part of his plan, she'd left without telling him. It would have been too painful to have him reject her when she needed him most. But even now, a wound opened whenever she allowed herself to think of him. *Don't go there,* she warned herself. *You need to move forward.*

Half an hour later, Lauren was in her kitchen putting together lasagna, while Bailey watched cartoons in the living room. As she worked, Lauren thought again about Devon's comment. All anyone had to do nowadays was google her and they'd find out the whole story. How had she gotten herself into such a mess? What the hell had she been thinking? It was bad enough she had breached attorney-client privilege, but the lies her client had told about her were even more damaging. Thank God she hadn't been disbarred. But how would her new clients feel if they found out? She was just getting her practice up and running.

You need to get in front of the story, Lauren told herself. *Put it out there before anyone else gets a chance.* Her friend Claire had warned her that the story might come to light someday. She would do that at the appropriate time. Thinking of Claire, Lauren realized she had promised to visit her. Claire had been suffering from postpartum depression since the birth of her baby six months before. It was so severe she couldn't even make plans to go back to work. *I've been neglecting her,* Lauren thought guiltily as she reached for the telephone.

—

Across town in Sycamore Heights, the telephone rang and rang. Claire Ste Denis struggled to open her eyes, but sleep dragged her down into a black well of oblivion. When she awoke some time later her baby was crying. Like a diver emerging from a murky lake, Claire fought her way to consciousness. She'd slept the afternoon away, she realized, feeling a stab of shame. How long had Ariel been crying? "I'm coming, baby," she called.

Groggy and disoriented, Claire stumbled into the nursery. She peeled off Ariel's soaked sleeper. Even the crib pad was wet. Overwhelmed and bleary with sleep, she managed to warm a bottle of formula and carry the wailing infant to the rocking chair.

As Ariel's sobs subsided, Claire felt a rush of tenderness. She loved this child; there was no doubt about that. Ariel was a good baby. It wasn't her fault that her mother was too tired to care for her. Kissing the sleeping infant's head, Claire gently placed her back in her crib.

In the full-length mirror at the bottom of the stairs, Claire winced at the sight of the exhausted-looking woman with deep lines of fatigue carved around her eyes. She hadn't expected motherhood to be this trying. Most days, she moved through her tasks like a sleepwalker. A sense of failure hit her like a physical blow. *Why does it have to be this difficult? Why do I feel so inadequate?*

On her way to the kitchen, Claire heard the doorbell ring and hurried to answer it. Mitch Cromwell, the university's director of drama, stood on the doorstep holding a gift bag decorated with kittens.

"Mitch!" Claire exclaimed. "Oh, dear, I forgot you were dropping by. Please come in."

Mitch stepped inside. His plaid jacket clashed badly with the pattern of yellow and purple owls on his tie. "I hope I'm not getting you at a bad time."

"Not at all," Claire said, giving him a quick hug. "It's good to see you."

"Is our girl around?" He held up the gift bag.

"Ariel's sleeping. More presents, Mitch? You're spoiling her."

Mitch put the bag on a table in the foyer and shrugged off his jacket. "I'm her godparent," he said. "It's my job to indulge her."

Shaking her head, Claire took Mitch's jacket. He doted on Ariel, always bringing her toys and books. He had even started a fund for her education.

Mitch pulled an envelope from his shirt pocket. "I brought something for you as well…for you and Bram, actually."

Claire took the envelope. Inside, she found tickets to the dinner theatre the drama department was putting on.

"It starts next Thursday and runs for three weeks," Mitch said. "I know Bram works most Thursdays so the tickets are for Saturday evening."

"Thanks, Mitch. That's very thoughtful of you. I'm looking forward to seeing everyone again."

"They've been asking about you," he said as he followed Claire to the sitting room.

She gestured to a seat near the fireplace. "Make yourself comfortable. Can I get you some tea?"

"No, thanks." Mitch lowered himself into the chair. "I just dropped by for a quick visit."

Claire took a seat across from him. "It's good to see you. I don't get out much."

"So I hear…." Mitch's face wrinkled with concern. "How are you, my dear?"

"Tired," she admitted.

Mitch nodded. "It can't be easy. My niece suffered from postpartum depression. It took her the best part of a year to recover."

Claire sighed. "My doctor tells me it will pass…I just wish she could put a time limit on it. God knows I'm taking enough drugs."

"You *will* get better again."

"I suppose I will." Still, Claire wondered if there would ever come a time when she didn't feel weary and strung out. A time when she didn't move in a stupor through an endless routine of feedings and diapers. Sometimes even the smallest chore seemed impossible.

"Are you getting enough help?"

"The students still come in from time to time," Claire said. "They run errands, help with the housework. They take Ariel for walks in her stroller. It helps. Bram is going to be at a medical conference in Ontario next week. I'm not looking forward to that, but I'm sure I'll be fine." Claire managed a weak smile, as if to demonstrate. "And how are *you*, Mitch? Still on the wagon?"

He nodded. "Nearly seven weeks now."

"Well, congratulations. Let's hope it's longer this time." The longest Mitch had been able to stay sober so far was three months.

"As you know, I'm retiring at the end of term." Frowning, he rubbed his chin with his thumb. "I'm pushing sixty-five. Don't know what I did to deserve *that*, but it happens. And," he added, "I'm beginning to feel my age."

Claire studied him silently, taking in his lined face, his shoulder-length hair as thin and wispy as cotton candy. She felt a surge of affection. They'd been friends for a long time. Mitch had taken her under his wing when she started working at the Shaw Theatre Festival. They sometimes acted opposite each other on stage—King Lear and Cordelia, Miranda and Prospero. After Mitch had come to St. Bridget's to set up the drama department, he'd sent Claire a brochure of the campus. *Come any time to visit,* he'd written. She had been busy writing her Ph.D. thesis at the time; however, the following year she took him up on his offer, and fell in love with the town. It was here she had met her husband, Bram Warren, a surgeon from Boston.

"I recommended that you be my replacement when I retire," Mitch said, bringing Claire out of her musings. "If anyone can make the department a success, it's you."

"Mitch, thank you," Claire said. "I'm so sorry but...right now, though, I just don't feel up to it."

"September is still months away," Mitch said, undeterred. "We can hire an acting director to take on your duties until you're ready." He glanced at his watch and rose from his seat. "Give it some thought."

Claire brightened. Maybe she could really make a difference in the future of the theatre, she thought as she followed Mitch to the door, build up its reputation.

Once she walked back into the kitchen, she noticed the blinking red light on her phone. She pressed the button.

"You have two new messages," a mechanical voice informed her. Claire punched in her password. The first call was from her mother. "'Allo, kids," she said in her broken English. "Papa and me...we leave to go home tomorrow. We will come visit you in Newfoundland soon. Is what...three months since we last see Ariel?"

Closer to four, Claire thought, but she smiled in spite of everything. After her father retired, her parents had gone to India on a spiritual retreat. They lived in an ashram, practicing hours of silent meditation. There was no access to television, radio, newspaper, or the internet. Claire had missed them terribly.

The other message was from Lauren. "Claire? I'm sorry it's taken so long to get back to you. I can come to see you next Thursday around three if that's a good time. Let me know if that works."

"Anytime is good for me," Claire muttered. "I hardly leave the house anymore." But the thought of seeing Lauren brightened her mood. They'd been friends since their undergraduate days at McGill. Even after Lauren went on to law school and Claire to the National Theatre School, they'd kept in touch. Claire was eager to tell her about Mitch's proposal. *He believes in me*, she thought. She imagined herself carrying out plans, making decisions about plays. She already had a vision for the future of the theatre. She and Mitch had discussed offering a master's degree. There was so much that could be done.

But will I be well enough? Claire wondered, reality hitting her like a splash of cold water.

CHAPTER

3

Jade frowned at herself in the bathroom mirror as she applied her makeup. No amount of concealer could hide the bags under her eyes. Only a good night's sleep could fix that. Her face was pale, her hair dull and lifeless. She swallowed back a wave of resentment. Who the hell did Professor LaVallee think she was? How dare she come here threatening to take away her bursary? Didn't she realize how difficult it was raising a baby while trying to get a degree?

Jade trembled with anger. She couldn't wait to graduate and get the hell away from this hick town. She glanced at her watch. And where was Patrick? He'd promised to babysit Cara this afternoon. Jade had an interview at the law firm of Bell Clarke; they were looking for a research assistant. Patrick knew how important the interview was. If she didn't leave now she'd be late. For a moment, she thought of taking Cara with her. No, she decided. Patrick would be here any minute now. Cara was sleeping; she would be okay until he arrived.

She worried that her clothes might not be suitable for the interview. Her one good blouse didn't look too bad with a pair of black jeans. It would have to do, Jade told herself as she grabbed the worn leather jacket she'd bought at Frenchy's. Minutes later she left the apartment, her résumé tucked inside a large shoulder bag.

At the end of the street, Jade saw Patrick approaching. "Hi," she called.

"I'm sorry I'm late," Patrick said, looking at his watch. "I would've called but your phone's disconnected."

"I left the apartment door open."

Patrick stared at her. "You left Cara alone? Christ, Jade."

"She's sound asleep." Jade checked her watch. "Look, if I don't hurry, I'll be late for my interview. Afterwards, I need to go to the library to get books for assignments I have due." She pursed her lips. "Buckle and LaVallee came here yesterday threatening to take away my damn bursary."

Patrick frowned. "You shouldn't go out and leave Cara alone, Jade. Anything could happen. What if I didn't show?"

"Whatever," Jade said dismissively. "I have to run."

"Good luck," Patrick said as he headed toward the apartment building.

"I'll be home around five," Jade called over her shoulder. "When Cara wakes up, give her the jar of food I left on the counter."

—

"Jesus," Patrick muttered as he walked up the two flights of steps to the apartment. He did what he could for Jade because she was on her own. Still, he didn't like some of the things he'd been witnessing lately. Jade's patience with Cara was starting to run thin. What if she snapped someday and hurt her? It happened all the time.

Cara was asleep in her infant carrier and didn't even stir when Patrick opened the door. *Poor baby,* he thought, tucking her blanket around her small shoulders.

He made himself a cup of tea and looked in the fridge for milk. *Christ, what does the woman live on?* There were a couple of wilted carrots, mustard, a few eggs, and a jar of pickles. He couldn't find any milk, but there were about half a dozen little packets of sugar—the kind you get in restaurants.

Patrick settled himself on the sofa and opened his textbook. For homework he had to read and summarize an essay on the stages of Freud's psychosexual theory of development. After reading the second paragraph, he put down the book and groaned. When he'd enrolled in the Early Childhood Development program, he hadn't expected to be studying all this theory crap. At least he was getting real experience at Kiddy Academy.

Patrick was the only male in the program, and only the third to enroll since it had begun five years ago. His father, an accountant who expected his sons to follow in his footsteps, wasn't happy about this career choice. Patrick could still hear his taunting: *You're borrowing thousands of dollars to learn how to babysit kids?* Miserable prick. No wonder his mother walked out on the son of a bitch. *I'm happy with what I'm doing with my life,* Patrick told himself. Someday he planned to open his own preschool. Screw the old man and his goddamn accounting. Patrick banged his fist down hard on the coffee table. The baby awoke with a start and let out a wail.

Patrick picked her up. "Hi, Cara," he crooned. "Mommy had to go out, but Uncle Patrick is here to take care of you."

She stopped crying and stared at him with wide, dark eyes.

"Poor baby," Patrick muttered. "You deserve better. You deserve a father. What's going to become of you?" He knew Jade was doing her best, but it seemed to him she still made some very bad choices. It broke his heart that Cara was being neglected.

—

Jade watched uneasily as a middle-aged woman—her nameplate read *Amy*—scanned her résumé. "Why do you want this job?" she asked without looking up at Jade.

Oh, for Christ's sake, Jade thought. What kind of a stunned arse was she dealing with here? She'd just finished telling *Amy* she was a single parent going to school full-time. Jade forced a tight smile. She needed this job. The landlord had already given her a second notice. Her mother had promised to send her a hundred dollars, but she still needed forty more. If she didn't come up with the full amount soon, she'd be evicted.

Amy glanced up at Jade, her eyes narrowed.

Jade took a deep breath. "I'm in the criminology program at St. Bridget's," she said. "I plan to go to law school when my daughter's a little older. I've been looking into the program at Dalhousie. This job will give me valuable work experience."

"You want to be a lawyer?"

Jade nodded. *Well, duh. That's usually why people go to law school.* Truth was, she had no intention to study law. But it sounded good coming from a single mother. "It's always been my dream," she said.

"And you have a sitter?"

"The university has an excellent childcare facility," Jade said, "and I have friends willing to help out. I promise to work hard," she added, trying not to sound desperate.

Amy stared at her without comment.

"I brought references." Jade inched a manila folder across the wide, polished table.

"Good. Good." Amy stood up, signalling the interview was over. "I'll be in touch."

Jade got a sinking feeling in her stomach. She wouldn't get the job. She could tell by the way the bitch dismissed her.

Sick with worry, Jade walked the five blocks to the library. How would she manage if she couldn't find a job? If she applied for any kind of assistance, she'd have to drop out of school. The system didn't make it easy for single mothers trying to better themselves. A social worker had suggested putting Cara in foster care until Jade could catch up on her rent and bills. Jade's eyes pricked with unshed tears; it was starting to seem like her only option.

In the small courtyard on the first floor of the library, Jade spotted Rebecca Taylor drinking coffee from a paper cup. She walked up to her table and pulled out a chair.

Rebecca was dressed in jeans and a red sweatshirt, her hair loose around her shoulders. She usually came to class straight from work, wearing her RCMP uniform. She looked much younger when she dressed casually and let her hair down, Jade thought.

They exchanged a few niceties. Rebecca told her about her son's obsession with changing his clothes every couple of hours. They talked about the difficulties of working and going to school while raising a child.

"Did you get your paper for LaVallee finished?" Jade asked after a while.

Rebecca nodded. "I wrote about the powerlessness of the police officer."

Jade laughed. "I didn't realize you were powerless."

"We have our limitations," Rebecca said. "And sometimes that can be a problem."

Jade sighed. "I'm still trying to find a topic. I was thinking about gun control, but…" she shrugged. "I don't know."

"You could write about a personal experience," Rebecca offered. "What I mean is...I was thinking, maybe about domestic abuse?"

Although she knew Rebecca meant well, Jade felt her face flush. The police had been called to her apartment on more than one occasion when she lived with Willy. He'd beaten the crap out of her when she was pregnant with Cara. They took him away in handcuffs that time. Rebecca had urged Jade to leave him.

"Or you could write about the burden of gun control in small communities like this one," Rebecca added quickly as if sensing Jade's discomfort.

Jade nodded, considering.

"That paper you did on effective partnership between law enforcement and the community was excellent." Rebecca took a sip of coffee. "I told some of the officers at work about it. As a matter of fact, I used some of your ideas when the subject came up at a meeting."

"Really?" Jade couldn't imagine her ideas being discussed among the police.

Rebecca peered at her. "Your paper was really good, Jade."

At that moment a couple of students, Erika Jansen and Megan Dillard, stopped by their table. They had just finished rehearsal and were going to Kelsey's to celebrate. "Drinks are half price for happy hour," said Megan. "Would you guys like to come along?"

Jade shook her head. How she wished she could, but she was down to her last eight dollars until Cara's baby bonus came at the end of the month. "I can't," she said.

"My mother-in-law is visiting," said Rebecca. "I have to leave in a few minutes. Have fun." As she watched the girls walk away, she shook her head. "I can't remember what it's like having that freedom anymore. A child really changes things."

"Sure does," Jade agreed. "When did your mother-in-law arrive?"

"Maggie came last evening. This time she plans to stay for two weeks."

"Is that a good thing?"

"Well...yes and no," Rebecca sighed. "Darren enjoys having her around. And she's good with Connor. I just wish she wouldn't harp on me all the time about my job."

Jade knew Rebecca's mother-in-law didn't approve of Rebecca's career. Before they came to Newfoundland, Darren had worked as a mechanic. He'd quit his job when Rebecca was transferred, and so far he hadn't been able to find anything in Paddy's Arm.

"It's great having Darren home with Connor," Rebecca continued. "When he goes back to work, I'm going to miss coming home to a cooked meal."

If only I could be so lucky, Jade thought. Rebecca's life was so different from her own. She would take a nagging mother-in-law any day if it meant not having to worry about money or babysitters, or finding a job. It would be nice having someone in her life to help take care of Cara.

Rebecca's cellphone rang and she glanced at the number. "Speak of the devil." She chuckled. "Probably wondering what I'm up to." She stood up, gathered her books and purse. "I should go before Maggie comes looking for me."

Jade gulped down the last of her coffee. "I should be going too. I need to pick up books so I can get this paper done."

"I'll see you in class," Rebecca said as she walked away.

Jade found the books she needed and brought them to the checkout desk. She'd get started on her assignments tonight, she promised herself. Get LaVallee and Buckle the hell off her back.

It was snowing lightly when Jade left the library. She felt a pinching headache. Her period was about to start, and there'd be unbearable cramps. What she wouldn't give for a little pot right now. Instead of going home, she headed toward the senior citizens' complex near the waterfront where her grandmother lived. Jade sometimes did her nan's grocery shopping and picked up her prescriptions. She let herself into the foyer with her spare key, and then she knocked on the apartment door before unlocking it. "Anyone home?" she called.

Nan was asleep in her rocker. There was a bottle of vodka on the coffee table, her false teeth next to it. She wore a cotton nightgown with a large brown stain down the front.

"Jesus, look at this place," Jade said. The table and counter were lined with dirty dishes, pots, and pans. Clothes and shoes were strewn on the floor.

Nan opened her eyes a moment then quickly closed them.

Shaking her head, Jade walked down the hallway to the bathroom. The strong smell of urine assaulted her nostrils. The tub and sink looked like they hadn't been cleaned in months. Wet towels littered the floor. In the medicine cabinet, she found Xanax and various pain medications. Taking some from each bottle, she slipped them into her purse.

When Jade came out of the bathroom, Nan was making little snoring noises through her open mouth. Christ almighty. No wonder the family was so screwed up. Nan had raised ten kids on her own. Jade's father used to talk about how his mother beat and neglected them. One time, he told Jade, Nan had thrown a junk of wood, knocking him out cold. Another time, when she was drinking, Nan broke her youngest son's arm. Children's aid took the kids away for over a year that time.

You're not doing such a great job either, Jade reminded herself. Would she end up like her grandmother, with her kid in and out of foster care? No, she decided, Cara's stay would be temporary. It would give Jade a chance to look for a job. She was nothing like Nan. Once she had a job and got Cara back, she would study hard. In another year she would finish her program, the only member of her family to achieve that. She thought of how Rebecca had praised her ideas and felt a ripple of pride.

Nan startled awake and gave a little cry. "Jade?"

Jade looked at her grandmother with disgust. "Ah, Nan. What did you do, spill booze all over yourself?" She shook her head. "Let me get you cleaned up."

In the bedroom, Jade was rummaging through a drawer for a fresh nightgown when she came across a small billfold. She opened it and found more than a hundred dollars inside. Nan must have just cashed her Old Age pension. Jade peeled off two twenties and stuffed them into her jacket pocket. Nan would only waste the money on booze, she reasoned. Better it was spent on keeping a roof over Cara's head. Despite her faults, Nan cared about her great-grandchild; she wouldn't want Cara to go without. Besides, she would never even miss it.

CHAPTER

4

Lauren had planned to pick Bailey up early from school so they could spend more time visiting with Claire. Just as she was leaving the house, the phone rang.

"Hello?"

"Professor LaVallee?" There was so much static and crackling, she could barely make out the words.

"This...Jade Roberts." More static, making it almost impossible to hear.

"Hello, Jade?" Lauren said. "Can you hear me?" Lauren didn't like students or clients calling her at home.

"I...wonder if...meet...you sometime?"

"You want to meet with me? Sure. We can meet early next week."

Jade said something, but the reception was so poor her words were lost.

"I can't hear you, Jade," Lauren said. "Can you hear me?"

More static.

"Jade, if you can hear me, give me a call tomorrow at the university. Okay?"

There was more static as Jade's voice faded in and out.

Lauren glanced at her watch. She had planned to pick Bailey up fifteen minutes ago. "I'm going to hang up now, Jade," she said. "I have to pick up my daughter from school. Call me tomorrow. Okay?"

She probably wants another extension on her term paper, Lauren told herself as she reached for her car keys. Jade had passed in one paper, on domestic violence, and gotten a B+. Lauren was impressed with how Jade made an argument for why women stay in abusive relationships and often don't report the violence. She was able to present her ideas in a clear, concise way. It was obvious she had put a lot of thought into it. She'd give her a couple of extra days to finish her other paper if that's what she needed.

Although Lauren got to the preschool forty minutes earlier than her usual pickup time, it was still later than she'd planned.

"We're going to visit Aunt Claire and Ariel," Lauren heard Bailey tell Patrick as he opened the gate. "That's why Momma's here early."

Patrick touched her curls. "I hope you have a nice visit." Turning to Lauren he said, "I went by Claire's house around noon to get the money she owes me for childcare. There was no one home."

"Was she expecting you?"

"She told me to come by when I could. Her car was in the driveway."

"That's odd," Lauren said. "I'll let her know that you dropped by."

"Will Aunt Claire let me hold Ariel?" Bailey cut in.

"Well, you could ask."

Bailey smiled. "I think she will."

Lauren took Bailey's hand, and they walked to the car. "Would you like to go out for supper?" she asked as she lifted her into her car seat.

Bailey nodded enthusiastically. "McDonald's?"

"McDonald's," Lauren groaned, feeling a pang of guilt. It would be the third time this week for fast food. Tonight was the premiere of the dinner theatre the drama students were putting on. She planned to arrive early, mingle, and have drinks with faculty members. The sitter was arriving around five-thirty. There wouldn't be time to cook a meal.

Lauren got into the car and started the engine. *I'm going to make more time for Claire*, she vowed silently. She had been a friend during some dark times in Lauren's life. It was Claire who had encouraged her to come to Paddy's Arm. She had been a longtime friend of David Beck, one of the partners at Beck Hayes, and recommended Lauren for the opening at their firm.

Although it wasn't yet three-thirty, heavy traffic was starting to build at Main. Lauren turned left on a side street and drove up the steep hill to Sycamore Heights. The houses in the area were newly built, elegant, two-storey brick on large treed lots. High rock walls and hedges separated properties with well-tended lawns and shrubbery. BMWs, Audis, and Mercedes were parked in the driveways.

As she turned right onto Sumac Lane, Lauren saw an ambulance in a driveway. Claire's driveway, she realized, gripping the steering wheel. As she neared the house, Lauren saw two paramedics slide a collapsed gurney through the rear doors of the ambulance. One of them climbed into the back; the other closed the doors and got into the driver's seat. The ambulance pulled away, lights flashing, as it sped down the street.

Lauren pulled into the driveway and got out of the car, her knees weak. She could feel her heart hammering as she unbuckled Bailey and pulled her from the car. She raced to the door and, with a trembling hand, rang the doorbell.

Dr. Anya Kaminsky, still wearing her jacket, opened the door. Had she just arrived? But why hadn't she gone in the ambulance with Claire? She was her doctor, after all.

"Is Claire okay?" Lauren asked, breathlessly.

Anya ushered them inside the spacious foyer. "The ambulance came for Ariel."

"What happened?"

"Come, have a seat," Anya said calmly. She had immigrated to Canada with her parents after the invasion of Chechnya, and had lived in various parts of Canada before settling in Newfoundland. She still had the hint of an accent and a slightly formal way of speaking. She took Lauren's coat and guided her into Claire's family room, filled with roomy chairs and sofas.

Lauren took a seat on a small sofa and pulled Bailey onto her knee.

"Claire called the clinic," Anya said. "She was distraught—so distraught the receptionist could not make out what she was saying. I took the call and was able to get her to calm down some. From what I could tell, there was something wrong with Ariel. I called 911 then left the clinic immediately. I got here just after the paramedics arrived."

"Where is Claire now?" Lauren asked. "Is she with Ariel?"

"Claire is sleeping," Anya said. "I gave her a sedative to calm her. Believe me, she was in no shape to go in the ambulance."

"Does Bram know?"

Anya nodded. "Bram is at the hospital. He will meet the ambulance there."

"Where's Ariel?" Bailey asked in a small, frightened voice. Lauren had momentarily forgotten her daughter.

Bailey wriggled out of her mother's lap and stood with her hands on her hips, her blue eyes troubled.

Anya knelt beside her. "Ariel had to go to the hospital, darling."

Bailey looked from the doctor to her mother.

"I'm sure she'll be fine," Lauren said, more to reassure herself than Bailey.

"Let's see if we can find something on television." Anya picked up the remote. "*Sandman Sam* is on. Do you like that show?"

Bailey nodded, still looking uneasy.

Anya surfed the channels, her long dark hair falling in her face. With her good looks, pale skin, and meticulous makeup, she looked more like a fashion model than a family physician, Lauren thought.

Once Bailey was settled, Anya turned her attention to Lauren. "Was Claire expecting you today?"

Lauren nodded. "I called last week."

"She must have forgotten," Anya said. "She has not been feeling well."

"Yes, I realize that," Lauren said, her head swimming with questions. Did Claire wake up and find the baby ill? If so, it would make sense to call Dr. Kaminsky, one of the few doctors who still made house calls. Anya had a reputation for going the extra mile for her patients. But what could have caused Claire to get so out of control she needed to be sedated?

"I asked Bram to call me as soon as he learned anything," Anya said, bringing Lauren back to the conversation. She peeked at her watch. "Would you mind staying with Claire until he gets home? My office is filling up with patients as we speak. Claire should not be left alone in her condition."

"Of course I'll stay," Lauren said. "Let me know if you hear any news about Ariel."

"I will do that." Anya buttoned her jacket. "I doubt that Claire will wake up anytime soon but if she does, give her one of the pills I left on her night table. And if you have any problems, please call me at the clinic."

After the doctor left, Lauren made herself a cup of tea and went to sit at the kitchen table. Thankfully, Bailey was engaged in her television program and didn't ask any more questions. Lauren stared out the window at the quiet, tree-lined street, her mind in turmoil. What could be wrong with Ariel? So wrong that she'd had to be taken away in an ambulance?

When Lauren finished her tea, she went upstairs to check on Claire. She looked small in the king-size bed, her face ashen. Her short black hair looked thin in places as if patches had fallen out. She stirred and moaned, but seemed to be sleeping soundly enough. Lauren closed the door softly.

Across the hall, the nursery door was ajar and Lauren entered it briefly. Pink and purple unicorns pranced across yellow wallpaper. A colourful mobile was suspended over a spacious white crib. Large framed photographs of Ariel hung on the wall. *Please God*, she prayed silently, *please let her be okay.*

By five, Lauren could no longer ignore her growing unease. Knowing she wouldn't be able to make it to the theatre, she called the sitter to cancel. It was growing dark outside the window, and from the light of the street lamp she saw it was beginning to snow. Feathery flakes fell against the window and onto the driveway. Had Emma heard the news? Lauren wondered. Emma and Claire were not just friends, but family. Emma had been married to Claire's first cousin. Should she call Emma at the theatre, fill her in on what had happened? No, she decided. She didn't know Ariel's condition and didn't want to alarm Emma unnecessarily. She'd wait until she heard from Bram. Any minute now, she expected him to walk through the door with Ariel in his arms.

Lauren made Bailey a peanut butter and jelly sandwich and poured her a glass of milk. She read to her from books that belonged to Ariel. By six-thirty, Bailey had fallen asleep on the sofa. Lauren turned off the television and tucked an afghan around her.

An hour later, she heard a car and went to the window. She watched as Bram pulled his Jeep Cherokee into the driveway. Snow was falling steadily now, slanting down through the glow of the headlights. It covered the street and driveway, clung to the branches of trees. Bram got out of the vehicle and started toward the house. Ariel wasn't with him, Lauren realized, her stomach tightening. She hurried to the door just as Bram stumbled into the foyer, his expression dark. Lines of exhaustion were etched around his eyes.

Lauren rushed to his side. "Bram!" she cried. "Where's Ariel?"

CHAPTER

5

It was intermission and student waiters served dinner rolls and plates of tossed salad. Audience members had left their tables to order drinks at the bar. Emma leaned back in her chair. The play, a comedy titled *My Son, Mac*, was a promising success. It had been written and work-shopped by students in Emma's playwriting class. Erika Jansen, the lead actress, was as skilled as any professional. In fact, all the students had done well. Too bad Lauren had missed it. *I wonder what happened*, Emma mused. Lauren hadn't even called. Maybe the sitter didn't show, she reasoned. Or maybe her car had broken down. Any number of things could have happened. Yet at the back of her mind was a nagging fear: Lauren always called if she couldn't make it.

About a dozen people were seated around the table, most of them from the drama department. Emma turned her attention to Frances Turple, who sat next to her partner, Annabelle Chandler. "Did you hear? Frances has just won an award for an article she published in *Crime Scene*," Emma announced.

"Impressive," said Lester Perry, vice president of the college.

Others around the table chimed in. "Good stuff, Frances," said Lester's wife, Charlotte. "I think a toast is in order."

Emma poured wine into glasses. "You must be proud, Frances."

"Well…I was surprised when they called me," Frances said, looking somewhat embarrassed by all the attention.

"She's a great writer," Annabelle said proudly.

Emma raised her glass. "To Frances and her success."

Glasses were raised. More toasts followed.

Emma sipped her wine, sneaking glances at Annabelle and Frances. Never had she met such an unlikely pair: Frances was at least sixty, her face lined. Her cropped iron-grey hair fell in uneven strands as if she'd hacked it off with a butcher knife. She had been an RCMP officer for twenty years, serving in various outposts across the country. She had a reputation for being tough on crime and had made a number of well-publicized drug busts. While working on the force, she had taken courses toward a Ph.D. in criminology and now taught at St. Bridget's.

Annabelle had long blond hair and eyes the colour of emeralds. Her smooth, delicate skin made her look much younger than her thirty-three years. Before she'd come to teach in the drama department she'd been a successful stage actress. She'd also had a part on a popular sitcom, *Down East*. Whereas Frances was gruff and crusty, Annabelle was quiet and soft-spoken. When they became a couple, people hadn't known what to make of it. Emma shook her head, remembering. No wonder students dubbed them "Beauty and the Beast." Despite their differences, however, it was obvious Annabelle and Frances were committed to each other.

"We have another announcement," Annabelle said. She laid a hand on Frances's shoulder. "Should *I* tell them?"

Frances smiled. "Go ahead."

"Well," Annabelle began, "as many of you know, Frances and I have been wanting to adopt." She looked around the table. "Today, we found out we will be getting a little girl."

There was more applause.

"Are you adopting an infant?" Emma asked.

"She's five months old," Annabelle said. "Her name is Dinah Marie."

At that moment, Mitch Cromwell dropped by their table holding a glass of wine. "May I?" he asked, indicating an empty chair.

"Yes, my son," Emma said. "We were toasting Frances and Annabelle. They just found out they're going to adopt a baby."

Mitch lowered himself into the chair. "Congratulations," he said, his voice slurred. "I'm sure you'll make great parents."

"Thank you, Mitch," Frances said. "And congratulations to you on the success of the play. As usual, you did a marvellous job."

Mitch beamed. "It wasn't all my effort," he said. "The students were wonderful. And, of course, Emma's students did an excellent job with the writing." He leaned toward Emma and she had an urge to fan her face with her hands. She thought of a line from a poem by Theodore Roethke: *The whiskey on your breath / Could make a small boy dizzy.* So much for all the time Mitch had spent in rehab. He often showed up at performances drunk. On one occasion, he'd fired the leading actor in the middle of a performance of *Hamlet* and the play had to be cancelled. For days, students and parents had called the university to complain. An article in the *Daily News* had called him "a drunk and an embarrassment to the university." But despite his behaviour, there was no doubting Mitch's skill as a director. The plays he didn't sabotage all got rave reviews. It was Mitch who had turned the drama department into the success it had become.

Mitch looked from Annabelle to Frances. "Are you still considering leaving us?"

"Leaving?" Emma asked.

"We've been thinking about moving to Arizona for some time now," said Annabelle. "A few days ago we sealed the deal."

There was a hum of excitement around the table, but before anyone could react to the big news, a cellphone jangled.

"Excuse me," Mitch said, pushing back his chair.

Annabelle shook her head as she watched him walk across the room. "Such talent," she said. "Too bad he's a liability."

"Yes," Emma agreed. "Looks like he's off the wagon again."

Minutes later, Mitch returned to the table, his expression grim. "Bram just called." He looked at Emma. "It's Ariel."

CHAPTER

6

"Bram, where's Ariel?"

Bram sank down on the sofa and covered his face with both hands. "Is she still at the hospital?" Lauren demanded.

Bram looked up at her, his face pale. "She's gone, Lauren. Ariel's gone."

"Gone?" Surely he couldn't mean….

But Bram's face told Lauren everything she needed to know. She felt the room swirling and gripped the arms of her chair for support. "What…happened?" she asked in a strangled voice.

"I'm almost certain it was SIDS. But we won't know for sure until the autopsy report is completed." He shook his head. "Jesus…. How could this have happened?"

Lauren stared at him, the weight of his words falling like blows. She knew sudden infant death syndrome was the most common cause of death in babies. But Ariel…no. She refused to accept it.

"How's Claire?" Bram asked.

Claire.

"Anya said she gave her a sedative."

"She's still sleeping," Lauren said.

Bram nodded slowly, pulled out his cellphone, and stepped into the hallway. Lauren listened as he made one gut-wrenching call after another to family and friends. *This can't be happening,* she told herself.

When Bram finished his calls, he returned to the living room. "I appreciate you staying with Claire, Lauren," he said as he collapsed onto the sofa. "I'm sorry I didn't get a chance to call from the hospital." He blew out a breath. "The medical examiner had questions. Then the police came and questioned me for nearly two hours. I thought it would never end."

Lauren nodded. "All standard procedure when someone dies at home."

At a loss for what to do with herself, she decided to make Bram coffee. "Is there anything else I can do?" she asked as he accepted a mug from her.

"I'll be fine, Lauren. Emma and Mitch are on their way. Maybe you should get Bailey home."

Numbly, Lauren went to get her coat.

Bram carried Bailey to the car and buckled her into her car seat. Snow now covered the streets and driveway. He kissed Lauren's cheek. "Drive carefully," he said. "It's getting slippery out there."

Lauren slid into the driver's seat and closed the door. As she pulled out of the driveway, Bram lifted his hand, snow falling around him.

Gripping the steering wheel, Lauren drove home, tears blurring her vision. Ariel was dead. Claire's beautiful baby was in the cold morgue. It all seemed so unreal.

Somehow, Lauren managed to get Bailey inside. Wearily, she climbed the stairs and put her daughter to bed. After slipping into a flannel nightgown, she went downstairs and took a bottle of chardonnay from the fridge. It was times like this when she most longed for Daniel, for the comfort of his arms around her.

Lauren sipped her wine, the events of the last few hours whirling furiously through her mind. Poor Claire, she thought, how would she take the news? It was unlikely she could have more children. Ariel was her miracle baby, the baby she thought she could never carry to term after three miscarriages. Lauren remembered the day Claire had called with the news of her pregnancy. She had waited until the second trimester just in case. Lauren had felt her friend's happiness as if it were her own. Why did this have to happen? What if—God forbid—something happened to Bailey? Could she go on with her life? Would she even want to? She shuddered, reaching for the half-empty bottle.

Lauren couldn't remember falling asleep. She awoke with a dull throbbing at the base of her brain. The realization of Ariel's death washed over her in a sickening wave. Dragging herself from bed, she pulled on her robe, went to the bathroom, and splashed cold water on her face. She barely recognized herself in the mirror; her eyes were red, her hair limp around her pale face. In the medicine cabinet she found a bottle of Aspirin and swallowed two.

She poured herself a cup of tea. For the best part of the next hour, she sat staring out the bay window that overlooked Paddy's Arm. It had stopped snowing during the night, and now a cold rain fell in a slow, steady drizzle. The ocean usually had a soothing effect on her, but this morning its greyness only added to her despair.

At seven-thirty, Bailey padded downstairs wearing a pink lace dress. "Good morning, Momma," she called.

Lauren held out her arms, and Bailey went to her. She held her daughter close, breathing in the sweet baby scent of shampoo and talc. How was she going to explain Ariel's death to her?

"Like my dress?" Bailey wiggled out of her mother's grasp and twirled around the kitchen floor.

Lauren smiled. Even at three and a half, Bailey was a diva when it came to fashion. They often had arguments about what outfits she would wear. The dress was entirely inappropriate for school. Today, however, it hardly seemed important.

"Taylor got a puppy." Bailey brushed tangled red curls away from her eyes. "Can we get a puppy, Momma?"

"I told you when we got Regis there'd be no more puppies."

Bailey ran into the living room and came back carrying a stuffed dog. "Momma, Regis is not *real*," she said, hugging the toy close.

"Right." Lauren set out cereal bowls and cut up fruit. She poured Bailey a glass of juice, all the while chatting with her daughter as if it were any ordinary day. Her thoughts kept drifting to Claire. She would have heard the news by now.

Lauren wanted to stay home in the safety of her rented townhouse, watch television, and bake cookies with Bailey. *That's not an option*, she told herself. She had a class at nine, a court appearance at eleven. Her afternoon calendar was heavy with appointments.

"Eat up, Toots," she told Bailey. "We don't want to be late."

After picking up her mail, Lauren grabbed a cup of tea from the faculty lounge and went to her office. Outside, the drizzle continued. She drew the curtains and switched on her reading lamp before logging onto her computer. There were twenty-six emails, the majority from students offering excuses for late term papers. There was a message from the president announcing Ariel's death, expressing condolences to Claire and Bram. Lauren stared at it for a long time. Reading about it on her screen took it out of the abstract, made it real. She went back to her inbox. There was an email from Jade Roberts:

> *Dear Professor LaVallee, I will not be returning to your class. I have been offered a job and the wages are too good to pass up. Cara and I will be moving away to make a new life. Sincerely, Jade Roberts.*

Lauren read the message twice. Was that why Jade had called her? To let her know she was leaving? But if that was the case, why would she have wanted to meet? And what kind of job had she been offered that would make it worth dropping out of school? Obviously, she had changed her plans about putting Cara in foster care. Maybe it was for the best. Still, Lauren wished Jade could have at least finished the term.

Before Lauren could reply to the email, a knock came at her door.

"Come in," she called, getting up from her desk.

Erika Jansen, a student from the drama department, opened the door. "Am I getting you at a bad time, Professor LaVallee?"

"Come in, Erika. I have a few minutes before class." Lauren cleared a mound of papers from a chair and motioned for her to sit.

"I heard the awful news," Erika said. Nervously, she raked her fingers through her blond curls.

"Yes, a terrible tragedy." Lauren went back to her desk.

"I can't believe it," Erika said, brokenly.

"I'm having difficulty believing it myself." Lauren stared at Erika for a long moment, surprised she had come to her. Erika wasn't one of her students. Lauren knew her enough to exchange greetings, but that was it. Everything she knew about Erika she had learned from Claire, who hired her to help out after Ariel's birth. Claire had described Erika as a natural when it came to children. She was also a very talented drama student; Mitch had called her his most promising actress.

"I figured something was wrong when Professor Cromwell and Professor Buckle left the dinner theatre early." Erika turned to Lauren, her eyes troubled. "It wasn't until this morning that I heard. What happened?"

"Bram thinks it was SIDS—crib death. It sometimes happens with infants."

"She was such a beautiful baby," Erika said, her eyes filling with tears.

"She really was."

Erika swiped at her eyes. "Professor Ste Denis must be devastated."

"I'm sure she must be. I was at her house last evening, but she was sleeping. I didn't get a chance to speak with her."

"Professor Ste Denis sleeps a lot," Erika said. "One day while I was taking care of Ariel, she slept for four hours. I tried to wake her before I left, but she was out like a light. I stayed until Dr. Warren got home that time." Erika stopped talking suddenly, as if afraid she'd said too much.

"I received an email from Jade Roberts this morning," Lauren said, steering the conversation away from Claire. "She won't be returning to my class. Have you heard from her?"

Erika frowned. "She just took Cara and left. I heard she left behind her furniture, dishes, everything."

"She told me she found a good job," Lauren said. "Do you know anything about that?"

"No, but she sent me a really strange email."

"Strange?" Lauren glanced up at her.

"The email…I mean, it didn't sound like Jade at all."

"How so?"

"Well…it was very formal for one thing: *Dear Erika*." She gave a short laugh. "Whenever I get a message from Jade it's like, *How ya doin'*. In this email, she *thanked* me for being her friend, *thanked* me for the times I took care of Cara."

"Well, it *was* an important message." Lauren folded her hands on her desk. "Jade probably wanted to sound sincere."

"I suppose so," Erika said, but Lauren could tell she wasn't entirely convinced.

CHAPTER

7

The following afternoon, Lauren stood outside Bram and Claire's house holding a chocolate cake she'd picked up at the bakery. Her stomach tightened as she rang the doorbell. What could she possibly say to Claire?

Emma answered the door wearing the vacant look of someone in shock. "Thank you for coming," she said.

Lauren hugged her. "I'm sorry, Emma. It must be a terrible blow."

Emma nodded. She accepted the cake and placed it on a nearby table that held platters of sandwiches, cookies, and squares. Another table had been set up with juice, pop, water, and bottles of wine.

Lauren shrugged off her coat and hung it in the hall closet. "How's Claire?"

"Still sedated." Emma lowered her voice. "I don't think she even realizes what's going on." She led Lauren into the living room where a dozen or more people were sitting on sofas and chairs, sipping drinks. A number of Claire's students were there, including Erika Jansen. There were professors from the university, as well as doctors from Bram's practice. Claire was sitting near the fireplace, staring blankly into space. Bram sat next to her, his face ashen.

Lauren approached them. "How are you, Claire?" she asked, kissing her cheek.

Claire gave her an empty stare.

Does she even realize I'm here? Lauren wondered, taking in Claire's glazed eyes and pale, drawn face.

Bram stood up. "Thank you for coming, Lauren. Can I get you something? Wine? Beer? Brandy?"

"I'll have a brandy," Lauren said.

"I'll get it," Emma offered.

"Thanks, Emma." Bram turned to an elderly woman sitting on a sofa across from Claire. "Lauren, have you met Claire's mother, Marie?"

Marie stood to embrace her. "Of course I meet Lauren. She come to my house often with Claire. How are you, Lauren? Is what… two years since I see you?"

"I believe it was. So nice to see you, Marie," said Lauren.

"Thank you for thinking of us."

"I'm sorry for your loss," Lauren said. "How's Pierre?"

"He is resting." Marie's voice wobbled. "Is taking Ariel's death hard."

Emma returned with the brandy, and Lauren gave Marie a sympathetic look before taking a seat on the sofa next to Mitch Cromwell. Anya Kaminsky sat on the other side of him. Mitch held a glass of amber liquid, but appeared sober. *Oh Lord, don't let him start crying,* Lauren prayed silently. Mitch could get pathetically maudlin after a few drinks.

For the next half hour, Lauren sipped her brandy, letting it soothe the disquiet within her. Around her, people spoke in hushed tones, everyone overly polite and cautious. All the while, Claire sat catatonically while Bram numbly acknowledged the sympathetic platitudes of colleagues, students, and friends.

"Can I get you another drink, Lauren?" Emma asked.

"No thanks. I'm driving, and I have to pick up Bailey from school."

Anya glanced at her watch. "I should be leaving soon," she said. "I have a plane to catch."

"Taking a vacation?" Mitch asked.

"I'm going to a medical conference in London, Ontario. Bram was supposed to go as well, but then——" She sighed. "I hate to leave while Claire is in such a fragile condition."

"She'll be fine," Mitch assured Anya. "Claire has friends and family, and everyone has been so kind."

Lauren nodded. In the short time she'd been there, a steady stream of visitors had brought baked goods and casseroles. Two florists had arrived with arrangements. Still, Claire hadn't said a word.

Half an hour later, as Lauren was putting on her coat in the foyer, a sharp authoritative rap came at the door. Lauren pulled it open. Two uniformed officers stood on the stoop. Rebecca Taylor from Lauren's criminology class was one of them. The other officer was a tall man sporting a thin moustache. They had never been introduced, but Lauren had seen him in court on various occasions.

"Hello, Lauren," Rebecca said soberly. "We need to speak with Claire Ste Denis."

Why are they here? Lauren wondered. Bram said the police had questioned him for nearly two hours at the hospital the night Ariel died.

Bram appeared in the foyer. "Hello," he said, his voice wary. "Can I help you?"

"I'm Constable Taylor," Rebecca said, "and this is Constable Harrison. We need to speak with Claire Ste Denis."

Bram frowned. "I'm Doctor Bram Warren, Claire's husband. Is there a problem, officer?"

"Yes, I'm afraid so, Dr. Warren," said Harrison.

"Come in," Bram said reluctantly. "We have visitors. We…we recently had a death in the family."

"Yes, I understand," Rebecca said. "I'm very sorry."

Harrison nodded. "Sorry to bother you at this difficult time, Doctor."

Bram led them into the crowded living room. The visitors fell silent, clearly startled by the arrival of the RCMP.

Harrison scanned the room, his gaze falling on Claire. "Mrs. Warren," he said as he approached her.

Dr. Ste Denis, Lauren corrected, silently.

"You are under arrest in connection with the death of your daughter, Ariel Elizabeth Warren."

Confusion spread throughout the room. Claire's mother gasped.

Was Claire being charged with neglect? Lauren wondered. It didn't make sense if the cause of death was SIDS.

Officer Harrison turned to Bram. "I'm afraid we're going to have to take her in."

"But—but," Bram sputtered, "Ariel died of SIDS."

"I'm afraid that's not true," Rebecca said, lowering her voice. "Your child died from abusive head trauma—shaken baby syndrome."

It's in the medical examiner's report."

Lauren felt a chill. Were they suggesting someone killed Ariel? Images too frightening to think about ran through her mind. *No*, she thought, *it must be a mistake*.

Anya stared at the officers, a stunned look on her face. She opened her mouth to say something, but stayed silent.

"Officer, I swear. My wife is innocent." Bram's voice was trembling, his words rushing out. "She would never harm our baby. She loves Ariel."

Claire stared at them, expressionless, still perched on her seat near the fireplace. A disapproving buzz seemed to vibrate throughout the room. Lauren looked around at the stricken faces. Claire's mother had her hand pressed to her mouth. Mitch was twirling an empty whiskey glass in his hand. Most people wore a stunned look of disbelief as the drama played out in front of them.

"Maybe it would be best if we had this conversation at the station," Rebecca said.

Claire's mother was on her feet, her eyes fierce. "How you can…accuse my daughter of such deed?"

"My wife wouldn't…" Bram began, his voice breaking.

Lauren watched as Rebecca pulled Claire's thin arms firmly behind her back.

"Is that necessary?" Bram asked.

"Police procedure," Officer Harrison said.

Claire's expression didn't change. Like a puppet being manipulated, she let Rebecca slip the handcuffs around her bony wrists.

"She'll need a lawyer," Lauren said, stepping forward. She looked at Bram, who gave a quick nod of confirmation. "I'll go with Claire to the station," she assured everyone. "I'll have her home as soon as it can be arranged."

CHAPTER

8

Bram placed a bowl of soup in front of Claire. "You should eat something, hon," he said. "You need your strength."

Claire pushed the bowl aside. "I want Ariel," she said, her eyes glistening with tears. "I want my baby."

Bram looked helplessly at Lauren, who was scrubbing pots and pans in the kitchen sink. In the five days since Ariel's death, she had been dropping by to help out. *What can I do?* Bram mouthed.

Lauren swallowed, not sure how to respond. Her heart went out to him. Claire seemed to be in a stupor, not really knowing what was going on. Today, though, she was fairly alert, certainly not in the comatose state she'd been in when they arrested her.

"I want to see Ariel, Bram," Claire insisted. "I want my baby."

Bram walked into the dining room. Lauren wiped her hands on a dishtowel and followed. "For God's sake, Lauren," he whispered, his eyes filled with anguish. "What the hell am I to do? Our baby's body hasn't even been released yet."

Lauren shook her head, feeling helpless.

"I've viewed the body," Bram continued. "Maybe Claire needs to see…I just don't know what it would do to her."

Lauren winced. "Maybe…Dr. Kaminsky might have a suggestion."

Nodding, Bram picked up a cordless phone and punched in the number. "Milly, it's Dr. Warren," he said. "Could you have Dr. Kaminsky call me when she checks in from the conference?… I'm at home."

Lauren glanced at Claire, who sat at the table, the bowl of soup untouched beside her. "Ariel," Claire murmured. "Where's Ariel?"

"I'll try to get her to lie down," Bram said.

Lauren nodded. "She could probably use a rest."

Taking Claire's hand, Bram pulled his wife to her feet as easily as if she were a child. He turned to Lauren. "If Dr. Kaminsky calls, could you take a message?"

Lauren went back to the sink, feeling a knot coil in her stomach. Although the police had released her after a few hours, Lauren knew Claire was still their number-one suspect. A team of investigators from the homicide division were collecting evidence against her. They had interviewed neighbours, colleagues, relatives, babysitters. Lauren was fully aware that when a child died under dubious circumstances, the parents were suspect, and in this case, all the evidence pointed to Claire. She had been alone with Ariel when she died—alone in a locked house. In fact, Walter Rodden, a neighbour who had a key, had let the paramedics in. Anya had arrived minutes later to find Claire in a desperate state; she was so incoherent she couldn't carry on a conversation. There was no indication of forced entry or that anyone else had come into the house that day. Claire would be under the umbrella of suspicion until they could prove otherwise. Lauren promised herself she would do everything she could to get Claire cleared. But it wasn't going to be easy.

The phone rang. Assuming it was Dr. Kaminsky, Lauren picked it up without checking the caller ID.

"*Baby killer,*" snarled a voice at the other end.

Lauren was so startled she dropped the phone. Bram had told her they'd been receiving nasty calls. Ariel's death had become headline news, both locally and nationally. Reporters had been calling and even showing up on their doorstep. She sometimes spotted them on the university campus. They sought out Claire's students and questioned them. Gossip and rumours were spreading. People who once supported Claire now doubted her innocence. There had been requests for Bram to appear on various news outlets, but he refused them all. Lauren picked up the phone and placed it in its cradle. What kind of people made calls like that?

She was wiping down the kitchen counter when the phone rang again. This time she checked the ID: *Paddy's Arm Medical Clinic.*

"Hello?"

"May I please speak to Bram Warren? This is Dr. Kaminsky returning his call."

"Bram can't come to the phone right now. This is Lauren." She explained the predicament they were in. "Claire's...insisting on viewing Ariel's remains. Bram is very concerned."

"I do not think that is even possible," Anya said. "In any case, it is not a good idea." Lauren could imagine Anya shaking her head, her long dark hair falling around her face. "I am just finishing up with my patients here. Please tell Bram I will drop by to check on Claire within the hour." She paused. "In the meantime, if she becomes agitated, he can give her one of the pills I prescribed."

Lauren replaced the receiver, jotted down Anya's message, and stuck it on the fridge. She had a client in half an hour and needed to get back to her office. She was putting on her coat when a loud knock came at the door. She glanced through the window, afraid it might be more reporters. Two police cruisers were sitting in the driveway.

—

Daniel Kerry was in his study when he learned of Claire's indictment on the evening news. "Professor Ste Denis is charged with aggravated assault in the death of her six-month-old daughter, Ariel," a reporter announced. "According to her lawyer, Ste Denis has already entered a plea of not guilty. A bail hearing is pending, and until that time she will be remanded to the correctional facility in Little Donegal."

Daniel sat up straighter in his chair. "Good heavens," he whispered, leaning forward. He hadn't seen Claire Ste Denis in years. She was a beautiful woman and a fine actress, but there had always been something hauntingly sad about her. Some years ago, Lauren had taken him to a production of *Romeo and Juliet* in which Claire played the lead role. He recalled Lauren telling him that Claire had graduated first in her class. At the time, she was dating a man twenty years older.

On screen, a sandy-haired man—Claire's husband, Daniel assumed—stood beside her on the courthouse steps. Claire looked dazed and disoriented as television cameras moved in like vultures.

"The child's body was discovered last Thursday afternoon by paramedics who had been called to the scene," the reporter continued in voice-over. "An autopsy revealed that the cause of death was abusive head trauma."

The image changed to a tight shot of Claire holding a dark-eyed infant. "Since her baby's birth, Claire Ste Denis has suffered from postpartum depression. It's not clear if her illness has in any way contributed to the child's death. Lauren LaVallee, lawyer for the defendant, says her client is innocent."

Daniel felt his heart stop. "Lauren," he whispered, leaning forward.

"Claire Ste Denis did not kill her baby," Lauren said with conviction. "She will enter a plea of not guilty to the charges. We will also be addressing the matter of bail at this time."

Daniel's heart doubled its beat. It was the first time he'd seen Lauren in nearly four years. She had not changed, he realized. The camera zoomed in on her as she spoke, and he watched her huge brown eyes light up her expressive face. She was still beautiful. Daniel reached for the remote and turned up the volume. Lauren must have moved to Newfoundland after they broke up. It made sense she had followed Claire there. Still as feisty as ever, he thought. She had let her chestnut hair grow long. He smiled now as she pushed strands away from her face.

Daniel leaned forward. He still loved her, he realized, fighting back the emotions that rose in him. Even after all this time apart, he missed her—missed waking up beside her.

A knock on his office door startled him out of his musings. His secretary poked her head into the dark panelled room. "Father Kerry, you have a call," she said. "Archbishop Delaney is holding on line two. He says it's important."

"I'll be right there, Hazel," Daniel said, but made no move to get up. He kept his eyes on the television.

"If convicted, Dr. Ste Denis could serve as much as twenty years without parole," the reporter continued.

"Unbelievable," Daniel muttered. Could Claire do something like this? He thought he'd heard just about everything in the confessional, but apparently he was still capable of being shocked.

CHAPTER

9

Claire stared at the unfamiliar ceiling, her mind hovering between dreaming and waking. The effects of the drugs were wearing off, the sharp edges of real life sinking in. She couldn't remember how many hours she'd been in this concrete cell, a space so small she wondered how it was possible to cram in the narrow cot, table, and toilet. The bright light shone overhead at all times. No sound came through the solid door with its small rectangle window. But none of this mattered to Claire: Ariel was dead. She had failed to protect her beautiful baby. She knew there was pain beneath her protective shell, but still she was unable to cry. She recalled the lockup at the police station, being photographed and fingerprinted, but she felt detached from her situation, an observer rather than a participant. It was as if she'd been cast as the lead in a badly written script.

Claire curled herself into the centre of the narrow bed and pulled her knees to her chest. Slowly the enormity of her loss was getting through to her. She would never see Ariel again. She would never see her baby take her first steps, never hear her first words. She would never see her start school. *I don't want to live without Ariel.* A ragged sob rose and caught in her throat, but her eyes remained dry. This was everything she imagined hell to be.

Bram had been allowed to see her briefly. "I'm sorry," she'd whispered, not knowing what she was sorry for. Sorry for being depressed? Sorry for letting someone come into their house and kill their child? Lauren had promised she would do everything in her power to keep her out of prison, but that wouldn't be enough. *It's up to me to find Ariel's* killer. *I will find out what happened,* Claire vowed, feeling a determination stronger than anything she'd ever felt before. *No more drugs. I need to keep a clear head.* She'd failed Ariel in life; she would not fail her in death. Finding her baby's killer would be her mission, her purpose.

—

"This way," the guard said as he led Lauren down a narrow grey corridor. As a defense lawyer, she was no stranger to the local jail. Still, she felt a tug of unease as the steel door clanged shut behind her. *What must it be like to wake up this place?* she wondered as she was led to a room at the far end of the corridor. "If you need anything," the guard told her, "I'll be just outside the door."

Claire, wearing orange prison garb, sat at a small metal table. Harsh fluorescent lights enhanced her pale face and the dark shadows around her eyes. "Thank you for coming, Lauren," she said.

Lauren took a seat across from her. "We need to get you out of here. The process is taking longer than I'd anticipated."

"I'm sure you're doing your best."

"I am, Claire, trust me." Lauren was pleased to see her friend so alert. "I've talked with the homicide police. Patrick Shaw says he rang your doorbell around noon. I'm sure they'll ask him to be more specific about the time."

"I went to bed shortly before noon," Claire said. "I didn't hear the doorbell." She frowned. "You say the police are questioning Patrick?"

"They are interested in the fact that you gave him a key at one time."

"That was months ago. Do they think he had a copy made?"

"I'm sure the police are considering that. In any case, Patrick was at your door that day. He may have noticed something unusual." Lauren reached for her notepad. "Is there anything at all that you remember?"

"Not much," Claire admitted. "I recall making a pan of squares for your visit. Afterwards, I felt tired and went to lie down. Ariel was already down for her nap." She shrugged. "I don't remember anything after that. I don't remember calling the clinic, or Anya coming to the house." Claire looked away. "Even after the police arrested me…it didn't seem real."

Lauren nodded, recalling how detached Claire had appeared that day. "The police haven't ruled out your neighbour, Walter Rodden, as a suspect."

"No, the Roddens are our friends. I gave them a key shortly after they moved here—more than a year ago now. Milly, Walter's wife, works at the clinic. Bram told me she was on duty when I called. Milly telephoned Walter in case the door was locked."

"Apparently, you wouldn't open the door," Lauren said. "Walter used the key you gave him to let the paramedics in."

Claire lowered her eyes. "I don't recall that."

"Walter says you were walking around the house clutching Ariel, calling out her name. The paramedics had to pry her from your arms."

Colour rose in Claire's cheeks. "I don't recall that either."

"You were so distraught Dr. Kaminsky had to sedate you," Lauren said.

Claire covered her face with her hands. "Dear God, I let someone murder my baby."

"It's not your fault," Lauren protested, her heart aching.

Claire shook her head. "I let Ariel down. The only thing I can do for her now is help bring her killer to justice. And I can only do that by staying alert. I'm not taking any more drugs. I need to be clear-headed."

Lauren stared at her. "How does Dr. Kaminsky feel about that decision?"

Claire shrugged. "Anya's away at the moment. Dr. Collins is taking her place."

Lauren wondered if stopping her medication was the best thing for Claire right now. Although she appeared to be more alert, she was obviously still fragile.

"Bram wants me to go with the insanity defense," Claire said. "Anya thinks I may have been suffering from postpartum psychosis."

Lauren nodded. She'd spoken briefly with Anya before she left for Ontario. "It would make a good defense, Claire, but you would have to give up your innocence."

"Never," Claire said fiercely. "If I plead guilty, they'll stop looking for Ariel's killer."

"It's entirely up to you. If you decide to fight this, I'm with you all the way."

"We *will* find Ariel's killer," Claire said with determination. "We have to. I keep imagining him coming into our house, picturing what he did to her." She covered her face with her hands. "We have to find out who did this."

"Yes, we will," Lauren agreed, sounding much more confident than she felt. "Claire, do you or Bram have enemies? Someone who might want get to you through your baby?"

Claire folded her arms. "Nobody could possibly hate us that much, Lauren."

"Did any of your students hold a grudge?"

"I've had disgruntled students," Claire admitted. "One even filed a formal complaint with the dean. That was more than a year ago. I believe the issue was resolved." She shook her head. "You think someone killed Ariel because of resentment they had toward me or Bram?"

"I'm trying to establish motive," Lauren said. "It's the lack of motive that's got me stumped. Were you expecting anyone else that day?"

Claire shook her head. "Just you and Bailey. I don't get many visitors."

Lauren briefly touched Claire's shoulder before rising to her feet. "I'll come back to see you in a couple of days," she promised. "Stay strong, Claire. Remember, we're all rooting for you. I promise I'll get you out of here." Claire remained silent as Lauren turned to leave. "I've left my contact information with administration," she said, turning back. "Have them call if you need me."

When she returned to the reception area, Lauren found Andrew Collins seated in a plastic chair, his black medical bag resting at his feet. He was staring at a small television suspended from the ceiling.

"Hi, Dr. Collins," Lauren said brightly as she approached him. She liked his quick smile, his gentle manner. He'd grown up in an outport not far from Paddy's Arm and had the most endearing accent.

He stood to take her hand. "I take it you're here visiting Claire. How is she?"

"Not too bad," Lauren said. "Still numb from shock."

"Shock is a wonderful survival mechanism," Andrew said. "It can distance the mind from the most horrific trauma."

"Dr. Collins?" A female guard clutching a clipboard approached Andrew and handed him a form. "You'll need to fill this out before you can treat the prisoner."

"Thanks." Andrew turned to Lauren. "Do you have to go straight home?"

"I have a meeting with a client, but not until one."

"I should be finished here in about half an hour. Can we meet for coffee? There's a café just off the highway. Bella's."

"I could use a cup of coffee," Lauren said. "But first I should get my car looked at. There's a rattle on the passenger side, probably the tire."

"Billard's Garage is just down the road."

"I'll meet you at the café in half an hour then."

"Good. I'll see you then." Andrew picked up his bag and followed the guard.

Lauren watched as he disappeared down the corridor. She didn't know Andrew well, but he struck her as a pleasant, thoughtful man. She found herself looking forward to having coffee with him.

—

Bella's was a quaint café with round glass tables and ice-cream-parlour chairs. The waitresses wore pink smocks under white bib aprons. When Andrew arrived, Lauren was already seated at a table studying a menu printed on a plastic placemat. "They have eighteen flavours of coffee," she informed him.

"Sounds good." Andrew pulled out a chair. "Get your car looked at?"

"It was the tire. The mechanic patched it up but said I should get it replaced."

A waitress came to take their order. "Just coffee, black, with cream on the side," Lauren said.

Andrew smiled at her. "Make mine decaf with double cream."

"How is your son?" Lauren asked. "I see him all the time at Kiddy Academy."

"Riley's a great little guy," Andrew said, proudly. "His mother and I are going through a difficult divorce right now, but he's adjusting."

"Divorce is never easy," Lauren sympathized.

Andrew traced the scalloped edges of the placemat with his finger. "I have Riley this week while his mother is at a medical conference."

"Is it the conference in Ontario that Dr. Kaminsky is attending?"

Andrew nodded. "Sylvia's giving the keynote."

Andrew's wife—soon to be ex-wife—was an obstetrician. Lauren had been referred to her during complications in her own pregnancy. She found her to be efficient, if aloof. There were rumours in town that she was making Andrew's life a living hell. Lauren recalled Claire telling her that Sylvia once came into the clinic yelling and screaming at him in front of a room full of patients.

"I'm fighting for full custody," Andrew said. "I feel like I'm walking a thin line. I don't want to make things more traumatic for Riley."

The waitress brought their coffee, and they talked easily. Andrew was one of nine children. After the fishing industry collapsed, most of his brothers and sisters had left home to find work. "I got a call the other day from my oldest brother, Glenn. He lives in Grande Prairie," he told her. "He says in twelve years he can retire." Andrew chuckled. "He made it sound like he's serving a sentence."

Lauren smiled. "One thing I've learned about Newfoundlanders is that they don't like to stray far from home."

"That about sums it up." His smile faded quickly and he switched to a more serious tone. "Listen," he said, "Bram called this morning. He says you gave Claire the option of going with the insanity defense."

"As her lawyer I have to put all options on the table."

"Anya thinks Claire might have been in a psychotic state at the time." Andrew spoke carefully, as if weighing his words. "I sensed Bram would like me to write a report favouring this." He shook his head. "I can't speak to what Claire's state of mind was at the time of her baby's death, but this morning she seemed coherent enough."

Lauren sighed. "I understand Bram's concern. He wants to keep Claire out of prison. But she'll never go along with it."

"I can't imagine her confessing to a crime she didn't commit."

Lauren met Andrew's gaze. "Claire's decided to go off her medication."

"She told me," Andrew said. "I warned her about going cold turkey." He shrugged. "It's her decision. I left a prescription with the prison doctor in case she needs them."

Lauren shuddered. "I'd need more than sleeping pills if I was in that place."

"My heart goes out to Claire," Andrew said sadly.

Lauren leaned toward him. "Andrew, the whole thing is so bizarre."

"I've been hearing all kinds of rumours." Andrew folded his paper napkin into tiny squares. "In fact, some of Dr. Warren's patients have come to me with questions. There's a rumour the baby was killed for the insurance money."

"Where do they *hear* such things? There was a small life insurance policy attached to a scholarship fund. The premiums will barely cover funeral expenses."

Andrew spread his hands in a helpless gesture. "I know."

Lauren added a dollop of cream to her coffee and stirred absently.

"What is it?" Andrew asked, picking up on her unease.

Lauren took a long sip of coffee and weighed her words. "I'm wondering if I'm doing everything right."

"What do you mean?"

"I keep second-guessing myself." Lauren frowned. "I mean, this issue with bail. Claire's been in a cell for almost two days now. I should have been able to convince the judge that she is not a danger to the community. She has no prior arrests or convictions."

Andrew leaned toward her. "I've heard all kinds of stories about Judge Dillard. They say he doesn't grant bail easily. Look at Rose Carson," he said, citing a well-known case. "She stayed in remand until her trial, and was found not guilty."

"I remember that case," Lauren said. Twenty-eight-year-old Carson was charged with abusing her infant son. During her trial, her lawyer called in medical experts who diagnosed the child as having brittle bones. Sighing, Lauren shook her head. "I'm starting to feel really frustrated. It's my job to see that Claire is with her family while she awaits trial."

"If you fight hard enough, the judge may come through," Andrew assured her. He studied her for a long moment. "Lauren, is there something else troubling you?"

She shrugged. "What do you mean?"

"It's not just bail that's bothering you, I can tell."

Lauren wondered how Andrew could sense her uncertainty. She looked him in the eye, and for the first time confessed her biggest fear. "I'm not sure I can help Claire," she admitted. Absently, she ran a finger around the rim of her coffee mug. "Unless I can find someone with a motive, Claire may go to prison for a very long time."

CHAPTER

10

Emma's daughter, Dylan, was standing in the window when Lauren pulled her car into Mae Buckle's driveway. Bailey waved excitedly and Dylan waved back. A moment later, Dylan disappeared from the window and came to stand in the doorway.

Lauren patted her daughter's knee. "Now, you be good for Mae and don't give her any trouble. It's kind of her to let you stay at her house while Momma is working."

"Where are you going, Momma?"

"Dylan's mom and I have to go talk to some people."

Lauren got out of the car and helped Bailey out of her car seat.

Mae had come to stand in the doorway behind Dylan. "There's our darling now," she said. "Dylan's been waiting for you, Bailey." She turned to Lauren. "Come on in, my love."

Lauren followed Mae into the kitchen. Dylan grabbed Bailey's arm, and they ran toward the living room.

Both Mae and Lauren smiled as they watched the girls.

"Thanks for offering to watch Bailey, Mae."

"No problem a'tall, my love. Sure, I'm only too glad to do it. And Dylan enjoys Bailey's company." Mae pulled a chair from around the kitchen table. "Emma told me you're going to canvass Claire's neighbourhood this afternoon."

"The police have already gone through the area conducting interviews," Lauren said. "Still, we're hoping someone might have seen something out of the ordinary that day."

"Sure, you never knows," Mae said.

Lauren nodded. "Emma told me you took a job at the Bay Wop Inn. How do you like working there?"

"Oh, my dear, I loves it. 'Tis only part-time, mind you. But it's the first job I had since I was a young girl working at Dunne's Boarding House."

Lauren smiled. "I'm glad it's working out."

"The money comes in handy too," Mae continued. "Jim had to give up fishing because of his back." She shook her head. "Not that there's much fish on the go."

"Nan," Dylan called. "Where did you put my new CD?"

"Excuse me, Lauren, my dear," Mae said. "Emma's in the basement looking for old photo albums. She'll be with you shortly."

After Mae disappeared into the living room, Lauren looked around the spacious kitchen. She loved these old outport kitchens, where family and friends gathered. There was an old-fashioned wood range and beside it, a large wood box. The walls were covered with photographs of Mae's children and grandchildren. Emma had eight brothers and sisters. Some lived in the area but, like Andrew's family, most of them had moved away after the fishing industry collapsed.

Jim and Mae were hardworking and unpretentious, Lauren thought as she studied the photographs. She knew the family well enough to know that they didn't engage in the games or power struggles her own family had always been so preoccupied with. Lauren saw none of the veiled hostility she had lived with most of her life. How ironic that her father gave relationship advice, yet had no idea how to create harmony in his own family. Despite his fancy degrees, Siggy, as they called him, didn't have Mae's wisdom or know-how. She felt a pang now recalling her mother's resentment and seething anger. Lauren had come to realize how much control her father had had over all of them. How much he'd damaged their lives. What she resented most was Siggy's attitude when she'd called to announce she was pregnant. He'd shown no emotion at the news of his first grandchild. The first words out of this mouth were, "Do you know who the father is?" When Lauren got off the phone, she had been in tears. She didn't dare tell her father about her law license being suspended.

"Lauren?"

Emma's voice startled Lauren back to the present.

"I didn't hear your car drive up," Emma said. "I hope I didn't keep you waiting."

"I just arrived, actually."

"Well," Emma said, "we should get a move on."

"Whenever you're ready."

They walked to the car in silence. Lauren caught sight of Bailey and Dylan in the window and waved. Once in the car, Emma turned to Lauren. "I heard you and Andrew had coffee at Bella's a couple of days ago"

"Really? Can't *anyone* do *anything* in this town without everyone knowing about it? We met for coffee. End of story."

"Ah…now that's not what I heard," Emma teased.

Lauren started the engine. "What exactly did *you* hear?"

"That you and Andrew were all cozy like you were on a date."

Lauren laughed. "That's stretching it."

Emma looked critical. "But seriously, don't you think Andrew's nice?"

"Of course."

"But not nice enough to date?"

"You're matchmaking again," Lauren chided as she backed the car out of the driveway. "Andrew's going through a messy divorce. He has a child and, from what I hear, a very disgruntled wife. This is no time for us to get involved."

"You need to focus on guys who are available," Emma said.

"I don't need *any* complicated relationships right now."

"Who says it has to be complicated?" Emma chuckled. "Not that I should be the one giving relationship advice."

Lauren shook her head, recalling Emma's last two disastrous relationships. A couple of years ago she'd dated a financial advisor who had cheated his clients and was now facing fraud charges. He had even tried to swindle Emma. After that, she'd had a brief relationship with Levi Stratton, an artist ten years younger than her; he ended up leaving her for an older woman, a divorcee with a sixteen-year-old daughter.

"Do you know who Levi's dating now?" Emma asked as if reading Lauren's thoughts.

"I didn't realize he was still around."

"I ran into him at one of our student productions. He's dating Hilda Wilson, Dr. Wilson's *widow*."

"Go on!" Lauren said. "Hilda must be at least sixty."

Emma laughed. "And here I was worried he would leave me for a younger woman."

Lauren turned the car onto Sumac Lane and stopped in front of a Tudor-style home down the road from Claire and Bram's. "Maybe we could start here."

As they got out of the car, Lauren was struck by how secluded Bram and Claire's house was. Only a few neighbours had a full view of it.

They walked down a long driveway and rang the doorbell. "I'm Lauren LaVallee from the law firm of Beck Hayes," Lauren told the grim-faced man who opened the door. "And this is Emma Buckle. I'm representing Claire Ste Denis, and we're investigating her daughter's death. Did you see anything out of the ordinary that—"

"We already told the police we were grocery shopping," the man said curtly.

"Just checking," Lauren said. "If you think of anything—" She was about to hand him her card when he closed the door.

"People from away," Emma said, shaking her head.

"Hey, I'm from away," Lauren said, laughing. She had to admit, though, that Newfoundlanders were a different breed entirely.

They made their way from one end of the street to the other. None of the people they talked with had witnessed anything unusual.

"Milly Rodden lives here," Lauren said, stopping in front of a two-storey brick house across the street from Bram and Claire's. "Her husband, Walter, is a retired engineer who teaches part-time at St. Bridget's."

"I've met them briefly," Emma said, "at a Christmas party not long after they moved here from St. John's."

"They're good friends with Bram and Claire. In fact, it was Walter who let the paramedics into the house the day Ariel died," Lauren explained. "And Milly was working at the clinic when Claire called." Lauren pressed the doorbell. "Hopefully, they can help shed some light on the situation."

Milly greeted them like long-lost relatives. "Come in. Come in," she said. "Good to see you." She was a short, small-boned woman with white hair. "Ah, don't bother with your shoes," she told Lauren. "I'll wash the floor later. Give me something to do, sure." She led them into a gleaming kitchen where a large window looked out on the street. An array of copper pots and pans were arranged on the wall. Canisters shaped like cows stood on the counter. "Let me put the kettle on," she said, turning on a burner.

"Oh, don't go to any bother," Emma protested. "We just finished lunch, sure."

"No bother, my love. With Walter gone, I got all kinds of free time."

"Walter's away?" Lauren couldn't hide her disappointment. "I was hoping to speak with him."

"He went duck hunting with Cal Parsons." Milly dropped two teabags into a rooster-shaped teapot and gestured to a breakfast nook by the window. "Have a seat."

They made small talk while the tea steeped, Milly filling them in on all the latest gossip.

"So you were at the clinic the day Claire called," Lauren said after Milly had poured the tea and had a chance to sit down.

"Yes, m'dear. I took the call. Claire was that upset I couldn't make out what she was saying. I handed the phone to Dr. Kaminsky, who'd just come on duty."

Lauren took a sip of tea. She'd read in the police report that the call came in around three. Anya had left the clinic shortly afterwards.

"Dr. Kaminsky barely had a chance to take her coat off before she was out the door again." Milly said. "Never seen a doctor so dedicated."

"It must have been upsetting for you, Claire being a close neighbour and all."

"I couldn't concentrate on my work," Milly admitted. "I kept making mistakes. We have a key to Dr. Warren's house, and I didn't know if the door was open or not."

"You called Walter," Lauren said.

"Well, m'dear, I tried to call him. I wanted to let him know the ambulance was coming. Walter was on the phone for the best part of an hour. Tilley Sampson called to tell him her granddaughter had a baby.

Seven pounds, fourteen ounces. Tilley belongs to our seniors' club. She's right excited about being a great-grandmother." Milly shook her head. "That Tilley. Talk the leg off an iron pot, that one. Sure, she—"

"But you did get Walter eventually," Lauren cut in. "He was at the house when the paramedics arrived."

Milly nodded. "Soon as he saw the ambulance pull into Bram's driveway, Walter got off the phone and went across the road to see what was going on. Good thing too, because the place was locked. When Claire didn't answer the door, Walter let the emergency team in."

"Did Walter see Patrick Shaw arrive earlier that day?" Lauren asked.

"No, he was in his study out back." Milly looked across the table at Lauren and Emma. "Never seen that woman arrive either."

"Woman? You mean Dr. Kaminsky?"

"Oh no, my dear. The woman who came to the door *before* the doctor."

Emma and Lauren exchanged puzzled glances.

"Guess you haven't heard, then. Flo Spencer"—Milly gestured toward the window—"lives up on Mountain Road in back of Dr. Warren. She claims a woman came to the door not long after Patrick left."

"I hadn't heard that," Lauren said.

"Flo and Herb left early the next morning for their cottage out near Bull Moose Pond," Milly continued. "Of course, they didn't know about the youngster's death then. Didn't learn about that 'til after they got home." Milly took a sip of tea and put down her cup. "Soon as they found out about little Ariel, they contacted the RCMP."

Emma stared at Milly. "Who was she…the woman who came to the door?"

"Nobody knows. Flo says she'd never seen her before and that she was…well…kind of strange. But maybe you should talk to Flo about that."

"Yes," Lauren agreed, "we'll go see Mrs. Spencer after we leave here." She met Milly's gaze. "How's Walter?"

Milly shook her head. "Oh, my dear. Right shook up, he was. Says he can't get the memory of the paramedics forcing the dead baby from Claire's arms out of his mind…. It still haunts him."

"I can only imagine," Lauren sympathized. She glanced at Emma. "We should be going," she said.

"Already? You got lots of time, sure," said Milly.

Emma pulled her chair away from the table. "We really need to get going, but thank you for the tea, Mrs. Rodden. You've been very helpful."

Lauren handed Milly her card. "If you think of anything else, please call."

Nodding, Milly walked them to the door. "Good luck with the investigation," she said. "And come back anytime. You don't need a reason to visit, sure."

—

The Spencers' Cape Cod looked as if it had been pressed into the side of the hill. The upper half of the house was above ground, while part of the lower half was embedded in the earth. Smoke rose from a brick chimney and the air was fragrant with burning wood. Taking a moment to look down the hill, Lauren realized the Spencers had an unobstructed view of Claire and Bram's house. From where she stood, she could see both the front and side doors.

Flo was a tall, serious-looking woman, not as friendly as Milly Rodden, but she invited them inside and politely answered their questions. She was a public relations consultant who ran a business from her home, she told them. She had been designing a logo the day Ariel died, and spent most of the day in her office.

"Did you see anyone else arrive at the Warren-Ste Denis house that day?"

"Well, like I told the Mounties, young Shaw came to the door around lunchtime."

"What time, exactly?"

"Must've been about ten past twelve."

"And what time did he leave?"

Flo shook her head. "That I can't tell you. It was a busy day for me. I happened to go out on the patio at twelve—it must've been around twelve-thirty when I saw a grey car pull into Claire's driveway. A woman got out and knocked at the door."

"Can you describe her?" Lauren asked.

"She's not someone I'm likely to forget," Flo said. "She was nearly six feet with platinum blond hair. She was wearing a red coat with white fur on the collar."

Lauren wracked her brain.

"When no one answered the door," Flo continued, "the woman went around back to the patio doors and peeked in. I thought it was kind of strange."

"And you have no idea who she is?"

"Never saw her before in my life," Flo said. "I don't think she was from around here."

"I don't know anyone around here who fits that description," Emma said.

"How long did she stay?" Lauren asked.

Flo shook her head. "I really don't know. I came back inside. I was busy getting ready for my trip, and I still had a lot of work to do."

"Did you notice the kind of car the woman drove?"

"It was grey. That's all I know. I don't know anything about makes and models."

"Thank you for all your help, Mrs. Spencer." Lauren handed Flo her card. "If you remember anything else, please call."

"Of course," she said, seeing them to the door.

"Well, what do you think of that?" Emma asked as they walked to the car.

Lauren shrugged. Although they'd come away with more information than she'd hoped to gain, there were still more questions than answers. "I know one thing," she said, opening the car door, "we need to find this mysterious platinum lady."

CHAPTER

11

What are you doing? Daniel chided himself. *Why are you driving so far out of your way to see a woman who walked out of your life four years ago?* He was on his way to New Wexford, Newfoundland, to help a friend celebrate his twenty-year ordination. From the time he rented a car at the airport in St. John's, he'd debated whether or not to stop at Paddy's Arm. *No harm in stopping to see an old friend,* he reasoned. Ever since he'd seen Lauren on the news three weeks before, he couldn't get her out of his mind. He kept seeing her wide, expressive brown eyes. He recalled the confident way she spoke into the microphone. At night, alone in his bed, he thought of her, missed her warm body beside him. *You're a selfish bastard,* he berated himself. *You know you can never give up the church.* Why then was he running to her now, when common sense told him to get back on the highway to New Wexford?

Distracted, Daniel almost drove past the Bay Wop Inn, a two-storey building set back from the main road. After a quick online search it had seemed the perfect spot, and he'd called immediately to book a room. He drove into the lot, parked his car, and got his duffel bag from the trunk.

"You must be Daniel Kerry," said the pleasant, heavyset woman who met him at the door. She had greying hair and spoke with a strong accent. "I'm Mae Buckle."

"Pleased to meet you," Daniel said, offering his hand.

"Come with me," Mae said. "I'll show yeh where yer room is to." She led him up a mahogany staircase. "The Bay Wop is listed as one of the finest inns in Newfoundland. Sure, we even gets movie stars staying here. A bunch of 'em came last summer to shoot a film over in Butler's Cove."

"Impressive," said Daniel. "May I ask, though, why it's called the Bay Wop?"

Mae chuckled. "My son, everyone who comes here asks that question. All I knows is that a bay wop is someone from the outports and bays. Sets us apart from the townies in St. John's, I s'pose."

"Interesting," Daniel said. On his way to the inn he'd stopped at a diner that offered a cheeseburger called the Bay Wopper.

"I knows some people who was born in the city but won't admit to being townies," Mae continued. "Sure, even Joey Smallwood would never own up to being one. He was born in Gambo, but I don't think he ever lived in an outport." She laughed. "One year, during a drive for heart disease, Joey walked nearly thirty miles just to 'show them townies what an outport boy could do.'"

"Really?" Daniel asked, amused.

They walked down a carpeted hallway past numbered doors. At the end of the hall, Mae opened the door to a bright room painted a sunny yellow. The four-poster brass bed had a bedspread that matched the curtains and lampshades. "We calls this the Harbour Room," she said, drawing open the curtains.

Daniel put his bag on the floor and looked out the window. "Magnificent," he said, taking in the unobstructed view of the harbour.

"My son, everyone who comes here just loves it," Mae said.

"I've never seen anything quite like it." Daniel stood for a few moments, taking in the long wharves that stretched over the water. A mountainous iceberg gleamed in the distance. There were fish stages piled high with lobster traps.

Mae switched on a light. "In here's the bathroom." The white-tiled floor was spotless. She pulled open a door to a large closet. "Towels, facecloths, and blankets is all in here. Breakfast is from seven 'til eleven, but if you like, I can have tea and scones ready in a few minutes."

"Sounds wonderful," Daniel said. "I'll come eat after I shower."

"What do you do?" Mae asked.

The unexpected question caught Daniel off guard. Usually, he would say he was a salesman or an engineer. But he couldn't seem to lie to this woman.

"I'm a Catholic priest," he told her. "I'm on my way to New Wexford to a friend's ordination anniversary."

Mae stared at him. "I never would've took you for a priest, my son."

Daniel looked down at his faded jeans and scuffed running shoes. He suddenly saw himself as Mae must see him: scruffy, dirty, and badly in need of a shave. He wore a T-shirt that said *Life is too short to drink bad wine*. His blond hair came down to his shoulders. Father Pierre and Father Luc were always telling him he needed a haircut. Daniel knew he was popular among his young parishioners. The older people in the parish didn't seem to mind either—at least the ladies. They brought him enough cakes and cookies to open a bakery.

"Why did you stop here?" Mae asked. "'Tis a bit out of the way."

"I dropped by to see a friend," Daniel said, "Lauren LaVallee."

"I knows Lauren well. She teaches at the college with my daughter, Emma."

"I didn't know Lauren taught," said Daniel. He immediately regretted telling her so much.

"Teaches law, my dear. Since they enlarged the college, we gets people coming from everywheres. Met a young girl the other day from Boston of all places. Come here to take acting lessons, she told me."

"How long has Lauren been teaching?"

"A few years now. But 'tis only part-time. She works at a law firm here in town." Mae gave him a curious look. "How do yeh know Lauren?"

"I met her in Montreal—at a fundraiser for a children's hospital."

Mae eyed him critically. "Must be a really good friend if you went this far out of your way to see her."

"Yes," Daniel said. "I haven't seen her in a long time, but we were good friends."

"Lauren's been in the news a lot lately," Mae said.

"The Warren case," Daniel said, grimly.

"Oh, my son, I gets right heartsick every time I thinks about it. That poor innocent baby."

"Is her mother still detained?"

"Yes, my dear, but Claire's innocent. She would never harm her youngster. I'm willing to bet everything I owns on that." She turned to face Daniel. "I prays every night that Lauren will get her off."

"Lauren's a great lawyer," Daniel said. He recalled when she had worked as a public defender. She would fret and worry about her clients, making sure they got the best defense. Sometimes when she was working on a case he would hardly see her. "I'm sure she'll do everything she can."

That's what Emma keeps telling me. " Mae smiled at Daniel. "Well, Father, I hope you enjoys your visit in Newfoundland. Do yeh plan to stay long?"

"A week." A cloud of sadness passed over Daniel's face. "Phil... um Father Noland, the priest who is celebrating his ordination, won't be with us long, unfortunately. He has stage-four cancer and the doctors gave him about six months. I want to spend some time with him before he passes."

"Oh, the poor soul," Mae said. "God bless him. Are you close?" Daniel nodded, thinking of how Phillip counselled him during his first couple of years in the priesthood. "We worked together at St. Theresa's Parish in Ottawa a number of years ago."

"I'm sorry, Father." Mae shook her head. "What a terrible disease that is. It takes so many of our friends."

"Stephen Coleman is on the line," Paula, the receptionist, told Lauren.

"*Coleman*? Isn't he that reporter with the *Daily News*?"

"It's The Hawk all right," Paula confirmed. It was a nickname Coleman had earned because of his ruthlessness and determination to get a story. Since Ariel's death, Lauren was used to reporters calling her at home and the office, but this was the first time she'd heard from Coleman. "Put him through, Paula," she said.

"How are you, Ms. LaVallee?" he asked when he came on the line.

"How can I help you, Mr. Coleman?" Lauren replied curtly.

"Well, actually...I need you to confirm a story. It's been brought to my attention that your friend and client Claire Ste Denis was adopted."

How is that a story? Lauren wondered, but she waited for him to continue.

"Not only did we learn that Claire was adopted, but that she'd been physically abused and neglected in her formative years."

Lauren drew in her breath. How had Coleman managed to dig that up? It wasn't something many people knew about. Claire was a very private person.

"My sources tell me she was adopted at age three," Coleman continued, "taken away from abusive parents."

Lauren didn't know how to reply.

"Are you still there, Ms. LaVallee?"

"What is your point, Mr. Coleman?" Lauren asked, although it was clear where he was going with this. If her mother was abusive, there was a chance Claire might also be abusive.

"Claire was suffering from a mental illness," Coleman went on. "I learned from students and faculty at St. Bridget's that she neglected her child."

"Claire suffered from postpartum depression. She has *never* neglected Ariel. She was a good mother. She would never have done anything to harm her child or put her in danger," Lauren knew she should stop talking, but she was enraged.

"Is it also true that she was drugged out of her mind the day her baby died?"

"I have nothing more to say, Mr. Coleman."

Lauren hung up the phone with shaking hands. This was all poor Claire needed. She looked at her watch. Bram would be here any minute now for an appointment. She would have to tell him what Coleman was up to.

—

Daniel's heart was racing as he approached an old Victorian house that had been converted into law offices. *Lauren is somewhere in this building,* he told himself. The receptionist sitting at a mahogany desk paid no attention when he walked in. *Paula* was engraved on a wooden plaque in front of her. The only other person in the waiting room was a man flipping idly through a magazine.

Daniel took a seat in a roomy chair and surveyed his surroundings. *Not bad*, he thought. The office was tastefully furnished with sofas and chairs in beige and gold. Tiffany-style lamps cast warm pools of light on polished tables. Reproductions and original paintings were scattered artfully on the soft grey walls. A stack of well-thumbed copies of *Law Yearly* and *Art Review* were stacked neatly on a glass table.

He glanced at the man across from him. He looked familiar, Daniel thought, taking in the man's sandy hair and square jaw. He was wearing a tailored suit, and an expensive leather briefcase lay at this feet.

Daniel thought again about the evening he and Lauren met at the children's hospital. She had read stories and played with the young patients for over an hour. Later, the two of them had gone to a café and talked for ages. Even now, he could recall their conversation almost verbatim. Both their fathers were psychologists, both control freaks. Lauren's father, who the family mockingly called Siggy, drove the family crazy with his psychobabble. "He puts the *fun* in dysfunctional," Lauren used to joke. Daniel's own father was a mean son of a bitch who'd become even meaner after he joined some fundamentalist religious outfit.

The phone rang. "Ms. LaVallee is ready to see you, Dr. Warren," the receptionist said.

Dr. *Bram* Warren, Daniel realized as the man picked up his briefcase and started down the hallway. That's why he looked familiar: Daniel had seen him on the news; he was Claire Ste Denis's husband.

The receptionist glanced at her calendar before turning her attention to Daniel. "Do you have an appointment, sir?"

Daniel got up from his seat. "I'm a friend of Lauren's, but I can see she's busy at the moment."

"She should be finished in—" Paula checked her watch "— about forty minutes. She usually picks Bailey up from preschool around that time."

"Bailey?"

"Lauren's daughter?"

Daughter. Daniel felt his mouth gape open. For a moment, he was too surprised to speak. "Ah, yes," he said, composing himself. "Bailey must be growing."

"She'll be four in August." Paula chuckled. "Keeps Lauren busy, that girl."

"I'm sure," Daniel said, surprised at how steady his voice was. "But then, I suppose Bailey's father is a big help."

Paula glanced up at him, her smile fading. "Who did you say you were?"

"I'm a friend...I haven't seen Lauren in years...I...."

The phone rang again and Paula picked it up.

Daniel turned to leave.

Paula placed her hand over the mouthpiece. "Can I give Lauren a message?" she called after Daniel, but he was already out the door.

Daniel walked to his car, stunned by what he'd learned. Lauren had found someone else. Well, what did he expect? She wasn't going to wait around for him. *But a child?* He felt a twinge of jealously. *She has a right to happiness*, he rebuked himself. Still, the sense of loss was hard to ignore.

Across the street was a brick building with a mural of a fisherman in a dory painted on its side. A sign in front said *Newfie B'ys Café*. He could use a cup of coffee, he decided.

Daniel took his coffee to a small table that looked out onto the street. For a long time he stared at the passing traffic. It hadn't taken Lauren long to get over their affair, he mused. Hadn't taken her long to crawl into someone else's bed. *Stop it*, he told himself. *You're being unreasonable*. Why shouldn't Lauren move forward with her life? She deserved to be happy and God knows he'd had little to offer her. Still, memories stirred. He recalled the trip they took to Europe. The quaint bed and breakfast in Ireland, where they'd registered as Mr. and Mrs. Kerry. The owner, a Mrs. Ryan, was a devout Catholic with seven grown children. She thought Lauren was too thin and loaded her plate with sausage, pancakes, and eggs each morning. She encouraged them to return, saying the next time they came to Ireland, she hoped they would have one or two little Kerrys in tow.

Daniel tried to imagine Lauren with a child. She would make a good mother, he knew. He recalled the time she'd taken care of her cousin's three young children while their mother was in the hospital. She kept them busy every minute, reading stories, baking cookies, and arranging treasure hunts. Daniel would leave the apartment exhausted, but Lauren, it seemed, never ran out of energy. He smiled at the memory. Now Lauren had a child of her own.

He'd go back to the inn, Daniel decided, collect his bag, and get back on the road. Lauren had a new life, a life that didn't include him. The realization pained him. Her child would be four in August, Paula said. She must have been conceived shortly after Lauren left him. He recalled the note he'd found after he got back from the special mass on St. Patrick's Day. As if a switch had been turned on in his brain, another thought occurred to Daniel.

"No," he said aloud, causing heads to turn at nearby tables. Lauren would have told him, surely. He counted years and months. He counted and re-counted. If his calculations were right, Lauren would have been three or four months pregnant when she left him.

For a long time, Daniel sat at the table, pulse racing. Stupefied, he walked to the counter and smiled. "Hi there, I'm looking for my niece's preschool—I know it's somewhere near here, but I can't remember the name," he said to the waitress.

"The only one I know of is Kiddy Academy."

"Yes, that's the one. Where is it located, again?"

"Actually, it's not far from here. Keep on Main until you come to Birch Street," she instructed. "Turn left on Birch. It's the second building on your left. Can't miss it."

CHAPTER

12

"What's on your mind, Bram?" Lauren asked. She could tell he was nervous from the way he kept wringing his hands.

"I feel we should reconsider the insanity defense."

Lauren leaned back in her chair, stifling a sigh. They'd been through this before. "It would make a good defense," she acknowledged. "Dr. Kaminsky says it's not uncommon for women suffering from postpartum depression to experience paranoia, delusions, even lose touch with reality. But Claire will never give up her innocence. She's determined to find Ariel's killer."

"I have no doubt my wife is innocent. But I don't want her going to jail." Bram absently ran his fingers through his hair. "I keep imagining the case from the perspective of a jury and it doesn't look good."

"The deck is stacked against her," Lauren admitted. "Claire was alone in a locked house with Ariel when she died. There's still no evidence linking anyone else to the crime. Even if we go with the insanity defense, there's no guarantee Claire won't get jail time."

Bram closed his eyes momentarily.

"Let's deal with this one thing at a time," Lauren said. "Right now, our main objective is getting Claire out of jail so she can attend Ariel's memorial service."

Bram nodded. "It's scheduled for next week, depending on whether Claire makes bail. Her parents feel it's important that she attend."

"Of course," Lauren said. She knew Claire's parents had already viewed the body before cremation took place.

"Did Claire tell you she went off her medication?"

"She seems to be doing well enough without it," Lauren said. "Dr. Collins doesn't seem concerned."

"She's very fragile."

"Claire's stronger than we realize. I'm amazed at how she's handling the situation."

"She's been through a lot," Bram agreed.

Lauren took a deep breath. "Bram," she said, "Stephen Coleman from the *Daily News* called this afternoon. He found out about Claire's adoption and the issues with her birth mother."

"How the hell did he find that out?"

Lauren shrugged. "I have no idea. But it's obvious he intends to connect Claire's past with Ariel's death."

Bram frowned. "I can't believe he's still writing for them! I've read some of the stories Coleman wrote for that rag he works for. He needs to be held accountable for what happened to that Baptist pastor over in Shelagh's Arm!"

"The Hawk can be ruthless," Lauren agreed. He'd made a career out of ruining marriages, businesses, careers, and families. Some months earlier, Coleman had written a story about a married pastor who was having an affair with a male member of his church. The pastor was so disturbed when the story broke that he committed suicide.

"He needs to be stopped," Bram said.

"I know how you feel," Lauren said, "but we have no control over sharks like Coleman."

Bram rose from his chair. A look of disgust came over his face. "I'm sick and tired of the press hounding us," he said. "They're harassing Claire's friends, her colleagues, her students. They've even approached my patients." He let out an exasperated breath. "I need them to go away." He grabbed his briefcase, knowing their time was up.

"I know how hard it is," Lauren said as she saw Bram to the door. "But that's what they do." She laid a reassuring hand on his arm. "You take care, Bram. I'll be in touch."

Lauren closed the door, feeling a sense of guilt. Would Claire be better off with another lawyer? It was true that Judge Dillard didn't easily grant bail. And this wasn't the first time a low-risk defendant had lingered in jail waiting for trial. Still, Lauren wondered if she had done everything possible for Claire. She'd been lingering in that cell for two weeks when she should have been home. There was another bail hearing in a couple of days. She had to get Claire home with her family.

The receptionist was putting on her coat when Lauren came into the waiting room. "I'll see you in the morning, Paula," she said.

"A man came by while you were in your meeting with Dr. Warren," Paula said. "He said he was a friend."

"A friend? Did you get his name?"

"No, I'm afraid I didn't."

"Did he say what it was about?"

Paula shook her head. "He didn't leave a message."

Just as well, Lauren thought. It had been a long day. She didn't like friends, clients, or even potential clients showing up unannounced. Bailey grew uneasy if she wasn't picked up on time, and Lauren was already running late.

—

Daniel had no trouble finding Kiddy Academy, a low brick building enclosed by a chain-link fence. He parked his car in the lot and got out. Children ran around the yard with balls and skipping ropes. Some rode tricycles and scooters. Daniel found the main door and went inside. Low shelves overflowing with puzzles, games, and books took up one side of the room. Paintings and crayoned drawings decorated the walls, each labelled with a child's name. A long window ran along one wall out of which he could see a sandbox, small tables, and chairs.

A teacher was putting away books and toys. "I'm a friend of Lauren LaVallee," Daniel told her. "She'll be here soon to pick up Bailey. Is it okay if I wait for her?"

"Follow me." The teacher led Daniel to a narrow room off the classroom. "You can wait in here," she said. The room had a sofa and a couple of armchairs. Daniel realized the window was actually a one-way mirror. "Good view," he commented.

"We had this installed a few months ago," the teacher explained. "Parents can observe their children discreetly. It comes in handy for instructors in the Early Education Program to evaluate their students."

Daniel settled himself on a sofa.

"She should be along soon. If you need anything, let me know," the teacher said and left the room.

A few minutes later, a group of noisy preschoolers came into the building. Daniel stood by the mirror, carefully scanning each little face. A boy with curly hair held hands with a younger girl. Two boys in baseball caps jostled to see who could reach the sandbox first. There were blond children and dark-haired children, some with curly hair, some with straight. He studied each child carefully. Then he saw her—a little girl wearing a white top and blue overalls. The eyes he recognized as clearly as if he were looking at his own. She kept pushing back her unruly red curls with a small hand. There was already a smattering of freckles across her pert little nose. A surge of emotion arose in Daniel. It took all his willpower not to go to her.

"Bailey," he whispered. This was his child. There was no doubt about it.

—

Lauren frowned at the line of cars in front of her. *Maybe I should start leaving the office earlier. I could avoid this traffic, spend more time with Bailey.*

She was about to turn onto Birch Street when she heard the *whump, whump, whump* of her damaged tire. "Great," Lauren muttered. Why hadn't she taken the mechanic's advice, had the damn thing replaced? She pulled off the road and dug her cellphone from her purse.

The garage promised to send a tow truck within the hour. Lauren could drop the keys off on her way home, the mechanic told her. She scrolled though her cellphone and found the number for Bert's Taxi. The line was busy. She'd walk. Probably be quicker than waiting for a cab, she decided.

It was raining a fine mist, and Lauren regretted not taking her umbrella. She was halfway to the school when the heavens opened. In no time, she was soaked, her hair plastered to her head. She was sure her new shoes were ruined.

Just then she heard the sound of a car horn. A pair of brake lights gleamed through the silvery downpour. Andrew Collins was behind the wheel. "Andrew, you're a lifesaver," she said, climbing aboard.

"What are you doing walking in a downpour?"

"That bad tire again. Glad you came along."

"Glad I can help. After we pick up the kids, I'll drive you home."

"I have to drop off my keys at the garage," Lauren explained. "They're going to send a tow truck."

"No problem. I'll swing by the garage."

"But it's out of your way."

"Happy to do it," Andrew said earnestly. "You look like you could use a friend."

Lauren shook her damp hair. Water dripped from her nose and chin. She winced at the sight of her mud-splattered trousers. "I must look like a drowned cat."

Andrew gave her an appraising look. "You look fine to me."

"Thank you." Lauren flushed. "So, been to visit Claire lately?"

"A couple of days ago," Andrew said. "Anya's back now and she'll be taking care of her, at least until the new doctor arrives. You realize she's moving to Alaska?"

"So, she's finally decided to make the big move," Lauren said. "I know she's been considering it for some time now." She made a mental note to call Anya. She would have to sign a sworn affidavit before she left. It might save her from having to testify if the case went to trial.

Andrew parked beside a blue car that had a string of rosary beads wrapped around the rear-view mirror. With a grin, he turned to Lauren. "Race you inside," he dared.

CHAPTER

13

"I've sent a letter of reference to Lance Rainer, the director of *Candlewood Lane*," Mitch told Erika Jansen. It was late afternoon and they were having tea at Newfie B'ys. "Lance is a good friend of mine, and he expects the pilot to do well."

"I appreciate you having so much confidence in me, Professor Cromwell," Erika said.

He smiled. "Who knows where this might lead?"

Erika brightened, feeling an excitement she hadn't felt in a long time. This could be her big break. "Do you think I'm ready for such a large part?" She looked up at Mitch. "I mean...I haven't even finished the program yet."

Mitch touched her sleeve. "Absolutely, my dear. I wouldn't have recommended you if I thought otherwise." He peered at her from beneath brushy white brows. "You have what it takes to make a successful actress."

"Thank you," Erika said.

"You've been through quite an ordeal for someone so young. But I know how determined you are." Mitch gave her an encouraging smile. "An actress's experience can be her best asset."

Erika was thoughtful. Instead of letting all her emotional baggage get in the way, she could use it to her advantage. She had a chance to start over, make a new life for herself.

She felt a stab of gratitude. Mitch was the only person she'd confided in about her past. She'd come to rehearsals one day in a bad state, stumbling over her lines, playing a less than enthusiastic

Lady Macbeth. Mitch had called a recess, demanding to know what was bothering her. When she shrugged it off, he'd requested she meet him after rehearsals. Before she knew it, she was spilling her guts. She was glad now that she had shared her burden.

"I think you'll make a perfect Daisy," Mitch said.

"I love Daisy." Erika smiled. "She's such a great character."

Mitch cleared his throat. "As you know, Erika, I'll be retiring next term," he said. "Professor Ste Denis may be taking my place."

If she doesn't go to jail, Erika thought. She knew things did not look good for Claire. "How is Professor Ste Denis?"

A shadow crossed Mitch's face. "As well as can be expected, considering the circumstances." He took a sip of tea. "She made bail and is home now, but it's not easy. She still has to face trial and the press is harassing her, making her life miserable."

Erika lifted a drowned teabag from her cup and placed it on a plate. "It must be very stressful. But at least she's made bail. You must be happy about that."

Mitch closed his eyes momentarily, opened them, and looked at Erika. "You remind me of her, you know."

Erika leaned toward him. "I remind you of Professor Ste Denis?"

Mitch nodded. "She's an excellent actress."

"Yes, I've seen her perform," Erika said, recalling the time Claire played Marsha in *The Three Sisters*.

Mitch locked his hazel eyes on her. "You're the only student in all the years I've been teaching who has shown as much promise."

She smiled. "I appreciate you saying that."

"It's true. I value your talent and dedication. Such gifts are rare." Mitch checked his watch and pushed aside his cup. "Well, I should go. I have a lot of work to do."

"And I have that paper to finish." Erika stood up and buttoned her jacket.

They walked to the front of the café together. Just as they reached the door, Erika nearly collided with Frances Turple, who was stepping away from the counter with two takeout coffees.

"Dr. Turple?" Erika said.

Frances gave a curt nod. "Hello, Erika. Mitch."

Mitch held the door open, gesturing for the women to go ahead.

"How are Dr. Chandler and the baby?" Erika asked as they walked outside.

"Fine. Fine. Thank you." Frances made her way toward a red SUV parked near the curb. Annabelle was in the driver's seat. She rolled down the window, and Frances handed her the coffee.

"Is Dinah Marie with you?" Erika asked, following. Before Frances or Annabelle had a chance to answer, she cupped her face with both hands and peered through the window. The baby was in an infant seat, blankets tucked around her face. Erika glanced quickly at Frances. "I haven't had a chance to meet her."

"Me either," said Mitch, now standing behind Erika.

"She's sleeping," Annabelle said quickly.

"She has a bad cold," Frances said, reaching for the door handle. Annabelle nodded. "She's been to the doctor."

"You should bring her by the department," Mitch said. "We'd all love to meet her."

"Yes," Frances said. "We've been meaning to do that." She climbed into the vehicle and closed the door, then gave a curt wave as Annabelle rolled up the window.

"They could've let us see her," Erika said as the SUV pulled away. "It's not like we can contaminate her from a distance."

Mitch chuckled. "Overprotective parents."

Erika nodded. "Yes, I suppose." She touched Mitch's elbow. "Thanks for the tea, Professor Cromwell, and for all your encouraging words. I'll see you at rehearsals this evening."

—

Mitch watched Erika walk away. Such a talented young woman, he thought. Who would have guessed she harboured so much pain? Carried so many secrets? Well, she wasn't the only one, he reminded himself. What would happen if people in this town found out what *he* had been hiding? *Erika's secrets are nothing compared to mine,* he thought as he walked toward campus.

Back at his office, Mitch logged onto his computer and went to ratemyprofessor.com. *Why am I obsessed with this?* he asked himself. He cast a guilty look at a pile of ungraded term papers on his desk.

I have so many other pressing things. But he couldn't help himself and constantly checked the site for new comments—not only to check his own postings but also those of his colleagues. The site allowed students to rate professors on helpfulness, clarity, and difficulty. Mitch's overall rating was 3.5 out of a possible 5. There were three new ratings since he'd last checked. He scanned them eagerly. *Not a terrible prof,* someone had posted, *but I wouldn't take his class again.* The other two comments were not as kind. *This guy has no sense of humour, but he is British, after all.* Another had posted: *God love him. He has a face like a garden gnome, and he's as crazy as a bag of farts.* Mitch felt a wave of anger. What the hell did any of that have to do with his teaching ability? Cyber bullying is what it was. And the cowards didn't have the decency to identify themselves. No doubt Jonathan Parsons had posted that last comment. Little bastard was probably pissed because he got a C last term. Well, this term he'd get an F, along with a letter from the dean.

To reassure himself, Mitch scrolled through previous comments. A number of them were positive: *Professor Cromwell made me see my potential. He is an amazing prof with a big heart. Dr. Cromwell is very helpful. He cares about his students, and he made me believe in myself.* Despite the encouraging posts, Mitch bristled at the negative. A few days ago, someone had posted: *He is stark raving mad, and belongs in the mental. I'm sure he buys his clothes at Frenchy's or the Sally Ann.*

Mitch pressed his lips together. Julie Langer or Kate Simpson, he guessed. Maybe they were both in on it. Thick as thieves, those two. Just last week, they'd come up to him in the student union building. "Professor Cromwell," Julie had said, "such a lovely jacket. Where did you get it?" He'd noted the amused look on their faces. He knew they mocked him behind his back.

Mitch checked Claire Ste Denis's ratings. Her overall score was 4.5, and most of the comments posted about her were positive: *Dr. Ste Denis supports and encourages her students. She is a great prof, nurturing and positive.* Another post: *She is definitely the best prof I ever had.* The only negative comments had to do with Claire's marking. *If you want an A, don't take Dr. Ste Denis's course. She's a hard marker and expects too much.*

Next, Mitch typed Annabelle Chandler's name. She had a 4.2 average and, like Claire, most of the comments were positive:

Professor Chandler is always so helpful. I just love her. This professor is a sweetheart. So kind and caring. A recent comment, however, was unsettling: *I had to drop out of Dr. Chandler's class. What she did is unforgivable. She is not as sweet as she appears to be. I urge students to be very cautious of this professor.*

Mitch reread the post. No hint of what Annabelle had done wrong. Strange, he thought. Usually, if there was a complaint against a professor in the department, it came to his attention. What had Annabelle done to cause a student to drop out of her class?

CHAPTER

14

"More coffee, sir?"

"Thank you." Daniel held out his cup to a waitress in a pale blue uniform. For the past half hour he'd been sitting in the hotel restaurant just outside New Wexford waiting for his friend Paul Dionne. Daniel looked anxiously at his watch. Paul should have been here by now. He gazed out the large window overlooking the ocean. The day was grey and overcast, the waves choppy with a smattering of whitecaps. Fishing boats and sailboats bobbed at their moorings.

Daniel had always assumed that Lauren left Quebec because of the scandal she was involved in at the time. It had hit her really hard, and nearly destroyed her. But it never dawned on him that she might have been pregnant.

He had wrestled with the decision to tell Paul about Bailey. Not too many priests—or people, for that matter—were as caring or as non-judgmental as Paul. He had cornered Daniel at the reception last evening. "What's wrong, my friend?" he asked. "You've been preoccupied since you arrived. Something is bothering you, I can tell."

At first, Daniel denied there was a problem.

"If you need to talk, you know where to find me," Paul assured him.

Daniel traced a finger along the rim of his cup. He'd been preoccupied, all right. All he could think about was the little girl with the red corkscrew curls. Last night, he'd lain awake for hours recalling Bailey's elfin face, the bright blue eyes that were so much like his own. He should have confronted Lauren before he'd left Paddy's Arm. Should have demanded to know why the hell she'd kept the child from him. He had been standing at the one-way mirror when Lauren burst into the room. There had been a man with her. An attractive man, Daniel thought. He had wavy dark hair and the build of someone who spent all his free time at the gym. They were laughing and playful. Never had Daniel seen Lauren so carefree. Bailey ran to her, and Lauren scooped her up in her arms. The man had a child too, a boy about Bailey's age. Daniel watched as they gathered jackets, hats, toys, and lunch boxes. To approach Lauren would be awkward at any time, but he couldn't do it while she was with a friend. She could be living with this man. He'd gone back to the inn, packed his clothes, and driven non-stop to New Wexford. *But that's not going to be the end of it*, he vowed. He would stop at Paddy's Arm on his way home. Bailey was his child too, and he had a right to see her.

"Daniel?"

Father Paul spoke with a heavy accent and pronounced Daniel's name *Danielle*. He was smiling down at him, a giant of a man with a ruddy complexion and mop of grey curls. He wore running shoes and a navy blue jogging outfit.

"Hi, Paul," Daniel said, relieved to see him. "Have a seat."

"Sorry to be late," Paul said, sliding into a chair across from him. "Hope I did not keep you waiting."

"It's okay."

No sooner was Paul seated than a waitress returned with the coffee carafe. "Ready to order?" she asked, filling his cup.

Paul picked up a glossy menu and gave it a quick glance. "I will have some toast—whole wheat."

"And you, sir?"

"I'm fine," Daniel told her.

"Did you 'ave a good time at the reception?" Paul asked after the waitress left.

"It was wonderful seeing so many old friends. Still, it was bittersweet."

"That's so true, mon ami." Paul said. "Poor Phillip."

For the next few minutes they chatted about the reception, their parishes, friends they hadn't seen in years.

The waitress brought Paul's order and refilled Daniel's cup. Paul reached for the jam and busied himself with his toast. He added cream to his coffee and stirred. "So," he said, giving Daniel a level look. "What is on your mind?"

A lump filled Daniel's throat, making it difficult to talk. "You know…I was seeing a woman some years ago," he began.

"Lauren?"

"Yes, Lauren," Daniel said, surprised Paul remembered her name. He swallowed. "She's living in Paddy's Arm now. She's a lawyer, involved in a high-profile case, and I…I saw her on the news. On the way here, I decided to drop by and see her."

Paul took a bite of toast, nodded for him to continue.

"I didn't get to see her…well, I *did* see her, but I didn't actually talk with her." Nervously, Daniel twisted his linen napkin. "But that's not the point…you see, I…" He realized he was rambling, probably not making much sense. "Lauren has a child," he said, taking the plunge. "My child."

Paul looked at him, a curious expression on his face. "Are you sure the child is yours? You said you did not actually speak to Lauren."

"Oh, she's mine all right," Daniel said, relieved to be able to talk about it. He explained about going to Lauren's office, visiting Bailey's school. "Paul, there's no doubt she's my child. She has my eyes, my face. Her hair is red and curly just like my sister, Maddie's. And she's beautiful." Daniel became aware of the pride in his voice. "I have a beautiful little daughter."

CHAPTER

15

Lauren threw the newspaper onto the kitchen table. "I'm sorry you have to deal with this, Claire," she said, pursing her lips in disgust. In his scathing article, Stephen Coleman had completely undermined Claire's competence as a parent. He had also revealed very private, personal information about her.

"I have no control over the media," Claire said. "Ever since I was charged they've been harassing me. It's gotten worse since I got out of jail. I don't know why they find this case so intriguing."

"I know," Lauren said. Reporters were digging up everything they could on Claire's early life. Old photographs of her were on the front pages of newspapers, and on the nightly news. Everyone had something to say about the case. Psychologists and psychiatrists who had never met Claire freely offered their opinions about her mental state. They diagnosed her as having an attachment disorder, abandonment issues, and various other problems. Some of her students and former babysitters had also given interviews.

"I have no idea where Coleman dug up the story of my adoption." Claire folded her hands on the table. "I have to admit, he did a good job of making me look like an unfit mother. It doesn't matter if things he said about me aren't true, it still looks bad in print."

"Unfortunately, most people believe whatever they read in the newspaper or see on television," Lauren said.

"Did you see the *Daily News*? The interview they did with Megan Dares?"

Lauren nodded grimly. Megan was a former student of Claire's who had been asked to leave the program because of her failing grades. However, she told a journalist that she'd quit because of Claire's violent temper. "I was scared to death of her," Megan claimed. "I didn't know what she would do from one day to the next."

"I just hope Megan's not called to testify in court."

"The truth always comes out," Lauren said. Still, she couldn't help but worry the prosecutor would make Claire's past an issue.

"My parents sent me to a psychologist at an early age," Claire said. "I don't know if they were afraid the abuse had damaged me, or if they thought I carried the same evil in my DNA as my biological mother."

"Your friends and family know who you are, Claire. We know you're not capable of harming anyone."

"I appreciate your loyalty," Claire said. "And I appreciate how hard you worked to get me out of jail in time for Ariel's memorial service. My parents are arriving this week. All of this has been very difficult for them." Claire bit her lip. "They wanted to stay here to support me, but I urged them to go home. Dad has a heart condition; he had an appointment scheduled with a specialist. I didn't think he should miss it…they're both getting up in age."

"I'm just sorry it took so long to get you out of that place. It must have been hell in there."

"It's hell no matter where I am." Claire's beautiful eyes, which once held so much vivacity, were now clouded with so much sorrow that Lauren found it difficult to look at her. Claire absently picked at her fingernails. "I have dreams where I'm searching for Ariel. Last night I dreamed I left her at the mall. I went back and searched every store, but couldn't find her anywhere." She levelled her gaze at Lauren. "And then I wake up to find that reality is worse than the dream." She shook her head. "There's no waking up from this."

Lauren struggled for words to lessen Claire's sorrow, but nothing came.

Claire forced a thin smile. "Enough about my problems. You said you had something to tell me."

"Yes," Lauren said, relieved to change the subject. "As you know, Emma and I have been investigating. We're hoping to find something the police might have overlooked. A couple of weeks ago, we went to see your neighbour Flo Spencer. She told us about a lady who came to your door the day Ariel died."

"A lady?"

Lauren nodded. "Mrs. Spencer says she was a platinum blonde, about six feet tall, wearing a red coat with fur on the collar. Do you know anyone fitting that description?"

Claire stared at Lauren, somewhat taken aback. "It's not unusual for strangers to come to the door," she said. "They come around trying to sell subscriptions, restaurant vouchers, long-distance bundles. And we get religious groups dropping by."

"None of your neighbours met this woman. If she was trying to sell something, I'm sure she would have stopped at other houses."

Claire shrugged.

"We'll continue to search for her," Lauren promised.

Claire rubbed her chin. "Mitch told me Frances and Annabelle adopted a baby."

Lauren nodded. "A little girl. I'm so happy for them. They had their hearts set on adoption. I haven't seen the baby, I don't think anyone has, actually—they're very protective."

"Annabelle and Frances were patients of Anya's. But Bram said that after the baby came they switched doctors, had their medical records transferred to the clinic in Jackson's Harbour."

"More than an hour's drive now that Annabelle and Frances have moved to Deep River," Lauren said. "Why would they stop seeing Dr. Kaminsky? From what I hear, she's an excellent physician."

Claire gave a derisive snort. "That's stretching it."

Lauren glanced up at her.

"Maybe I'm being unfair," Claire admitted, "but I really resent Anya for prescribing me so many drugs. Had I not been so drugged the day…that day…well, things might have been different."

"I'm sure Anya had your best interests at heart, Claire." She looked skeptical. Lauren tried another track. "How does Bram feel about it?"

"In hindsight, he feels the prescribing might have been excessive. But she said it's not unusual to prescribe large doses for patients with PPD." Claire shook her head. "Anyway, that's beside the point. If Frances and Annabelle didn't like Anya, there are other good doctors in the area. No need for them to go so far away."

"True," Lauren agreed.

Claire glanced at the clock on the kitchen wall. "I wonder what's keeping Bram."

"You never know with doctors," Lauren said. "He could have been called out on an emergency."

"Yes, I suppose," Claire said, not sounding entirely convinced. "Bram's been staying away from home more and more these days."

Lauren wasn't sure how to respond to this news.

"He's such a private person," Claire continued. "He doesn't show emotion, and it's difficult to know what he's feeling. His childhood experience has had a profound effect on him. He doesn't trust readily."

Lauren nodded. "For sure, it hasn't been easy for him." Bram's parents and two sisters had been killed in a car accident when he was ten. Bram, the only survivor, had spent a year in a rehabilitation centre recovering from his injuries. Relatives had taken him in, only to squander his inheritance and educational fund. With no family, Bram had moved out on his own when he was just sixteen.

"He blames me for Ariel's death," Claire said.

"Has he told you that?"

"No," Claire admitted. "Not in so many words." Absently, she looked out the window. "Bram's restless at night, up at all hours. And he's started drinking."

"I'm sure he doesn't blame you." Lauren put a reassuring hand on Claire's arm.

"Most marriages can't survive the trauma of losing a child," Claire said in a matter-of-fact tone. "I don't know the statistics, but I can understand why. In the past when one of us was in crisis, we drew strength from the other. But now both of us are in so much pain, we just avoid each other."

"Have you considered professional help?" Lauren asked. She should have realized Ariel's death would put a strain on their marriage.

"I have an appointment with a grief counsellor after the memorial service," Claire said. "Bram refuses to see her. In any case, I doubt anyone can restore the wreckage our lives have become."

CHAPTER

16

As Lauren drove her car into the university chapel parking lot, photographers aimed cameras with telescopic lenses in her direction. *At least they won't be allowed inside,* she told herself as she searched for a parking space. The lot was full and she had to drive around campus looking for a place to park. After some time, she found a spot near the Student Union Building.

It was cold, and a raw wind bit her face as she made her way to the chapel. As she neared the building, television reporters rushed toward her with their black bubble microphones. "Ms. LaVallee, do you think the killer will show up at the service today?"

Although Lauren had expected this, she was at a loss for words.

"Killers often show up at the funerals of their victims," another reporter shouted.

Before Lauren could reply, Cyril Hynes, a security guard who worked for the university, appeared. "Come with me," he said, taking her arm. "It's really crazy around here." By this time, more people were walking across the lot, and Cyril gestured for them to follow.

A swell of organ music greeted Lauren as she pushed open the heavy wooden doors to the chapel. The air was thick with the mingled aromas of burning candles, wood polish, and altar wine. An usher handed Lauren a program and led her to a seat at the back. She slid quietly into the polished pew and looked around. The chapel was already packed, and more people were streaming in. A poster-sized photograph of Ariel stood near the pulpit. Next to it was a small brass urn. Teddy bears, balloons, and flowers festooned the foot of the altar. Lauren studied the program, sadness washing over her. Ariel's picture was there again on the front page, along with the dates of her birth and death.

It had been a long time since she'd attended church, Lauren realized as she watched ushers lead mourners to their pews. When she lived in Montreal, she used to enjoy watching Daniel "celebrate mass," as he called it. Most of his sermons were about feeding the poor and taking care of "the least of these." A deacon had once criticized him for being too liberal.

She watched as Patrick Shaw and Annabelle Chandler were led to a pew a couple of rows ahead of her. Annabelle was wearing a dark dress with a black shawl. Patrick wore a suit and tie, his blond hair carefully slicked back.

Lauren looked around the packed chapel. Bram and Claire sat in the front row with Claire's parents, Emma, and Father Barry Williams, the priest. Anya Kaminsky, Mitch Cromwell, Andrew Collins, and a couple of Bram's colleagues sat in the pew behind them. Not far behind were Claire's students and faculty from the university.

Reverend Hunt, the chaplain, followed by a procession of chapel assistants, made his way to the altar, and the congregation rose. "Let us pray," he began, and the mourners bowed their heads. "Dear God, you have called from this earth Ariel Elizabeth Warren."

While the chaplain led the mourners in prayer, Lauren scanned the bowed heads. Was Ariel's killer among them as the reporter had suggested? The thought unsettled her and she tried to banish it from her mind.

The chaplain finished praying, and the children's choir sang "Jesus Loves the Little Children." Then, one by one, various relatives and friends made their way to the altar.

Mitch said Ariel was the granddaughter he never had, that he would miss her sunny smiles. After Bram, Emma, and Claire's parents expressed what Ariel's short life had meant to them, Father Williams took the podium. "I baptized this precious child," he began. "Little did I know that less than a year later, I would be eulogizing her." He opened his arms as if embracing the congregation. "There is nothing more devastating than the death of a child. We have heard the heart-rending testimonies of those who knew and loved little Ariel. Her death seems so senseless, so contradictory to the natural order of things. At times like this, our faith is truly tested; we wonder, where is God?"

Claire spoke last. "Ariel was our gift from God," she said. "Not only to Bram and me, but to all the people who knew and loved her." She recited a poem she'd written for her daughter, her voice trembling, nearly breaking, as she read. By the time she finished, the congregation were dabbing at their eyes.

Following the service, Bram and Claire, along with Father Williams, stood by the chapel door. People stopped to offer condolences as they passed. Lauren remembered the priest; he had once come to the law firm to show support for a member of his flock whom she was representing. He'd been a great help to Claire during this difficult time and had often visited her at the jail.

Lauren was waiting to have a word with Bram and Claire when she felt a hand on her shoulder. She turned around to see Andrew Collins. "I was going to call you," he said. "I was hoping we could get together."

"Oh?" Lauren said, taken by surprise.

Andrew lowered his voice. "There's something I'd like to talk to you about. Can I take you out to dinner tomorrow evening?"

Lauren thought of the things she had planned for the rest of the weekend: a meeting with Anya, clients to see. She and Emma were planning to drive to St. John's to see the production of *Othello* playing at The Hall. "Tomorrow's not good for me, I'm afraid. How about next Friday?"

"Can we meet sooner? This is something I don't want to put off for too long."

Lauren raised an eyebrow. "Well, we can have dinner at my house on Tuesday. Bring Riley if you want."

"I was actually hoping to talk with you in private…without the kids."

"Sounds serious," Lauren teased.

"It *is* serious," Andrew said, his voice grave.

"Come anytime after seven-thirty. I'll have Bailey in bed by then."

He nodded his head and turned to leave.

Lauren watched him walk away, his gait weary. What could he possibly have to tell her that was so important?

CHAPTER

17

Lauren rang the doorbell outside Dr. Kaminsky's condo, taking in the SOLD sticker plastered across it in bright orange letters.

A moment later, Anya answered the door looking smart in a red blouse and black pants, her long hair swept back in an elegant French braid. "Come in, Lauren," she said brightly.

"Thank you for seeing me so early on a Sunday," Lauren said. "I'm sure you have better things to do on your day off."

"This will benefit me as much as it will you."

Lauren slipped off her shoes. "You were able to sell your home, I see."

"Yes, but unfortunately my house on Duffy's Mountain is still on the market. I may have to lower the price again."

"It's beautiful up there. I'm sure someone will be interested."

"It is a long way from town," Anya said, "and the price of gas keeps going up."

Lauren followed Anya into the dining room. Cartons and boxes were stacked against the walls, dishes and ornaments piled on a sideboard. "Doesn't Andrew Collins have a cottage on Duffy's Mountain?"

"Andrew is my nearest neighbour. When he and Sylvia were together, they came to the mountain nearly every weekend. He seldom comes anymore." She pulled out a chair from around the dining room table. "Have a seat," she said. Anya was about to sit down when her cellphone rang. "I better get that," she said. "It might be the hospital." With the phone to her ear, she walked into the kitchen.

Lauren opened her briefcase, found the document she needed, and placed it on the table. While she waited for Anya, she studied the pictures on the wall. A photograph of a teenage Anya hung over the dining room table. Sitting next to her was a boy who looked to be a couple of years older—Anya's brother, she guessed. There was also a photograph of a man and woman who she assumed were Anya's parents. On another wall was a painting of a country house surrounded by birch trees; it looked amateurish, kind of folksy.

Amid the clutter on the table, Lauren noticed a set of nesting dolls. Instead of the typical stylized image of a woman in a red peasant dress, the outermost doll depicted Joseph Stalin. Lauren picked it up and pulled apart the middle. Inside were dolls depicting Gorbachev, Brezhnev, Lenin, and other Soviet and Russian leaders.

Lauren had no sooner reassembled the set when Anya came back into the room.

"I was just admiring your nesting dolls."

"A gift from a friend in Russia."

"A clever idea," said Lauren.

Anya took at seat at the table. "Yes, I thought so."

Lauren gestured to the painting of the country house. "Is that your work?"

"I dabbled in art," Anya said, "but ballet was my true love. I wanted to take lessons, but my parents scoffed at the idea."

Lauren smiled. "They wanted you to have a more practical career."

"No, they wanted me to get married," Anya said without emotion. She gestured to the photo of the teenage boy on the wall. "My brother, Dmitry, was groomed to be the doctor in the family. After we fled to Canada, he applied to as many as fifty medical schools but was rejected every time." She smiled wryly. "I was accepted into St. James, the first school I applied to. I did it simply to show my parents I was more capable than their darling son."

Lauren didn't know how to respond, so she said nothing.

Anya pointed to the portraits on the wall. "We moved from St. Petersburg to Chechnya when I was a baby."

"I've read about the war there. It must have been horrible."

"It was hell," Anya said. "One day we were living a normal life and the next, thousands of armed soldiers had invaded our city.

The images are still with me like scenes from a bad movie. Bombs, gunfire, armoured vehicles in the streets. My family tried to flee to Dagestan, but its borders were closed. We camped on the border and went without food for days on end." Anya shook her head as if to clear away the memories.

Lauren stared at her, unable to come up with an adequate reply.

Anya smiled. "It is all behind me now. I am excited about my new life in Alaska."

"Claire said you've been planning this move for over a year. Where in Alaska are you going?"

"Savoonga. It's an Inuit village that is very remote. I saw a photograph of it in *National Geographic* and decided I wanted to live there."

Lauren looked at Anya with admiration. "You *are* an adventurous one. The people of Savoonga are lucky to get you as their doctor."

"Thank you, Lauren. I will try to live up to that."

"The worst thing about living in a college town is watching people move away," Lauren said. "Even in the short time I've been here so many friends and colleagues have left. Frances and Annabelle are moving at the end of the term." She turned to the document in front of her. "And speaking of moving away," she added, picking it up, "an affidavit will allow you to give a sworn statement without going to court. By signing it you're simply attesting, under oath, that your statement is true."

"As long as I do not have to return from Alaska to testify."

"The affidavit should be enough," Lauren said. "However, there are no guarantees. The prosecutor may want to cross-examine you. I need to go over your statement to make sure everything is accurate." She began to read: "On February 12, around 3:00 P.M., Claire Ste Denis called the clinic. She was very distraught—so distraught the receptionist could not understand what she was saying. I took the phone, and was able to get her calm enough to tell me that her baby, Ariel Elizabeth Warren, was not breathing. After calling 911, I decided to drive to the Warren-Ste Denis home."

Lauren stopped reading and glanced at Anya, who gave a nod of confirmation.

"I arrived at 33 Sumac Lane at approximately 3:15," Lauren continued. "Paramedics were already on the scene. They tried to revive the infant, but she had been dead for some time. The mother, Claire Ste Denis, was in a desperate state. Because she was so agitated, I gave her a sedative and helped her to bed. At the time, I concluded the cause of death was sudden infant death syndrome."

Lauren looked at the doctor. "You knew Ariel was dead before the ambulance left," she said. She'd often wondered why Anya had left the house that afternoon, letting Lauren believe the baby was still alive.

"I am sorry about that," Anya said. "I know you and Claire are close and...well, I did not know how you would take the news."

You thought I'd become hysterical, and you didn't want to have to deal with that along with everything else, Lauren thought. But in a way, she could understand Anya's decision.

"I now wonder if I made the right call by sedating Claire," Anya said. "But she was incoherent and distraught."

Lauren nodded, recalling what she'd read in the police report. "I'm surprised the paramedics didn't call the police, considering that Ariel died at home under dubious circumstances."

"I suppose the fact that I was a medical doctor who felt certain the cause of death was SIDS factored into their decision."

"That makes sense," Lauren said. She shoved the papers back in her briefcase and rose to her feet. She could see by the clock on the dining room wall that it was nearly 11:00. She and Emma were driving to St. John's to see a play at The Hall. The play was at 1:00, and it was nearly an hour and a half drive. She would have to get a move on if they were going to make it.

Anya walked her to the door. "Take care, Lauren," she said.

"You too, Anya, and good luck with your move."

Lauren was walking to her car when her phone rang. She looked at the number: *S. Roberts*, long-distance. "Hello?"

"Lauren LaVallee?" the caller asked.

"Yes, this is she," Lauren said, as she opened the car door and got in.

"This is Stella Roberts. My daughter Jade was a student in your criminology class."

"Oh, yes, Ms. Roberts. How can I help you?"

"I was wondering if you'd heard from Jade."

"I had a call from her the day before she left. Must be...oh... almost a month ago now. She wanted to meet with me. But the next morning she sent an email saying she wouldn't be coming back to my class. That's the last time I heard from her."

"I'm very worried about Jade and Cara," Stella continued. As she talked, Lauren became aware of the distress in her voice. "None of her friends have heard from her. It's like she dropped off the face of the earth."

Lauren felt a familiar dread. "Have you notified the police?"

"They said Jade was an adult, that she didn't have to inform me of her whereabouts."

"Maybe Jade needs some alone time right now," Lauren said. "Maybe she'll call once she's settled."

"I don't know. I'm very concerned. I hope Jade didn't...leave Cara with someone."

"I'm not sure I follow you, Ms. Roberts."

Stella hesitated a moment before answering. "Jade mentioned that someone offered her money for Cara. At the time, she told me she'd never give up her baby, but...I'm worried."

Lauren recalled what Jade had said the day she and Emma went to visit her: *I could have got thousands of dollars.*

"It's a terrible thing," Stella went on, "to think your own daughter could do something like that."

Lauren gripped the phone. "You believe Jade sold her baby?"

"Jade can be impulsive, and...well...I did consider that possibility."

"Do you know who offered Jade money?"

"Jade didn't say who the person was, but I know for certain that she received a sum of money from someone in the drama department. She said it was a loan."

Lauren gasped.

"I won't keep you," Stella said, "but if you hear from Jade, could you please call me?" She rattled off a number where she could be reached.

"Of course," Lauren told her.

Lauren stared at the phone for a long moment, her mind racing. Was it a coincidence that Frances and Annabelle had adopted a baby around the time Jade and Cara had gone missing? Dinah Marie was around the same age as Cara. So much about the adoption was odd. Claire said Annabelle and Frances had switched doctors. Had they moved to Deep River so no one would recognize the baby? Lauren knew she wasn't the only one who thought it strange that the couple never brought their new baby around the university. Come to think of it, she had never even seen a picture of Dinah Marie. And whenever there was mention of a baby shower, Annabelle or Frances would come up with some excuse for why they couldn't have people over: the baby had a cold; they were too busy. Lauren frowned. *Had* Jade sold them her baby? Frances and Annabelle were leaving for Arizona at the end of the term. If they had Jade's baby, no one would ever know.

Lauren was approaching Emma's house when her phone rang again. This time it was Emma. *Probably wondering where I am*, Lauren thought as she answered.

"Lauren," Emma said in a strangled voice, "I have some bad news."

CHAPTER

18

"Bad news?" Lauren felt panic building in the pit of her stomach. "Bailey?"

"No, no," Emma assured her. "Bailey's fine."

Lauren's body went limp with relief.

"I hate to tell you this, Lauren, but The Hawk found out about *Nelson vs. Little* and your suspended license."

Lauren let out her breath. "Oh god," she said. "I should have prepared for this. I just left Anya's house. I'll be there shortly."

By the time Lauren pulled into Emma's driveway, her mind was in turmoil. *If it's not one thing, it's something else,* she thought. She should have got in front of the story like Claire suggested. Her stomach was churning as she got out of the car.

Emma met Lauren at the door, and gave her a quick hug. "Ah, damn, girl, I'm sorry. Looks like the creep went and done it again."

"I should have expected it," Lauren said. She followed Emma into the kitchen, where a copy of the Sunday *Daily News* lay on the table. On the front page in block letters ran the headline: CLAIRE STE DENIS'S DEFENSE LAWYER INVOLVED IN UNLAWFUL AND SHADY CONDUCT. With shaking hands, Lauren picked up the newspaper. Not only had Coleman resurrected the story, but he'd managed to make it about Claire. She scanned the article, words and phrases jumping out at her. *License suspended. Bribery charges. Breach of confidentiality. Not fit to practice.* Coleman had interviewed Greg Nelson, the former client who'd brought the charges against her. "Patty and I were in love," he was quoted as saying. "If it wasn't for LaVallee we might still be together. The woman is evil." Lauren put down the paper, feeling sick to her stomach.

Emma came to stand beside her. "Are you okay? We can postpone the play if you like. It's on all next week, sure."

"No, it's okay." Lauren glanced at her watch. "We should get going if we want to get there on time."

They drove in silence for nearly thirty minutes, Lauren deep in thought. She realized how little Emma, or any of her friends, knew about the case. The shame Lauren felt ran so deep that she'd never been able to share the full story with even her closest friend. *And after everything Emma and I went through together,* she thought now.

When Lauren first arrived in Paddy's Arm, she had never felt so alone in her life. Claire had introduced her to Emma, who was also single and pregnant. Emma had broken off her relationship with André, Dylan's father, a few weeks before she found out she was pregnant. It was perhaps because of their similar situation that a strong bond had developed between Emma and Lauren. They had often shared their concerns about being single parents, shopped for baby clothes and furniture, and spent hours talking about cribs, strollers, and breastfeeding. They pored over baby magazines, clipping articles on nutrition, parenting, and toys suitable for infants. Both wanted girls and were overjoyed with the results of their sonograms. But whether they had boys or girls, names had already been decided. Emma was set on Dylan after Dylan Thomas, her favourite poet. Lauren chose Bailey after a male cousin she was close to.

Lauren silently stared out the window at the passing scenery. Long sections of forest were punctuated by picturesque coves and inlets. A tall lighthouse stood on a rocky cliff. She recalled how happy Emma had been after she'd gotten back with André. He had been offered a job in Ottawa and Emma and Dylan went with him. Although Lauren had missed them terribly, by this time she was teaching and busy taking care of her new baby. When Dylan was still a toddler, André was killed during a home invasion. The incident had shaken Emma to the core, and she'd immediately moved back to Paddy's Arm.

"A penny for your thoughts, Lauren," Emma said now.

Lauren turned to look at her. "Emma, I never really told you the full details of *Nelson vs. Little*," she said. "You only know the bare facts."

"I've read the article," Emma said, "and I can't believe some of the things you were accused of." She turned to look at her. "I'm sorry. I know how much you wanted to put all of that behind you."

"It's not something I've wanted to rehash," Lauren admitted, "but I think it's time I told you what really happened."

Emma nodded.

"Right after university, I worked as a public defender," Lauren began. "It was good for the most part. I was able to give a voice to the wrongly accused. I defended people who were in danger of falling through the cracks. However, I also had my share of child abusers, wife beaters, and murder suspects. Some of them I simply couldn't stand, but I had no choice but to take them on."

"You're not required to like the people you have to defend."

"True," Lauren agreed. "Even the vilest among us is entitled to a fair trial. I was at the firm less than a year when I was handed *Nelson vs. Little*. Greg Nelson, thirty-six, was charged with assaulting his twenty-one-year-old girlfriend, Patty Little." Lauren shook her head. "I disliked Nelson from the start. He was always angry, it seemed. One day he came into my office in a rage. He was so mad he was foaming at the mouth. 'I'd like to kill that little bitch,' he told me. He often bragged about beating up a younger stepsister. You can imagine how I feared for his girlfriend's safety."

"Wouldn't that be reason enough to forfeit attorney-client privilege?"

"Nelson said he'd *like* to kill her, not that he was *going* to kill her," Lauren clarified. "A couple of evenings later, Patty came to my office. She was very upset." Lauren paused, recalling the wisp of a girl with pale features who showed up, her face a mass of bruises. "'You're defending a monster,' she said. 'Look what the son of a bitch did to me. If he gets away with this, he'll kill me.' Patty then told me she'd been receiving threatening phone calls, and she believed it was Nelson. She was afraid to go home."

Emma waited.

"I suggested she go to a motel," Lauren continued, "but she had no money." She rubbed her forehead. "I don't know what the hell I was thinking. I should have shooed her away, told her I couldn't talk with her. Instead I gave her money for a motel, warned her to be careful. I let it slip that he beat his stepsister too." Lauren shook her head. "As soon as the words left my lips, I regretted them. That was a clear violation of attorney-client privilege."

"Word got back to Nelson?"

"Yeah," Lauren said grimly. "A week later he and Patty got back together. Nelson filed a complaint with the barrister's society. I was accused not only of breaching attorney-client privilege but of bribing the plaintiff to keep silent. No doubt Patty was coached by Nelson, maybe even coerced. There was a hearing. The bribery charges were dropped, but I was charged with breach of confidence."

Emma touched Lauren's arm. "I'm sorry," she said.

"I'm worried about my clients at Beck Hayes," Lauren admitted. "I'm afraid of losing their trust." She looked down at her hands. "And I hate that they made the story about Claire."

"It's not your fault," Emma said, loyally. "And I'm sure Claire will understand."

"I hope so," Lauren said. "But let's not talk about it anymore. Let's try to enjoy the ride and the beautiful scenery."

"It doesn't get much better than this," Emma said, gesturing through the window. They had moved into an area of jagged cliffs and headlands. Offshore islands could be seen in the distance. Every couple of miles they passed little fishing villages filled with wharfs and boats and lobster traps.

"So much natural beauty," Lauren said, drinking it all in. For a little while, at least, she tried to forget the unpleasant things happening in her life.

—

After the performance, Lauren and Emma stopped to have coffee and bagels outside a café on Duckworth Street. The weather had unexpectedly turned warm and the mild day had brought people out of their homes. Couples strolled arm in arm. Families with children and dogs walked past the café. Young mothers pushed babies and toddlers in strollers.

Lauren leaned back in her chair and blew out her breath. There was something else Emma needed to know. "I got a call from Stella Roberts this morning."

"Jade's mother?"

Lauren nodded. "She's very concerned about Jade and Cara. She thinks someone in the drama department might have her granddaughter." She told her about the loan Jade's mother had mentioned.

Emma stared at her. "Frances and Annabelle?"

"There does seem to be an air of secrecy around Dinah Marie's adoption."

"I hope Jade wasn't coerced into anything."

A brief silence passed between the women as they considered this.

"I'm going to visit Annabelle and Frances next week," Lauren said.

"They *invited* you to their home?"

"No, I wasn't invited. I'm going to"—Lauren made air quotes—"'just happen' to be in Deep River. I'll drop by with gifts for the baby."

"Sneaky," Emma said. "But what makes you think they'll let you see her?"

"If they refuse, I can only assume they have something to hide." Lauren wiped her hands on a napkin. "I may even alert the RCMP, let them know what I suspect. Frances and Annabelle are leaving the country at the end of the summer."

A waiter came out of the café and stopped by their table. "Can I get you ladies something else?"

Emma drained her mug and looked at Lauren.

"Nothing for me, thanks." Lauren checked her watch and saw it was nearly four. "We should be heading home." She opened her purse but Emma beat her to it.

"It's on me," she said, handing the waiter a twenty.

"Thanks, Emma." Lauren buttoned her coat, and was reaching for her glasses when Emma gave her a sharp nudge. "It's her," she whispered.

"Who?" Lauren asked, looking around.

Emma pointed across the street at a woman heading in their direction.

"My God!" Lauren said, taking in the woman's platinum blond hair and red coat. She was exactly as Mrs. Spencer had described her.

The woman saw them and stopped abruptly, her mouth a perfect O. She turned, making a hasty retreat.

"Ma'am," Lauren called, starting after her. "We need to talk with you."

Upping her pace, the platinum lady stumbled in her high heels. Lauren and Emma hurried after her down Duckworth Street. The woman wove in and out of traffic, a car missing her by inches. The driver blew his horn, mouthing obscenities. When a metro bus stopped across the street, she followed the passengers aboard.

"Damn!" Lauren cursed as the bus started down Duckworth.

"Let's get the car and follow," Emma suggested.

By the time they reached the car, the bus was long gone. *Trust it to be Sunday with no traffic to slow it down*, Lauren thought. She pulled her cellphone from her purse and googled the number for the transit company. It took several minutes for someone to take her call.

By this time, Lauren and Emma were heading down Water Street, the bus far ahead of them. "It's the number nine bus, and it's headed for the Village Mall," Lauren said, putting her phone away. "Hopefully, we can get there before Miss Platinum gets off." She frowned. "Who in the world is she?"

Emma shrugged. "It's obvious she knows us—or one of us at least. She must have something to hide or she wouldn't have bolted the way she did."

The sun was low in the sky and tall shadows were gathering by the time they reached the mall ten minutes later. They pulled into the parking lot where a number of other buses were waiting. The driver was standing near the number-nine bus smoking a cigarette. "Bus leaves in seven minutes," he said as they approached.

"My mother got on your bus at Duckworth," Lauren said. "She forgot her heart medication. It's very important that she take it the same time every day. She was wearing a red coat with white trim. Do you remember her?"

"I remember her," the driver said. "Got off somewheres near Arthur Street. I forgets where to." He gestured toward the bus. "Gary might know. He's our driver in training."

They found Gary—who looked barely out of his teens—near the rear of the bus talking with a young woman. They fell silent as Emma and Lauren boarded.

Lauren described the platinum lady, giving Gary the same story she'd given the other driver. "It's important that we find her," she added.

"I remember her," Gary said. "The one with the big…" he held his hands about a foot away from his chest.

The girl slapped at his hands. "Geez, Gary, that's her mother you're talking about." She turned to Lauren, shaking her head apologetically.

"She got off at the seniors' building on Arthur," Gary said. "Is that where she lives?"

"Umm…she's probably visiting a friend," Lauren lied. She turned to Emma. "We should be going if we want to find her."

They reached the manor in less than five minutes. In the lobby, seniors were sitting around small folding tables, playing cards and checkers. They all seemed to be eyeing Lauren and Emma.

"Can I help you?" asked the security guard behind a desk near the entrance.

Emma described the platinum lady.

"No one living here fits that description," the guard told them.

"Sure, I remembers her," said a lady with a cane who'd been listening to the conversation. "She got off the bus about twenty minutes ago."

"Did she come inside?" Emma asked. By this time, most of the residents had put down their cards and were listening intently.

"I seen her get into a City Wide Taxi," said a woman in a wheelchair.

"Did she say where she was going?"

"I didn't speak with her."

Lauren looked around the room. "Has anyone seen her before today?"

They shook their heads.

"Please call me collect if you happen to see her again," Lauren said, doling out her business cards. But even as she spoke, she knew it was unlikely the woman would return. Miss Platinum had gotten on the bus to avoid talking to them. Most likely, the taxi had taken her to her actual place of residence.

CHAPTER

19

Lauren lowered the heat on a pot of spaghetti sauce. Andrew had said to expect him between seven-thirty and eight o'clock. It was now ten past eight. She had set out her best dishes and lace tablecloth. A Caesar salad was waiting in the fridge. All she had left to do was cook the pasta and put garlic bread in the oven.

Lauren had gone back to Beck Hayes that day for the first time since Coleman's article had appeared in Sunday's *Daily News*. Only a couple of her clients mentioned it. Charlie Dayton, a dentist accused of groping a patient, made it very clear that what he told her was confidential. Lauren assured him it would be. Tomorrow, she would have to face the students in her criminology class. She wasn't looking forward to that. The phone rang, startling her out of her thoughts. She picked it up, expecting Andrew. "Hello?"

"Lauren?" The voice was deep, familiar.

"Yes?"

"It's Daniel."

Daniel? Lauren's breath caught in her throat. She lowered herself into a nearby chair, her heart pounding.

"Lauren? Are you still there?"

"Daniel," she croaked.

"I'm in Newfoundland…New Wexford, actually. I'll be leaving in a few days, and I intend to stop at Paddy's Arm tomorrow on my way home. Can we get together?"

"Well…I…"

"We need to talk, Lauren. Can we meet for coffee?"

"Well, I suppose," she said, sensing urgency in his voice.

"I'll call you when I arrive."

"Okay." Lauren gave him her cell number.

"I'm looking forward to seeing you again, Lauren."

"Me too, Daniel."

With trembling hands, Lauren replaced the receiver, already regretting her decision. *Why didn't I have the good sense to say no?* All the physical and emotional longing she felt for him came rushing back. There was an ache inside her she knew would never go away. *Will Daniel always have this hold on me?* she wondered as she went to the window. Staring out at the blackness, she thought of all the years she and Daniel had sneaked around in motel rooms, remote cabins, and cottages. She recalled their visit to Europe when Daniel visited the Vatican. He had joked about introducing her to the Pope as his mistress. In Rome they strode hand in hand through narrow cobblestone streets, giddy and silly. They stood outside in rainy weather, getting drenched. Mornings they slept late and ate breakfast in bed. It seemed as if nothing could come between them there. *I'm a fool for love*, she thought, *forbidden love.* When she was sixty-five, would she still yearn for a man she couldn't have? Or worse, would she grow bitter and resentful?

She would see Daniel, she decided. She would make it clear their relationship was over. And there was no way she was going to tell him about Bailey. She didn't need more complications in her life.

Lauren turned away from the window. *Where's Andrew?* she thought irritably. It was quarter to nine. He should have called if he was going to be this late. She poured herself a glass of wine and went into the living room, her heart still racing.

At nine-thirty, Lauren called Andrew's office. She got the standard message announcing that the clinic was closed. She called his cellphone and it went to voice mail. His home number rang and rang. Lauren poured the spaghetti sauce into plastic containers. She put away the dishes and folded the tablecloth. She knew there was a chance Andrew had been called out on an emergency. Still, he could have called her. The evening had been a total wash.

Lauren was in bed by eleven but was unable to sleep. The phone call from Daniel had unsettled her more than she cared to admit. What could he possibly want to talk with her about?

No sooner had she fallen asleep when the ringing telephone jolted her awake. Groggily, she switched on the table lamp. Squinting at the clock, she saw it was 1:56 A.M. Her caller ID displayed Andrew's name and number. Why would he be calling her in the middle of the night? "Hello," she said sleepily, a touch of annoyance in her voice.

"This is Constable Taylor with the RCMP."

Rebecca? Lauren was too confused to say anything.

"Could you identify yourself, please?"

Identify herself? Rebecca had called *her*. Why was she calling so late and from Andrew's phone? "It's Lauren LaVallee," Lauren said. "Is something wrong?"

"Lauren. I'm sorry to bother you at this late hour," Rebecca said, the formality in her voice dissipating. "Apparently, you were the last person to call Dr. Collins's cellphone."

Lauren pulled herself to a sitting position. "Is Andrew okay?"

There was a moment's hesitation "I'm afraid not," Rebecca said. "We have a, um…situation here. Why did you call Dr. Collins this evening?"

"We were supposed to have dinner, but he didn't show."

"Have you talked with him this evening?"

"No, I tried to reach him but—"

"We need to come by and talk with you."

"Now?"

"We will see you shortly."

"What—"

Rebecca had already hung up.

Twenty minutes later, Lauren watched through parted curtains as a police cruiser pulled into her driveway. Rebecca got out, followed by Kyle Harrison, the officer who had come with her to arrest Claire. She went to the door.

"Come in," Lauren said, trying to quell the knot of anxiety that curled in her stomach. Lauren led them into the kitchen, where they sat around the table. Rebecca pulled a notepad from her pocket.

"What's going on?" Lauren asked, her voice wobbling with nervousness.

"Earlier this evening, you called Dr. Collins's cellphone," Harrison said. "Do you mind telling us the nature of the call?"

"As I explained to Reb—Constable Taylor, he…we had a dinner date, and he didn't show. I called to see if he was okay."

"Why did you think he *wouldn't* be okay?" Harrison asked.

"He said he'd be here between seven-thirty and eight. When he didn't show, I…I assumed there was an emergency at the clinic or at the hospital."

"You didn't speak with him at all this evening?" Rebecca asked.

"I already told you I couldn't reach him." Lauren looked from Rebecca to Harrison. "Is someone going to tell me what's going on?"

Harrison ignored her request for information. "Were you and Dr. Collins a couple?" he asked bluntly.

As much as she resented the question, Lauren knew he was only doing his job. "No," she replied. "I barely knew him."

Harrison cocked an eyebrow. "But you invited him to dinner."

"He said he had information I might be interested in."

"Information?" The officer looked at her with interest.

Lauren shrugged. "I assumed it was relevant to a case I'm working on."

"The Claire Ste Denis case?" Rebecca asked.

Lauren folded her arms across her chest. "Did something happen to Andrew?" she demanded, her frustration building toward anger.

The officers exchanged a quick glance.

"Earlier this evening, Dr. Collins was taken to the hospital," Rebecca said.

Lauren felt a cold sensation spread through her chest. "What happened?"

Leaning toward her, Rebecca took a deep breath. "He was shot in the head."

CHAPTER

20

When Claire awoke in the darkness, her first thought was to check on Ariel. Then, like a sharp jab to the heart, she remembered Ariel was dead. Grief crashed down. The ache was unlike anything she'd ever known. It always crept up on her. Nighttime was the worst. She was often startled awake from a fitful sleep filled with nightmares. She had an overwhelming yearning for her baby. Would she ever get used to the fact that Ariel was gone forever?

It took Claire a moment to realize Bram was not beside her. Glancing at the clock, she saw it was nearly one. Trembling, she got out of bed and started toward the nursery. In this room she felt close to Ariel. She sometimes came here just to sit quietly. Outside the window it was pitch black as if someone had smothered the light. Nights were always darker now, the house more silent.

After some time, Claire went downstairs. Bram was in the living room staring at the television, the sound barely audible. His eyes were bloodshot, his face stubbly from a two-day-old beard. On the table beside him was a glass of whiskey. Bram had never been a heavy drinker, but since Ariel's death Claire had noticed the bottles in their well-stocked liquor cabinet rapidly disappearing. She knew how much Bram had loved Ariel. She had witnessed his grief, watched him toss through sleepless nights.

Claire stood in the hallway for a few moments watching the man she'd been married to for seven years. Was she imagining it, or did he look older? His hair had more grey, and deep lines had set in around his mouth. They'd both been mortally wounded, she realized. *Will we survive this,* she wondered, *or will we become another statistic? Sometimes it seems that this house is too small to hold all of our grief.*

The television was tuned to the CBC. On screen, a picture of Ariel popped up. Bram, who was staring off into space, didn't seem to notice. Claire strained to listen to the newscaster. "Bombshell today in the baby Ariel case," she said dramatically. "It's been learned that the mother, Claire, has a history of psychiatric problems."

Claire shook her head. Pundits, psychologists, lawyers, even psychics—all had judged her. Most of the time there was no basis for their claims.

"We also learned that she has a violent temper," the newscaster continued. "With us tonight is Megan Dares, a student who claims she had to leave her university studies because of Dr. Ste Denis's bad temper."

Claire blew out a breath. *Megan Dares again. Is there anyone that girl won't talk to?* She walked into the living room, picked up the remote, and turned off the television. Only then did Bram notice her. He gave her a sad smile.

She sat beside him on the sofa. "Bram," she said, "we *need* to talk about our baby."

Bram regarded her with haunted eyes. "I love Ariel dearly," he said.

Present tense. She recalled her grief counsellor's warning: *In order to heal, you must mourn and accept your child's death. You must learn to say goodbye. Don't get caught up in what-ifs. Don't fantasize about how things could have been.* In the days following Ariel's death, Bram had become sullen and unapproachable. Claire understood how he felt. Whenever she looked at her husband, she was reminded of their loss. It had to be the same for Bram.

"Bram, I need to ask you something."

He turned to look at her. "What is it?"

Claire swallowed before asking the question that had been on her mind since their child died: "Do you blame me for Ariel's death?"

Bram hesitated for a beat. His eyes were full of pain and something else—reproach, Claire realized. The look cut her to the core. "No, of course not," he replied.

The momentary pause told Claire all she needed to know. "I know I haven't been the best wife."

"You were not available," Bram said shortly.

Again, his words, even if he had not meant them to be cruel, cut deeply.

"I was not well," Claire said, hating how defensive she sounded.

Instead of answering, Bram reached for his glass. "Would you like a drink?"

"It's late. Don't you have surgery in the morning?"

Bram shrugged and looked away.

Claire folded her arms across her chest as if to shield herself from her husband's callousness. A chilling loneliness filled her. It was like a part of her had been amputated. New wounds opened as the cold truth crept in, carving a hollowness within her. *Not only does he blame me for Ariel's death, but he no longer loves me.* It was something she'd believed for a while but could only now admit.

Taking a deep breath, Claire got up from the sofa. She couldn't do this anymore. She couldn't stay in this house another minute. For her own sanity, she had to get away. She went upstairs, found a small bag, and threw in a nightgown, toothbrush, and change of clothes. It was not the first time she'd considered leaving. Things had been falling apart for a long time. Even before Ariel's death.

When Claire went back downstairs, Bram was asleep in front of the television. She scribbled a note, telling him she would return tomorrow for the rest of her things.

—

Claire drove around for nearly an hour, thinking about her encounter with Bram. Did he really hold her accountable for Ariel's death? *Maybe I'm being paranoid,* she told herself. *Maybe it's about the guilt I feel for not protecting my baby.* In any case, she needed to get away. She still loved Bram; that hadn't changed. But she couldn't live with him if he resented her.

At 2 A.M., Claire turned onto a side street near the college. Mitch had turned his attic into a bachelor apartment that he rented to students. His last tenant had moved out weeks ago. With any luck the apartment might still be available.

Except for the light above the door, the house was dark. *Maybe I should have called first*, she thought as she strode up to the front door and rang the bell. In the stillness, she could hear chimes echoing through the house.

A few minutes later, a light came on. Through the frosted pane of glass in the door, Claire saw a figure moving down the hallway. The door opened, and Mitch stood in the foyer wearing a red silk robe. "Claire?" he said groggily, squinting though the blackness.

"I'm sorry to barge in this late," she said, feeling a surge of guilt for waking him.

"It's quite all right, my dear. Are you okay?"

"Well…not exactly," she admitted.

Mitch waved her inside and helped her with her coat. He led her down the hallway to an old-fashioned kitchen. "I'll make us some hot chocolate."

Claire sat at the large wooden table while Mitch poured milk into a saucepan. He got mugs and envelopes of hot-chocolate mix from the cupboard. "Did you hear the sirens earlier?" he asked.

"Yes," Claire said. "Not another accident, I hope." Just a few months ago, a car carrying a load of students had crashed into a truck. One student was killed, two others seriously injured.

Mitch added the mix to the milk and stirred. He filled two mugs and brought them to the table along with a plate of homemade cookies. "Now tell me," he said, taking a seat across from Claire, "why are you here at this hour?"

"I've left Bram."

Mitch nodded as if he'd known this all along.

"Since Ariel's death things have not been right between us."

"I can see why that would put a strain on your relationship." Mitch took a sip of hot chocolate and put down his cup. "Can you work it out? I always thought you and Bram were good for each other."

"We're making ourselves miserable," Claire said. "Bram has retreated into himself. We're not much comfort to each other." She didn't tell Mitch that she feared Bram no longer loved her.

"Maybe you both need some time apart." Mitch reached across the table and covered her hand with his. "I care about you,

Claire. You're the daughter I never had, and I can't bear seeing you unhappy."

"Thank you," Claire said, already feeling better. "I have to find a place to stay. Is your apartment still available?"

"A young lady came to look at it yesterday. She said she'd get back to me. If you like, I'll call her and tell her it's taken." Mitch shrugged. "It's kind of small."

"It's perfect," Claire said. "Maybe I can move in tonight."

"It will take a day or so to get it ready. Stay here tonight." Mitch got up from the table and put a hand on her shoulder. "I'll make up the guest room."

CHAPTER

21

In the faculty lounge the following morning, Lauren found a discarded copy of the Daily News. As she expected, Andrew's shooting was front-page news. PADDY'S ARM DOCTOR SHOT IN HEAD ran the two-inch headline. With shaking hands, she spread the paper on the table. The details were sketchy, outlining the barest of facts, information she'd already learned from the police: *The thirty-five-year-old family physician was found in his office by a cleaning crew. Police believe the shooting was the result of an armed robbery. Any persons with information are asked to call the Paddy's Arm RCMP detachment.*

Lauren folded the newspaper. Was the shooting random, as the police believed, or was it something more personal? Andrew had information he'd wanted to share with her. She recalled how determined he had been to speak with her at the memorial service.

"Lauren?"

"Emma." Lauren put her hand over her heart. "Don't sneak up on me like that."

"I didn't realize you had a class this morning."

"I was waiting for you." Lauren held up the paper. "Have you read this?"

Emma squinted at the headlines, her eyes widening in surprise.

A couple of students came into the staff room, talking and laughing. "Let's go to my office," Emma whispered, "so we can talk in private."

They walked in silence down the hallway. Emma took off her coat and hung it on the rack in the outer office. She unlocked the door, flicked on the lights.

Lauren sat across from Emma in a chair reserved for visitors. "My God, girl. What happened?" Emma asked. "Didn't you and Andrew have a dinner date last evening?"

"That was the plan." Lauren explained about the late-night visit from the RCMP. "They informed me that someone had shot Andrew."

Emma stared at her. "Who would do such a thing?"

"The police believe it was an armed robbery. A glass cabinet in Andrew's office had been broken into. They assume it was someone looking for drugs."

"Is Andrew going to be okay?"

"I'm not sure," Lauren answered. "His condition is critical. I called the hospital and left a message for Gina." Andrew's older sister taught design at the college and Lauren had met her a handful of times.

"My God...."

"I guess he was in the wrong place at the wrong time," Lauren said.

Emma leaned back in her chair. "Lauren, you should go home and get some rest. You look like something the cat dragged in, sure."

"I couldn't get back to sleep after the Mounties left."

"No wonder, after what happened."

"That wasn't the only reason." Lauren took a deep breath. "Daniel called last night from New Wexford. He wants to see me before he returns to Quebec."

Emma looked shocked. "And you agreed?"

Lauren folded her arms. "I'm meeting him this afternoon. I want him to know that our relationship is over."

"What about Bailey?"

"There's no reason he has to know about Bailey."

Emma eyed her skeptically. "You're not afraid the good father will lead you once again into temptation?"

"We're meeting for coffee," Lauren said with a hint of annoyance. But deep down she knew Emma was right.

On the drive back to Beck Hayes, Lauren chided herself for being so foolish. Why on earth would she allow Daniel to come back into her life again? She needed to move on, she told herself. How could she do that with Daniel around?

Back at the firm, Lauren found a message on her voice mail from Andrew's sister: "Lauren, Gina here. Just wanted to let you know that Andrew is in a medically induced coma. It's to help decrease the swelling on his brain." Her voice faltered. "They want to prevent any brain damage from occurring. His condition is still critical…but we are all trying to stay positive. Thanks for your concern, Lauren. I'll keep you updated."

This sounds serious, Lauren thought. She sat down at her desk, exhaustion enveloping her like a net. The events of the past twelve hours were taking a toll. She looked at her calendar. Her eleven o'clock client had cancelled. Since she didn't have to be in court until one, she decided to go home and grab a nap. She was relishing the thought of snuggling under her down comforter when the receptionist approached her. "I got a call from Josephine Shaw," she said. "Her son was taken into custody this morning. She asked if you could meet her at the police station."

Lauren groaned inwardly. "Tell her I'll be there in a few minutes."

Which one of Josephine's boys is in trouble now? she wondered as she reached for her coat. Justin, most likely. Poor Josephine. A single mom with five sons, three of them teenagers. And trouble seemed to follow sixteen-year-old Justin wherever he went.

Despite the traffic, it took only a few minutes for Lauren to arrive at the police station. She was walking up the concrete steps to the front entrance when she spotted Josephine through the glass doors. A short, heavyset woman with spiked white-blond hair, she gripped the handles of a stroller that held her youngest boy, Noah.

"Thank God you came," she said, grabbing Lauren's arm.

Lauren studied Josephine's anxious face. "What's wrong?"

"They've arrested Patrick."

"Patrick? What happened?" Of all the brothers, mild-mannered Patrick was the one Lauren least expected to be in trouble. She had gotten to know and like him in the months since he started his internship at Kiddy Academy.

"You must have heard about the shooting at the medical clinic."

Lauren nodded.

"Patrick was there last night. He cut his hand and thought he needed stitches. He found Dr. Collins lying on the floor. He panicked and ran."

"Has he been charged?"

Josephine bent to pick up the toddler, who was starting to fuss. "They're saying at this point, he's a person of interest."

Lauren put a reassuring hand on her arm. "You did the right thing, calling me."

Noah started to cry, twisting in his mother's arms. "It's past his naptime," Josephine said, trying to soothe him.

"Take Noah home," Lauren suggested. "I'll take care of things." She took papers from her briefcase and handed them to Josephine. "I'll need you or Patrick to sign this representation agreement and get it back to me," she said. It wasn't the usual way she did business, but Patrick needed her counsel now. She would worry about the paperwork later.

"Thanks." Josephine put the papers in Noah's diaper bag. "I'll be in touch."

Patrick was being held in a small windowless room in the bowels of the station. A rough wooden table and a few straight-backed chairs were the only furniture. Two officers, a male and a female, were perched at either end of the table. Heads turned when Lauren opened the door.

"Your *counsel* is here," the male officer said, not bothering to disguise the mockery in his voice.

"Hi, Patrick," Lauren said. She took a seat across from him, and placed her briefcase on the table. "I'll be representing you today."

"Thanks," Patrick mumbled, looking sheepish.

"I'm Detective Grant," the female officer said. "And this," she gestured across the table, "is Detective Wilson."

"Lauren LaVallee, Beck Hayes," she said as she opened her briefcase and took out a pen and notepad. "Shall we get started?"

Detective Wilson scanned the report in front of him before turning to Patrick, asking him to state his full name, birthdate, and other identifying information.

"What were you doing at the clinic last evening?" Wilson followed-up, signalling an end to the simple questions.

"I cut myself." Patrick held up a bandaged hand.

"Was this before or after you went to the clinic?"

Patrick looked confused.

Realizing where the detective was going with this, Lauren turned to Patrick. "You went to the clinic to have your wound treated, isn't that right?"

"Yes," Patrick replied.

"And you found Dr. Collins lying on the floor?" Detective Wilson said.

"Yes, sir."

"And you fled the building, doing nothing to help."

Patrick stared at him. "I thought he was dead…and I…panicked."

Detective Wilson raised an eyebrow.

"I thought the person who killed—hurt Dr. Collins might still be in the building."

The officer narrowed his eyes. "Did you see anyone?"

Patrick looked down at this bandaged hand. "A woman was coming around the corner of the building when I parked the car. Must have come from the back entrance."

Lauren's head shot up.

Both detectives were looking at Patrick with interest.

"What did she look like, this woman?" Wilson asked.

"I only saw her from behind. She was wearing a long red coat."

"What colour was her hair?"

"I…I didn't really notice."

"Was she driving a car?"

"I don't know. I mean…I didn't see one."

Lauren knew the clinic had parking lots at both ends of the building. It would be logical for whoever shot Andrew to leave through the back doors.

"There was no one around when you went into the clinic—no nurse or receptionist?"

Patrick shook his head. "No one."

"It's odd the clinic wasn't locked after the patients and staff had left," Lauren said.

Detective Wilson nodded in agreement.

"The door was open," Patrick said. "The clinic was empty. I sat a few minutes and waited. After a while, I walked down the hallway. That's when I saw Dr. Collins. The cabinet in his office smashed, glass everywhere."

Detective Wilson eyed him suspiciously. "What did you do then?"

"I got the hell out of there."

"You didn't bother to call the police. Not even *after* you left the clinic?"

Patrick shook his head.

"I can't hear you," the detective barked.

"I didn't call anyone," Patrick said. "Like I told you, I thought the doctor was dead. I drove around a while longer, drove past the clinic twice. The second time I drove by, I saw a van with *Bartlett's Cleaners* on the side. I figured they'd call for help, so I went home."

"Did you shoot Dr. Collins?"

Patrick recoiled. "No!"

"You have a history of drug use, don't you, Mr. Shaw? In fact, you were arrested twice for possession and trafficking."

Lauren sat up straighter in her chair and looked hard at Patrick. This was the first time she'd heard of a drug arrest. Had the director at Kiddy Academy known this when she allowed him to work there? Didn't they do background checks? When she'd enrolled Bailey, she'd trusted they would screen their staff. She didn't like the idea of a convicted drug offender working with her child.

"I've only sold to friends," Patrick said.

"Mr. Shaw's prior drug use is not an issue at this time," Lauren said, the lawyer in her kicking in. Still, she continued to stare at Patrick. He'd also been at Claire's house the day Ariel was killed. Had he gone inside? Was he intending to rob the place to get money to buy drugs? *Enough*, she told herself. *You're a lawyer. You deal with facts, not speculation.* But she couldn't shake her uneasy feelings about Patrick Shaw.

CHAPTER

22

Lauren had arranged to meet Daniel at three o'clock at Newfie B'ys. It was now six minutes past, and the butterflies in her stomach were multiplying. Twice she'd gone to the window to look out. Why am I putting myself through this all over again?

A few minutes later, Daniel strolled into the café. Dressed casually in blue jeans and a red V-neck sweater, he looked even more attractive than Lauren remembered. Still taut and trim. He looked around the restaurant, his face lighting up in a smile when he spotted her.

Lauren felt her heart speed up as he approached her table. "It's good to see you, Lauren." He gave her a quick peck on the cheek before taking a seat across from her. "You look wonderful, by the way. How have you been?"

"Busy. My practice is growing, and I'm teaching a course at the university this semester." Lauren became aware of her leg bouncing under the table.

"Well, you look great." Daniel smiled. "Can I get you anything?"

"Water."

He got up from the table and returned a few minutes later with coffee for himself and a bottle of Perrier for Lauren. "Do you need a glass?"

"No, this is fine." Lauren twisted the lid.

The first few minutes were filled with idle chitchat about Lauren's job, Daniel's trip, and the Newfoundland weather. "Well," Daniel said, "I'm glad I found you, finally." He smiled. "I thought you'd disappeared forever."

"How *did* you find me?"

"I turned on the television one day and there you were."

"I see…. Well then, you must know about what happened with Claire."

Daniel stared into his coffee cup. "Yes, I was very surprised. How is she?"

"As well as can be expected, considering…."

"I'm very sorry," Daniel said.

Lauren picked at the label on her water bottle. "To add to Claire's anguish, the press is harassing her." She sighed. "And harassing me. Stephen Coleman, a local reporter, ratted me out in an article. Claire's case has become high-profile, and I guess he figured I was fair game. He dug up information on *Nelson vs. Little*, and wrote an article about how I handled the case."

Daniel frowned. "I know that wasn't easy for you. But I also thought you were much too hard on yourself. You made a mistake, but you were able to move on. I wish this Coleman guy, whoever he is, would write about something else." Daniel fixed his eyes on her a moment before he spoke again. "I dropped by your office last week. You were with a client."

"That was you? Why didn't you leave a message?"

"I would have waited, but the receptionist—Paula, isn't it?"

"Yes, Paula's our receptionist."

"Paula said you had to pick up your daughter from school." He gave her a searching look.

Lauren took a breath. "It's been more than four years since we broke up, Daniel." She struggled to keep her voice even. "Yes, I have a daughter. I wasn't the one who took a vow of chastity."

A smile played around Daniel's mouth, but his eyes were sad. "That's exactly what I told myself. But Paula said Bailey would turn four at the end of August." His eyes locked on hers. "I did some quick calculations."

Lauren stared at him, her eyes wide. "You think—"

Daniel held up his hand. "Lauren, I went to Bailey's school. I *saw* her."

"You went to her *school?*" Lauren stood up. "You can't prove a thing, Daniel."

Daniel laid a restraining hand on her arm. "I don't *need* to prove anything. That child is mine. I knew it the moment I saw her."

Lauren sagged back down into the booth. "What do you want, Daniel?" she asked, her voice weary. "You made it clear there's no future for us. The only good thing to come from our relationship was Bailey."

Daniel looked down at his hands. A few moments passed before he spoke. "She's beautiful," he said, his voice thick with emotion. "Why didn't you tell me about her?"

"What would be the point?"

A flash of pain crossed Daniel's face. "I'm her father. Do you think you're being fair to Bailey, keeping her from me?"

Lauren lowered her eyes. She'd lost many a good night's sleep pondering the same question. She had always justified her decision with the rationalization that Daniel would not want a child in his life. But now he was here, questioning her.

"Let me take you and Bailey out to dinner tonight."

"We're on a very rigid schedule. Bailey's usually tired when she gets home. I have to get her clothes ready for school. Usually she's in bed by seven-thirty."

"I'm leaving for Nova Scotia on Friday to visit my sister. I'd like to meet Bailey before I go. How about tomorrow night?"

Lauren's hands were trembling, and she gripped the edge of the table to steady them. "Well…I guess tomorrow evening will work. Bailey likes Ma Taters, a restaurant not far from my office. We'll meet you there."

"Thanks, Lauren." Daniel reached across the table and touched her hand. It was a small gesture, but one that evoked strong memories. She recalled the gentleness of his hands when they made love. Unwanted tears filled her eyes, and she blinked them away. How could she get over Daniel if he was right in front of her?

CHAPTER

23

As Lauren browsed the racks of dresses and sleepers at Hansel and Gretel's, she thought of Daniel. The simple explanation she had given Bailey was that Momma's friend wanted to take them to Ma Taters for dinner. As usual, Bailey was thrilled to eat out.

"Can I assist you?" a woman asked. Her name tag read *Ruby, Store Manager.*

Lauren held up a yellow sleeper with a pattern of panda bears. "I'm looking for a gift for a…umm…she's probably seven…maybe eight months old," Lauren said.

"I'd go with a larger size," Ruby said. "Kids grow fast at that age."

"You're right," Lauren said, thinking of Bailey's growth spurts. "I'll take it in a size eighteen months."

Ruby removed the outfit from its plastic hanger and folded it neatly. "Will there be anything else?"

"I'll just take a quick look around," Lauren told her.

Ruby nodded. "Take your time."

What a wonderful place, Lauren thought, taking in the racks of frilly dresses. Child-size mannequins flaunted spring coats and jackets. A glass case held silver spoons, fancy rattles, and china dishes. She went through an archway into a separate room where the toys and books were kept. There she found games, stuffed animals, dolls, Lego, puppets, and various other toys. Lauren browsed through a shelf of books, settling on Margaret Wise Brown's *Goodnight Moon.* She also found a glass-eyed teddy bear with soft brown fur.

Back in the main section, she was surprised to see Dr. Kaminsky browsing through a rack of baby dresses. "Hello, Anya."

"Lauren, it's nice to see you, again." Anya smiled. "I'm looking for a gift for Elena Petrov. Perhaps you know her. Her husband, Nicholas, teaches at the college."

"Yes, I've met the Petrovs. Elena must be nearing her due date."

"Any day now." Anya held up a couple of little dresses. "Aren't they adorable?"

Lauren nodded. "This is a wonderful shop."

"I was surprised that such a posh store would come to Paddy's Arm. I doubt I will find anything as fancy in Alaska."

"Not in Savoonga, anyway," Lauren said, hoping she'd got the name right. She turned to face Anya. "Have you heard anything more about Andrew?"

"His condition hasn't changed. He's still in the induced coma."

Lauren frowned. "How long do they usually keep patients in a coma like that?"

"It can be anywhere from a few days to two weeks, depending on the seriousness of the situation. Rarely do they keep a patient induced for more than two weeks."

"I went to the hospital to visit, but only family members were allowed. I've been in touch with his sister Gina, but I haven't been able to reach her lately."

"Andrew's family is very concerned," Anya said. "His brothers and sisters have all come home to visit."

"Can I help you?" the store manager asked. This time the question was directed at Anya.

"I'm still trying to decide," Anya said, holding up the dresses.

"The pink dress is from an exclusive line," Ruby said proudly. "They came in this week. We're one of the first stores in Canada to carry it."

Anya checked the price tag. "That explains it," she said, winking at Lauren.

"Well, I should run," Lauren said. "Good luck with your shopping, Anya." Clutching her purchases, she headed to the counter at the front of the store.

The cashier ran Lauren's credit card through the electronic scanner, then carefully removed the tags from the sleeper with nail scissors. She expertly folded it into a box, and laid the book and teddy bear on top.

Lauren peeked at her watch and saw it was nearing three o'clock. She had to stop at the university for some papers before picking Bailey up from school.

Moments later, she was walking across campus when she spotted Frances Turple in Motorcycle Alley, the area under the fire escape where students parked their bikes. Erika Jansen was standing next to her, both women puffing on cigarettes. The alley was the only place on campus where smoking was allowed. *What would Frances think if she knew what I was up to?* Lauren wondered. *How would she feel if she knew I was scheming to see her baby?*

"Hi," Lauren said pleasantly, approaching the women.

"Hi, Professor LaVallee," Erika greeted.

Frances looked up at her and nodded. She was wearing a brown jacket, and with the hood pulled up she looked like a wrinkled monk.

"It must be hell in winter having to come out here to smoke," Lauren said.

"Yes," Erika agreed, "but I only smoke when I'm stressed."

Frances said nothing.

"How's Dinah Marie?" Lauren asked.

"She's teething. Got two little teeth coming in."

Lauren smiled. "She's what…seven months?"

Frances blew out a plume of smoke. "Nearly seven months."

Lauren did a quick calculation. Jade's baby would be nearly nine months now. But was Frances telling the truth about the baby's age? She could be lying to deflect suspicion. "That's a precious age," she said.

Frances flicked an ash off the end of her cigarette. "Dinah Marie is very bright."

"You should bring her in to see us before you leave for Arizona," Erika said.

Frances smiled tightly, and took a deep drag from her cigarette.

"I have to ask: have either of you heard from Jade?" Lauren said. "Her mother called me and she's very concerned."

Erika nodded. "Ms. Roberts called me too. She's coming to Paddy's Arm in a couple of days." She turned to Frances. "She may drop by to see you."

"You never stop worrying about your children," Frances said.

She had two grown children, Lauren remembered. "How are your children?" she asked.

"Sonya's doing well. She's finishing up her Ph.D. at Memorial. Rick, on the other hand…" Frances frowned. "Now he's a different story. Don't have sense enough to tie his own shoelaces, that one."

Lauren knew all about Frances's wayward son. He'd been busted for drug possession, and had been in and out of rehab. Lauren wondered how his mother, an ex-RCMP officer, felt about that. Frances had raised her children on her own after her fisherman husband drowned off the Grand Banks.

"It's not only Jade that Ms. Roberts is concerned about," Lauren said. "She's worried about her granddaughter." She looked pointedly at Frances. "She thinks Jade may have left Cara with someone."

Frances tightened her lips. "From what I hear, Jade didn't deserve to have a baby." She sounded disgusted.

Lauren stared at her, waiting for an explanation.

Frances threw her cigarette butt in the dumpster. Without another word, she walked away.

CHAPTER

24

"Momma, there's Ethan from my school." Bailey waved at a boy across the restaurant who was sitting with his parents. "Can I go see him?"

"Not now," Lauren said. "Stay with me until we're seated." It was quarter to six by the clock above the cash register. Daniel had said he'd meet them around six. Usually they had to wait at least ten minutes for a table. This evening, however, there were only a few people ahead of them.

Ma Taters was a family-style restaurant, best known for its seasoned potato skins. Lauren usually took Bailey there a couple of times a month. It had a good kids' menu, and Bailey loved Bully the mechanical bull. For a loonie, kids could ride Bully for a full five minutes.

"Just the two of you?" the waiter asked.

"A friend will be joining us shortly," Lauren said.

"Would you like a table or a booth?"

"I'd prefer a booth. By the window if there's one available."

"Follow me." The waiter was leading them to a booth when Bailey let out a squeal. "Patrick's here!" Before Lauren could stop her, she scampered across the restaurant to a table in the corner.

"Bailey, come back here," Lauren called, going after her. She stopped suddenly, gaping in surprise when she saw Patrick Shaw sitting at a table with Annabelle Chandler. On the table were platters of seafood and an opened bottle of wine. Patrick, dressed in a tan jacket and dress pants, looked more self-assured than he had at the police station.

"Hey there, Bailey," he called.

"I'm sorry," Lauren said, reaching for her daughter's hand.

"No problem," Patrick said, good-naturedly.

Annabelle smiled. "Nice to see you, Lauren. You look good."

Never as good as you, Annabelle, Lauren thought. Although the restaurant had a relaxed atmosphere and most patrons dressed casually, Annabelle wore a fancy dress. As usual, her lipstick and eyeliner were meticulous. "Good to see you too," Lauren said.

After a few moments of polite chatter, Lauren said, "I'll let you two finish your meal in peace." Holding Bailey's hand, she led her to their booth. By this time, a server had arrived at their table with a paper placemat that looked like a page ripped from a large colouring book. He handed it to Bailey along with a small package of crayons.

"Know what I like best about this restaurant?" Bailey asked.

Lauren smiled. "The nuggets?"

"Nope. I like the crayons."

While Bailey coloured a picture of Cinderella, Lauren glanced nervously out the window. Would Daniel demand his rights as a father? Would he demand weekends or holidays with his daughter? He was hardly in a position to do so, she argued with herself.

From where she sat Lauren had an unobstructed view of Patrick and Annabelle's table. She watched as Patrick poured wine into Annabelle's glass. When had the two become friends? Lauren wondered. When she'd seen them sitting together at Ariel's memorial service, she'd assumed it was because of the seating shortage. Now, it seemed more likely that they had arrived together. What could they possibly have in common? Annabelle was nearly old enough to be Patrick's mother. Was she a relative? No, Lauren told herself. She recalled Patrick's mother telling her how difficult it was not having family in the area. Not even a cousin, she had complained.

A couple of minutes past six, Lauren saw Daniel pass by the window. He was wearing a blue shirt under a brown wool sweater and blue jeans. "Daniel's here," she told Bailey.

"Is he your boyfriend, Momma?"

Lauren laughed. "No, Daniel's a friend."

After a brief exchange with the waiter, Daniel headed toward their table. "Hi, Lauren," he said as he approached. "Good to see you again." He squatted down next to the booth where Bailey was sitting. "And you must be Bailey."

"Yup." Bailey giggled.

Smiling, Daniel continued, "Is it okay if I sit next to you?"

Nodding, Bailey shifted to make room.

"Well," Daniel said. "It's not often I get to dine with two beautiful women. You look lovely, both of you." He turned to Bailey, taking in her pinafore dress. Lauren had brushed her red curls into pigtails. "Is that a new dress?"

"Momma buyed it at Hansel and Gretel's."

At that moment, the server came by with three large menus. "I'll have the usual," Lauren said without opening hers.

"What's the usual?" Daniel asked.

The server smiled at Lauren. "Breaded pork chops, a salad, and potato skins. Right?"

Lauren nodded. "Good memory, Kevin."

"That sounds good," Daniel said. "Make that two breaded pork chops."

Kevin turned to Bailey. "And will you be having your usual nuggets and fries, missy?"

Bailey nodded. "And a chocolate sundae with a cherry on top."

Lauren saw Daniel nod and smile.

After the server left, Bailey picked up a crayon and began working on her placemat.

"That's really great colouring," Daniel said, watching her.

"I draw really good pictures too," Bailey said.

Daniel patted her arm. "I'm sure you do."

Bailey smiled. "Do you want to come to Arts and Crafts Day at my school?"

"Arts and Crafts Day?" Daniel turned to Lauren.

"Bailey's school has an open house where they display the children's arts and crafts," Lauren explained. "The next one is Tuesday afternoon." Turning to Bailey she said, "Daniel will be gone by then, darling. He's going to Nova Scotia."

"That was my original plan," Daniel said, "but this sounds pretty important. Why don't I change my flight and stick around for a couple more days. How does that sound?"

"You're staying here…in Paddy's Arm," Lauren said, incredulous.

"You like it here?" Bailey asked without looking up from her colouring.

Daniel nodded. "I've met some really great people."

"Who?" Bailey asked.

"Well, there's your mom. And there's that lovely lady Mae, who works at the Bay Wop Inn where I'm staying."

"That's Dylan's nan," Bailey said.

"And of course, there's you," Daniel said, smiling at Bailey. "I would love to come to Arts and Crafts Day at your school. Thank you for inviting me."

Bailey grinned. "They have cookies and squares and Kool-Aid."

"Well, I hope they have cherry Kool-Aid," Daniel said. "That's my favourite."

"My favourite is grape," Bailey said.

While they waited for their orders, Daniel peppered Bailey with questions. Did she like school? Did she have any pets? What games did she like? What were her favourite books? What were her favourite TV programs? As he listened, Daniel nodded and smiled, amused by her answers.

During the meal, Lauren kept sneaking glances at Annabelle and Patrick. After a while she saw Annabelle get up from the table. She kissed Patrick's cheek and then went to pay the tab. Patrick remained seated even after she left the restaurant.

The server came with their food, and for the next few minutes they busied themselves with applying ketchup, buttering rolls, and tucking in napkins.

"Do you have any little girls or boys?" Bailey asked Daniel after a while.

Daniel shot Lauren a startled look. "No, I…have no little girls or boys."

After they finished dessert, Daniel and Lauren ordered coffee. Bailey had finished colouring her placemat and was starting to get antsy. Lauren was thinking of some way to engage her when Patrick appeared at their table. With him was the kid from Bailey's school. "Sorry to disturb you," Patrick said. "I was wondering if Bailey wanted to go on Bully with Ethan." He pulled a fistful of change from his pocket. "I have all those loonies I want to get rid of." He smiled at Lauren. "I also have a lot of time to kill until my friend gets here."

Bailey's eyes lit up. "Can I, Momma?"

Lauren nodded. "That's very kind of you, Patrick. Thanks for the offer." Turning to Daniel, she said, "This is Patrick Shaw, Bailey's favourite teacher. Patrick, this is my friend Daniel Kerry."

Bailey was practically skipping as she walked away. Without Bailey to distract them, Lauren suddenly felt uneasy with Daniel. Sipping her coffee, she tried to make small talk. "Patrick is great with the little ones," she said, gesturing toward the bull. Ethan and Bailey were on Bully's back, squealing with delight.

Daniel nodded. "He seems like a nice guy." He peered at Lauren. "Thank you for having dinner with me," he said. "I hope you'll let me be part of Bailey's life."

Lauren sighed. "How do I explain to Bailey that you're her father? How do I explain why you haven't been in her life all these years?"

"The reason I haven't been in her life before now is because you didn't tell me about her." Daniel covered Lauren's hand with his. "We'll work it out. You'll see."

"Are you going to tell your superiors about Bailey? What will your bishop say?"

"He won't be pleased," Daniel admitted. "But God knows I'm not the first priest this has happened to. It's more common than you think." He rubbed his chin with his thumb. "That's the least of my concerns right now. Bailey is my daughter, Lauren. I want to be in her life."

CHAPTER

25

Lauren arrived at the open house much later than she'd planned. Bailey was excited that Daniel would be attending. He had been to visit at the house twice since their dinner at Ma Taters. No sooner had she opened the door than Bailey came running. "Momma!" she called. When Lauren dropped her off at school that morning, her face was scrubbed, her hair combed neatly into pigtails. Because it was a special occasion, Lauren let her wear her good outfit with the white frilly blouse. Now, Bailey's hair was flying in all directions. There was a rim of chocolate around her lips. She had spilled purple Kool-Aid down the front of her blouse. "Look what Daniel buyed me," she said, proudly showing off a new doll.

"I hope you don't mind," Daniel said, coming to stand beside her. He had a camera slung over his shoulder. "I picked it up at that store you mentioned."

"Don't you have enough dolls?" Lauren asked, stooping to kiss her daughter.

"She can bend her arms and legs." Bailey twisted the doll's legs backward to demonstrate.

Lauren looked around the room, at the walls plastered with children's drawings, finger paintings, collages, and other artwork. A couple of small tables held projects made from pottery, playdough, and papier mâché. "Come see my pictures, Momma," Bailey said, tugging at Lauren's sleeve. She led her mother to the back of the room.

"Wow!" Lauren exclaimed, taking in Bailey's drawings and finger paintings.

"That's Regis." Bailey pointed to one of the drawings.

"Awesome!" Lauren couldn't help smiling at the image. Bailey had painted the dog purple. Its head was twice the size of its body. The only resemblance to an animal was its four stick legs.

"I think Regis will like it." Bailey ran to a nearby table and picked up a small clay bowl with an imprint of her hand at the bottom. "I made this for you, Momma."

"Well, thank you, Bailey. It's wonderful."

"I think we have an artist on our hands," Daniel said, proudly.

Although Lauren smiled, she was a little uneasy with Daniel's choice of words: *we, our.* At that moment, a teacher appeared with a platter of egg sandwiches. Daniel and Bailey each took two and settled down at a small table to eat.

"Aren't you going to have some?" Daniel asked Lauren. "Or are you afraid of ruining your supper?"

Supper. Lauren shook her head."I forgot to take the bean casserole from the freezer this morning." Unless she ordered out, there'd be no dinner.

"Can I buy you and Bailey dinner?" Daniel asked. "Mae told me there's a great deli in town that delivers."

Lauren hesitated. Did she want Daniel coming to the house again?

"Mae says the lasagna's really good."

"Really, Daniel, you don't have to go to any trouble."

"No trouble," he assured her.

"Well. Thank you. Bailey and I love lasagna."

"I'll show you the pictures I took of Bailey's artwork."

Lauren smiled. "I'd forgotten what a great photographer you are." She was about to sit down at the table when she noticed a familiar-looking woman across the room. It was Gina, she realized. She was with Riley, Andrew's son. Lauren watched as Riley proudly showed his aunt a ceramic figure he had created. "Excuse me," she told Daniel, "I'll be right back."

Gina smiled as Lauren approached her. "That's Bailey's mom," Riley told her.

"That looks interesting," Lauren said, studying the ceramic figurine. Whereas most of the kids' creations were unidentifiable blobs, Riley had actually added details such as hair, eyes, nose, mouth, and even eyebrows.

"It's Daddy," he said. "And see this here." He pointed to the figure's head, which had a hole as round as a pencil. "That's where a bullet went through his head."

Lauren involuntary took a step back. Before she could form a response, Riley put down the figurine and ran across the room. "Mommy," he called. Lauren looked to see his mother, Sylvia, standing by the door. Riley threw his arms around her legs.

"Oh, my," Lauren said, turning to Gina. "I wasn't expecting that."

Gina looked like she was going to cry. "We tried to protect him," she said. "He learned the details of his father's shooting from a neighbour's kid." She shook her head. "It's been very hard on him. Sylvia says he's been having nightmares."

"Poor kid. I can only imagine how difficult it must be," Lauren said. "Is there anything new with his father?"

"I was going to call you tonight," Gina said. "Andrew's been taken out of the induced coma. He opened his eyes yesterday for the first time. He hasn't spoken yet, but the doctors say he's conscious of what's going on around him." She picked up some of Riley's artwork from the table. "It's too early to tell if there's any brain damage, so he's not out of the woods yet, but the prognosis looks good."

"Well, that's good news. You must be relieved."

"My God, I've never felt so scared in my life." Gina swiped at her eyes.

"Well it sounds like the worst is over," Lauren said. She looked across the room to where Daniel and Bailey were seated. They had finished their food and were waiting for her. "I have to go," she said, casting Gina a sympathetic smile. "Keep in touch, and let me know if there are any changes."

"I will do that," Gina promised. "Thank you for your concern."

—

While Lauren tore lettuce and cut up vegetables for a salad, she stole glances at Bailey and Daniel; they were sitting at the dining room table, which was littered with Barbie dolls and accessories. "We need to get our dolls dressed," Bailey said.

"Right," Daniel said, reaching for a pair of pink shoes.

Those two have sure bonded, Lauren thought, not exactly thrilled by the revelation.

"Would you like a glass of wine?" Lauren asked.

Bailey giggled. "I'll have a glass of wine."

"I'll have wine with dinner," Daniel said. "The deli said delivery would take about forty minutes."

Bailey handed Daniel a Barbie. "My dolls like pretty dresses."

"They're lucky to have such a fine wardrobe." Daniel picked up a frilly dress and pulled it over a Barbie's naked body. "This one has pretty red hair like yours."

"Her name's Kerry."

"Kerry?"

Bailey nodded. "Like me. I'm Bailey Kerry LaVallee. And this one," she said, holding up another doll, "is Ariel. Like my friend." Her voice grew sad. "Ariel went to heaven. Now God won't let her come back home." She made a face. "The *meanie.*"

Daniel raised an eyebrow.

Lauren shook her head, realizing she had not done a very good job explaining Ariel's death to Bailey. She grated cheese and added it to the salad. "You need to clear the table for supper," she said.

During dinner, Daniel included Bailey in the conversation as much as he did Lauren. He told funny stories that made them laugh. The lasagna was delicious and even Bailey—picky eater that she was—cleaned her plate.

It was nearly six-thirty by the time Lauren got around to serving dessert—canned pineapples with whipped cream.

Bailey turned to Daniel. "You want to come for supper again tomorrow?" She picked up half a pineapple ring with her fingers and stuffed it into her mouth.

Daniel handed her a napkin. "I'm going home tomorrow," he said. "But if it's okay with Mom, I'll take you to McDonald's for breakfast. Would you like that?"

Bailey, her mouth full, nodded enthusiastically.

After Bailey had left the table, Lauren pushed back her chair. "I'll make us some coffee."

After a few minutes, she poured a cup for Daniel and one for herself. No sooner had she sat at the table than Bailey came rushing into the dining room. "Momma," she shouted, "you're on the TV. Come see."

Lauren got up from the table and went into the living room, Daniel close behind.

"Momma, the lady on the television says you're in hot water." Bailey giggled. "You're not in hot water."

The TV was tuned to the CBC evening news. Lauren's picture was in the upper left hand corner of the television. "LaVallee, the lawyer for Claire Ste Denis, the woman charged in the death of her infant, is alleged to have been involved in unethical behaviour. According to a report—"

Lauren grabbed the remote and turned off the television. *That's old news*, she thought. *Why bring it up after more than a week? And why do they keep involving Claire in this?* She reached for Bailey's hand. "Bath time," she said.

"After your bath, would you like me to read you a bedtime story?" Daniel asked.

"*Madeline?*" Bailey said eagerly.

"*Madeline.*" Daniel ruffled her hair.

After she had given Bailey her bath, Lauren gathered old newspapers to start a fire. From upstairs, she could hear Bailey giggling. Unexpectedly, she felt a tug of guilt for keeping her from her father. She remembered the excitement she'd felt when Bailey was first born. She would stand over her bassinet for hours staring at her while she slept. Her baby was a miracle she couldn't believe had happened. Was that how Daniel felt now? He didn't have the early memories she did.

The phone rang and Lauren picked up the extension in the kitchen. "Hello?"

"Lauren?" came the muffled voice.

"Claire? Are you okay?" It sounded like she was crying.

"I'm just having a bad day."

"I'm sorry. Is there anything I can do?"

"I just need to talk. Is this a good time?"

"Of course. I've been meaning to call you."

Lauren heard Claire draw in a deep breath. "I've left Bram," she said. "I'm renting the apartment in Mitch's house."

Lauren let the information sink in. She knew Claire and Bram were having problems, but was surprised that Claire had actually moved out.

"How does Bram feel about this?"

"He's called a couple of times asking me to come back. I explained that I can't do that right now." She sighed. "I think he's accepted the fact that I won't be coming home anytime soon."

"I'm sorry," Lauren said again, at a lost for words.

"I miss Ariel so much," Claire said, her tone muffled. Again, Lauren wondered if she was crying. "It's hard to face the reality that she's never coming back."

"Would you like me to come over?" Lauren knew Daniel would be more than willing to sit with Bailey.

"I think I'll be okay," Claire said. "But if you could come by tomorrow, I would really appreciate it?"

"I can come around nine tomorrow morning if you like."

"I'll cook you breakfast," Claire said. "It will give me something to do, take my mind off things."

"Sounds wonderful."

"Did you watch the news tonight?"

"No, I didn't get a chance."

"CBC reported on the article Coleman wrote about me." She paused. "And I'm afraid you've been dragged into it again. I'll tell you more about it when I see you in the morning."

They chatted for a few more minutes and Lauren hung up the phone just as Daniel was coming downstairs. "Bailey fell asleep while I was reading to her," he said.

"Probably exhausted. I know I am."

"She's a great girl," Daniel said, smiling.

"Yes," Lauren agreed. "I'm very lucky."

"We're both lucky."

"Would you like some wine?" She grabbed a nearby bottle and held it out.

Daniel picked up his glass. Lauren filled it, and refilled her own. "Let's go into the family room," she said. "I'll light a fire."

Lauren sat on the sofa. Daniel took a seat across from her in a wing chair. "This is nice," he said, nodding toward the blazing fire.

"And necessary," Lauren said. "Can you believe how cold it is?"

"Well, as the saying goes, 'April is the cruellest month.'"

Lauren laughed. "It's still March. But the problem is that every month is cruel in Newfoundland."

Daniel studied her a moment. "Are you okay, Lauren?"

"It's just…I should have gotten in front of that story before Coleman had a chance to write about it." Lauren shook her head. "A lot of crap has been happening, Daniel. I just got off the phone with Claire. She left her husband."

"That's rough. You'd think she'd want his support right now."

Lauren took a sip of wine. "She's charged with aggravated assault, and honest to God, Daniel, I don't know how I can get her exonerated. It keeps me awake at night."

"You can only do your best, Lauren."

"You sound like my grandmother."

Smiling, Daniel raised his glass. "To the wisdom of grannies."

"I'm going to see Claire tomorrow morning," Lauren said. "Could you give Bailey a ride to school after McDonald's?"

"Sure thing."

Lauren refilled their glasses. For the next while they talked easily. Lauren told Daniel about the problems they were having with the press. "You never know when they're going to ambush you," she said, "and they call at all hours."

"Must be very stressful for Claire," Daniel said.

"And you probably heard about the doctor who got shot a couple of days ago."

"I recall reading something about that. Was he from Paddy's Arm?"

Lauren nodded. "In fact, we had a dinner date the night it happened. Of course, he never showed."

Daniel cleared his throat. "Were you close?"

Lauren sensed something in Daniel's voice. Was it jealousy? Regret? "I was just getting to know him. I was shocked when the police called."

"A lot *has* been happening."

"It's been one thing after another," Lauren said. Then, to her surprise, she burst into tears.

In an instant, Daniel was beside her, his voice gentle. "Are you okay?" He took a handkerchief from his pocket and handed it to her.

"I'm fine." She laughed shakily, wiping her eyes.

"You've had a bad day," he said soothingly.

"Yes," she agreed. "Not one of my best."

Daniel put his arm around her shoulder. His familiar scent enveloped her as she sank into him. His hand moved over her back, stroking her, soothing her. He massaged her shoulders, his fingers moving to the tender nape of her neck. Lauren closed her eyes, enjoying his touch.

He kissed her earlobe, the hollow above her collarbone. Lauren felt his breath warm on her neck as he whispered close to her ear. She turned toward him and he put his mouth on hers. Four years of separation melted away, and passion that had lain dormant was stirred back to life.

Daniel fumbled with the buttons on Lauren's blouse. One hand found her breast, the other slid across her lower abdomen. "Daniel," Lauren moaned, lost in a wave of desire. She clung to him.

Unbidden, reality crashed in with ruthless clarity. It took all of Lauren's willpower to float from the depths of her physical sensation. *No*, she told herself. *I will not be drawn into another love affair with no happy ending. I will not let Daniel take physical pleasure from me and offer me nothing more.* She pulled herself away, shaken by what she had almost let happen.

Daniel stared at her, a confused look on his face.

Straightening her clothing, Lauren rose to her feet. "Daniel, you have to go."

"Lauren...I'm sorry...I didn't mean...I—"

"Daniel, please. Just go."

CHAPTER

26

By the time Lauren pulled into McDonald's, the parking lot was nearly full, the drive-through clogged with cars. Daniel had called earlier to say he was running late, and Lauren decided it would be best to drop Bailey off instead of having him come to the house. Now, as she walked toward the restaurant holding Bailey's hand, she wondered if she could face him.

"There he is, Momma!" Bailey exclaimed when they walked inside.

Daniel started toward them. He was wearing blue jeans and a grey tweed jacket. Despite the shadows under his eyes, he was still strikingly handsome. Lauren felt a pain so sharp she blinked back tears.

"Good morning, ladies." He briefly squeezed Bailey's shoulder. "You look chipper this morning. All ready for breakfast?"

Bailey nodded. "I'll have the hash browns."

Lauren and Daniel exchanged amused looks in spite of everything. "Be good," she told Bailey, bending to kiss her. "Daniel will drive you to school."

"Can we go to the playground again?" she asked, glancing from Daniel to Lauren.

"Daniel has to go home," Lauren said quickly.

Bailey grabbed his hand. "Will you come back to visit?"

"I'm sure it can be arranged," Daniel said.

Lauren didn't answer.

"Let's go order those hash browns." Daniel put a reassuring hand on Lauren's arm. "I'll take good care of her."

Lauren nodded.

Damn him, she thought as she drove down Main Street. She'd been doing fine. But what did she expect? Her love for Daniel had only brought her sorrow. There could be no happy ending. What was she thinking, letting him buy dinner, drinking wine with him? She slid a CD of Beethoven's piano sonatas into her car stereo and turned up the volume. The music usually had a calming effect, but this morning nothing could lift her dark mood.

When Lauren pulled up in front of Mitch's house, she saw a police cruiser parked on the street. A news van was parked not far behind. Had something happened to Claire? Lauren felt a stab of anxiety. She got out of her car just as two officers came out of the apartment. Lauren donned a baseball cap and large dark sunglasses. She expected the press to be all over her, but they were more interested in the RCMP.

"Can you tell us why you are visiting with Claire Ste Denis at this time?" Lauren heard a reporter ask one of the officers.

"Routine questioning," the officer said, and moved on. From his tone, it was clear that he didn't want to discuss it.

Lauren knew Ariel's case was out of the hands of the local police, turned over to the crime unit. Still, she didn't like the idea of Claire talking to the RCMP without her being present. *Why are they here?* she wondered as she made her way to Claire's entrance.

"Hi, Lauren," Claire said when she opened the door. "Come on in."

Although there were shadows under her eyes, Claire seemed okay. There were no signs of the distress she had expressed on the telephone last evening.

Lauren stepped inside the small sitting room with sloping ceilings. She hugged Claire briefly. "How are you?"

"I'm much better this morning," Claire said. She took Lauren's jacket and hung it on a coat rack.

Lauren took a moment to look around the room. There was barely enough space for a sofa, reclining chair, and coffee table. Claire led her into a narrow kitchen that ran parallel to the living room. A small table was set for two. "Something smells good," Lauren said.

"Breakfast is ready." Claire pulled out a chair from around the table. "Have a seat."

"I saw the police leave."

"They had questions." Claire opened the oven door, and took out a pan of biscuits.

"You reminded them that I'm your attorney."

"Oh, it had nothing to do with me." Claire dumped the biscuits into a wicker basket and placed it on the table. "They had questions about Patrick Shaw." She turned to face Lauren. "Patrick's a suspect in Andrew's shooting."

Lauren nodded.

"I trusted Patrick," Claire said, "but I'm beginning to wonder if he…hurt Ariel."

Lauren felt sick. "What are you trying to say, Claire? Has he ever given you cause for concern?"

"No," Claire demured, "in fact Patrick has always been good with Ariel. But with all this new information coming out about him… well, I can't help but wonder."

"I can certainly understand your concern," Lauren said, calming slightly. "Still, Patrick doesn't strike me as the violent type. I trust him with Bailey."

"I suppose you're right." Claire placed a pan of bacon and pancakes on the table, and sat down across from Lauren.

"Everything looks delicious," Lauren said, filling her plate.

Claire took a small bite of her pancake. "It's nice having someone to eat with."

Lauren fixed a stare on Claire, taking in her gaunt frame. She must have lost twenty pounds since the death of her baby.

"I don't have much appetite since Ariel…left," Claire said, as if reading Lauren's thoughts. She gave her a weak smile. "You look tired."

"I've had an emotional couple of days. Daniel came to see me."

Claire glanced up at her with interest.

Lauren told her everything, beginning with Daniel's phone call.

"You're still in love with him," Claire said. It was a statement, not a question.

"Maybe," Lauren admitted, her voice sad. "But I refuse to be his mistress."

"I can't blame you. You deserve better."

"Yes, I deserve much better." Taking the conversation in a new direction, she apologized again. "I'm very sorry that they've involved you."

"Don't worry about it," Claire said. "I'm used to the press."

"I'm sure you are." Lauren looked around the small kitchen. "How long do you plan to stay here?"

Claire looked down at her plate. "I'm not sure. I don't know if things can be the same between us again."

"Don't give up on your marriage, Claire. You've both been through a lot but Bram is still the same man you married."

"Bram's changed," Claire said. "He's shut me out."

"I'm sorry," Lauren said.

"Enough about that," Claire said, attempting a smile. "What's been happening at work?" For the next while, Lauren filled her in on the latest gossip. Before she knew it a whole hour had passed. Lauren wiped her hands on a paper napkin. "I should get back to the college," she said. "My class—my last class, I'm happy to say—starts in half an hour."

"You sound relieved."

"It's a mad time of the year," Lauren said. "The students are getting ready for final exams. They're all keyed up and edgy."

"I know what that's like," Claire said as she went to retrieve Lauren's coat. "You were brave to take it on."

"I can't say I didn't entirely enjoy it," Lauren said. "It's just that I'm so busy."

Claire helped Lauren into her coat. "I don't know how you manage it all."

Lauren buttoned her coat, then turned to hug Claire goodbye. "Take care," she said, "and keep in touch."

Maybe a temporary separation from Bram is not such a bad thing, Lauren thought as she walked outside. She knew Claire would never get over the horror of losing Ariel. Time would deaden that pain, but wouldn't erase it entirely. But if Claire went to prison for Ariel's death, it would destroy her. Destroy her *and* Bram. *I can't let that happen*, she told herself.

Lauren was pleased to see the sun had come out. It was turning out to be a nice day, and she felt her mood lift. As she rounded the corner to go to her car, she stopped abruptly. "It's you," she gasped, finding herself face to face with the platinum lady.

CHAPTER

27

"Hello, Ms. LaVallee."

The strange woman stared at Lauren beneath false eyelashes, her broad face caked with makeup. Her hair, which Lauren realized was a wig, came down to her shoulders. She wore a royal blue dress with small white buttons down the front. A string of pearls was wound around her thick neck.

Lauren took a step toward her.

"You seem surprised to see me," the woman said, her voice deep and familiar.

Lauren stared, dumbfounded. "Mitch?" she said, nearly choking on her words.

They stood for a moment in awkward silence.

"I suppose I owe you an explanation," Mitch said, motioning toward the house. "Please, come inside."

Lauren followed him inside. Mitch led her into a large room furnished with antique sofas and chairs. "Make yourself comfortable," he said, gesturing to an elegant love seat. "I'll be with you in a moment." He turned and retreated down the hallway.

The room was eerily quiet, the ticking of the grandfather clock ominously loud. A skinny black cat jumped up on the sofa and silently regarded Lauren with narrowed eyes.

After a few minutes, the door opened and Claire walked in. Lauren could tell she was upset. "Lauren, I should have told you."

It took a moment for Lauren to realize Claire was referring to Mitch. He must have called her from an upstairs telephone. "Yes," she said with a note of reproach. "I asked *specifically* about a platinum blonde. You denied knowing any such person."

Claire lowered herself onto a sofa. "Mitch would never harm Ariel," she said. "He loved her as much as Bram and I did. She was like a granddaughter to him."

"That's not the point, Claire, and you know it."

"I didn't want Mitch to be embarrassed." Claire lowered her voice. "Only a few of our close friends know." She gave Lauren a pleading look. "People in this town would never understand."

Claire was right, Lauren realized. If this got out, Mitch would be shunned and ridiculed. She turned to Claire. "If he's so concerned about people finding out, why does he take such chances? Why does he go out in broad daylight dressed as a woman? I ran into her…him in St. John's, for heaven's sake."

"He usually stays around the house," Claire said. "But he came to our house on a couple of occasions. He…" she stopped when they heard Mitch's footsteps on the stairs.

Mitch joined them in the living room, his face wiped clean of makeup. He had changed into a pair of tan pants and a button-down blue shirt. "The secret's out," he said, fixing an accusing stare on Lauren. "You can tell everyone that Mitch Cromwell, director of drama, is really Mrs. Doubtfire."

"I'm not out to embarrass you, Mitch," Lauren said, feeling some empathy for his predicament. "But the police consider you a suspect right now. You have to let them know you were at Claire's house the day Ariel died."

Mitch sank down on the sofa. "I suppose you're right," he conceded.

"If you like, I'll go with you while you give a statement," Lauren offered.

"That won't be necessary," Mitch said. "I'm innocent. I don't need a lawyer."

―

"Well, it's not a secret anymore," Mitch told Claire. Lauren had left, and they were having coffee at the kitchen table.

"Lauren will be discreet, I'm sure," Claire said. "I had a talk with her, and she realizes that you don't want this getting out."

"It's not Lauren I'm worried about." Mitch folded his hands in front of him. "I may have to testify in court. I'll be the laughing-stock of Paddy's Arm. I dread having to go to the police station. You know they'll question why I was lurking around your house in a dress."

"Even if people do find out, it's not such a bad thing," Claire said. "More people now are going public." She laid a hand on his arm. "It's never too late to be yourself."

Mitch shook his head. "I'm too old for that. I've lived my whole life pretending to be something I'm not. I don't know how to live any other way."

Claire stared at him. "It must take a lot of energy keeping a secret, hiding who you are."

A cloud of pain passed over Mitch's face. "I've paid a price," he admitted. He thought of his father. Even if Mitch lived another sixty-five years, he would still feel the sting of his father's disappointment. James Cromwell was a high-ranking army officer. He had no use for men who were "soft," as he put it. When Mitch was ten, he'd asked if he could take ballet lessons. "Christ," his father had muttered, "what am I raising, a goddamn pansy?" The disgust in his eyes had cut Mitch to the core.

"It doesn't matter what that hateful man thinks of you," Claire said, knowingly. She'd heard about Mitch's father and his cruelty.

Mitch nodded, absently. He recalled the day he and two girls were acting out *Snow White*. Mitch, who was playing the queen, had donned one of his sister's dresses. He had been using a lace curtain as a veil. His father had come home early that day. He tore the curtain off Mitch's head and ordered him inside the house. Later that evening, Mitch heard him talking on the phone to his uncle. "I believe the lad's a faggot." A few weeks later, Mitch was shipped off to a military academy.

Mitch stared down at his coffee mug. "For the longest time, I believed I was gay," he said, speaking his thoughts aloud. "It would have been much easier if I were. But I'm a woman." He looked down at his massive bulk and gave a bitter laugh. "A woman imprisoned in this...this ghastly body."

"Do you think other members of your family knew?"

"My mother, god bless her, said she knew I was *that way* from the time I was a child." Mitch paused momentarily. "'Don't ever tell your father,' she warned me. She sent me to a psychologist who specialized in my"—he made quotes with his fingers—"'disorder.' The military academy was the worst. I hated everything about it. They cut my goddamn hair so short they might as well have shaved my head. It was just after the Beatles became popular and I'd let my hair grow down to my shoulders."

Claire shook her head in disbelief.

"I had a secret tote where I kept silk dresses and night gowns, lace panties, bras, eye makeup, lipstick, and jewellery," Mitch continued. "I called it my survival kit. Every evening before I went to bed, I would get dressed up. One time, when I thought everyone was asleep, I went into the bathroom wearing one of my nightgowns. I had on lipstick and eye shadow." He smiled, remembering. "When I came out of the stall, Charlie Burgess was standing by the sink. I thought that was the end. But Charlie only laughed. Called me a nut and punched me in the shoulder."

"Did you have anyone to confide in?" Claire asked.

"My best and only friend—well, only *real* friend—was Vera Mills. She was a closet lesbian who grew up in a strict, religious family. They would have disowned her had they known she was gay. We stuck together, Vera and I. Everyone thought we were a couple. We went to movies and dances. She was my date for the prom." He laughed. "My mother began to push the relationship. I think she hoped if I became interested in a woman it would cure me of my *disorder*. I still recall the talk I had with Vera's father," Mitch continued. "I think he was afraid I would take advantage of his daughter. With a straight face, I had to assure him that I was not that kind of a bloke."

Claire smiled in spite of everything.

"Acting is what saved me," Mitch said. "I could escape into the role of whatever character I was playing. Of course, I was given roles as Romeo and Mark Anthony when I really wanted to play Juliet and Cleopatra."

"I'm sorry," Claire said.

"Ah, it's okay," he said, dismissively. "I had Vera, and I had my good friend Johnny."

"Johnny?"

"Johnny Walker," he said, raising his coffee cup.

—

"That's where I keep my stuff." Bailey led Daniel to a row of brightly painted lockers that held jackets, boots, books, and toys. Bailey's orange locker had her name printed on yellow construction paper taped to the door.

Parents dropping off their children shot Daniel curious glances.

"Are you coming back again?" Bailey asked as he hung up her coat.

Daniel knelt beside her. "Would you like for me to come back?"

Nodding, Bailey threw her small arms around his neck. "When you come back, I'll draw you a picture," she whispered.

"I could use a picture for my bedroom wall."

"I draw good snowmen."

Daniel smiled. "Then why don't you make me a snowman?"

"Bailey?" someone called.

Daniel turned to see a woman and a little girl walking toward them. The little girl smiled as they approached.

"Hi, Auntie Emma," Bailey called brightly. "Hi, Dylan."

"How *are* you, sweetheart?" The woman knelt beside Bailey. "You must come visit us. Sure, we hardly get to see you anymore." She rose to her feet and held out her hand to Daniel. "I'm Emma Buckle," she said, "Lauren's friend."

"Daniel Kerry," he said, taking Emma's outstretched hand.

"This is my daughter, Dylan. She and Bailey are good friends."

Daniel took Dylan's small hand in his. "I'm pleased to meet you, Dylan."

"Hello," Dylan mumbled shyly.

Emma gave Daniel a curious once-over that made him uneasy. No doubt she'd heard about him from Lauren.

"You'll have to excuse me," he said. "I have a long drive to catch my flight, and I need to get an early start."

"It's been nice meeting you," Emma said pleasantly. "Have a safe trip."

"Thank you."

Daniel turned to Bailey and kissed the top of her head. "I have to go now," he said, "but I'll come back for my picture."

Bailey grabbed his hand and pulled him close. "Promise?"

"Promise," he whispered, folding her in his arms.

It took all of Daniel's willpower to walk away. As he headed toward the door, he noticed Emma Buckle watching him.

Things can never be the same, Daniel thought as he walked to his car. It was uncanny how much his life had changed in such a short time.

He had taken his calling to the priesthood seriously. There had never been any doubt about his vocation. He felt privileged to be able to comfort the sick, offer hope to the poor and downtrodden. He couldn't find words to describe the joy he felt each time he celebrated mass. He felt both humbled and honoured with the ritual of preparing the Eucharist. But now, recalling Bailey's small trusting arms around his neck, he wondered if this might be a higher calling.

Lauren had done a good job with Bailey, Daniel thought as he got behind the wheel of his rental car. She was a bright child, happy and confident. But would she grow into a sullen, angry teenager, scarred by his absence? He'd seen kids in his parish acting out in anger because they felt their parents had abandoned them. God knows, he loved Lauren. Would God want him to sacrifice the woman and child he loved? What had he been thinking last night to behave in such a manner? He could only imagine what Lauren thought about it. She had loved him and he had brought her nothing but pain. Now he had come back into her life offering her nothing again.

CHAPTER

28

Emma glanced at her watch. Lauren would be arriving in about ten minutes. She had called earlier saying she'd drop by after her class. Leaning back in her chair, she stared out the window overlooking the campus. The grounds were scattered with dead leaves, ice, and slush. Emma knew that in a few weeks the groundskeepers would have them manicured to perfection. The trees would be in full bloom and colourful flowers would flourish in bark-mulched beds.

What's Lauren up to? Emma wondered. She'd been adamant about not letting Daniel Kerry back into her life, yet there he was this morning dropping Bailey off at school. Not that Emma faulted her for letting Bailey get to know her father. She never thought Lauren should have kept them apart. And Bailey seemed so at ease with Daniel—as if she'd known him all her life. It was easy to see why Lauren was attracted to him. He was handsome and charming. Those blue eyes. No wonder Lauren was so conflicted.

A knock at the door roused Emma from her thoughts. *Lauren's early,* she thought. "Come in," she called through the partially opened door.

Emma looked up, surprised to see Erika Jansen walk in.

"I hope I'm not disturbing you, Professor Buckle," she said.

"I have a few minutes," Emma said. "Have a seat."

"I'm hoping to get another extension on my assignment. I'll have it to you by noon tomorrow, I promise."

"That's no problem, sure." Emma studied Erika. "You're looking a lot better than when I last saw you. How are you feeling?"

"I have a handle on my depression, but I'm still not sleeping. My anxiety attacks are still a big problem."

"Well, I'm glad the depression has lifted at least. That can be a terrible thing."

"A real bitch," Erika agreed. She looked at Emma. "Have you ever been depressed?"

Emma paused. "I have," she admitted. "In the months after my husband died. It took me a long time to come out of it. It can be really challenging." Usually, Emma didn't share private information with her students, but she felt it was important for Erika to realize she understood what she was going through.

"Really?" It was clear that Erika wasn't expecting to hear this. "I appreciate your honesty, Professor Buckle. People who haven't been depressed can't understand what it's like. Sometimes it feels like I've fallen into a deep, dark hole with no way out."

Emma nodded. Her own depression had totally incapacitated her. Her mother had come every day during that dark time; she'd done the housework and taken care of Dylan. During that period, Dylan spent more time with her grandmother than she did with Emma.

"I don't know when a panic attack is going to hit me," Erika said.

Emma knew what that was like too. After André was killed, she would sometimes feel an overwhelming sense of fear. The world was fragile, no longer a safe place. A loved one could be gone in the blink of an eye. She no longer felt safe in her own home. Emma leaned toward Erika. "I hope you'll be feeling better soon," she said.

"Thank you for your understanding, Professor Buckle. And thank you for giving me another extension."

"Take as much time as you need," Emma said. "That assignment you took on is more elaborate and complex than anything your classmates have committed themselves to."

"I did go a bit overboard," Erika admitted.

Emma smiled. "You certainly did." While most of her students had written one-act plays for their final assignment, Erika had chosen to write a stage adaptation of *The Victory of Geraldine Gull*, a novel by Joan Clark. The book, shortlisted for the Governor General's Award back in the eighties, was one of Emma's favourites.

"I appreciate you offering me extra time," Erika said, "but I really do plan to have it in by tomorrow. I need to be able to move on to other things." She met Emma's gaze. "You're so caring, Professor Buckle. Not like some professors I could name."

Emma knew Erika was referring to Annabelle Chandler; the two had butted heads on more than one occasion. Although Emma felt Annabelle had been unreasonable not to take Erika's depression into account, she wasn't about to discuss her colleague with a student. "I'm happy to help in any way I can if it will make things easier," she replied.

"You know that Lisa Hare dropped out of the program because of Dr. Chandler," Erika continued.

"What? Why?" Emma asked, taken aback by the news. Lisa had been a talented student with the potential to make it as a professional actress. Barely a month into the second term, she'd quit the program without a word to anyone.

"She humiliated Lisa in front of the whole class."

"What happened?"

"Lisa was playing Joan of Arc and she was having trouble with her lines. Professor Chandler told her if Joan's voice had been as weak as hers France would have been lost to England forever."

Emma frowned. Annabelle should have known better. She was a great actress and a fine professor, but she could be insensitive at times. Still, for Lisa to drop out of the program over this was a bit extreme.

"I'm sorry that she quit the program," Emma said. "Like you, Lisa was a very promising actress. I wish she could have worked it out."

"I miss her," Erika said.

"Me too." Emma smiled. "Well, I must tell you, Professor Cromwell is very impressed with your adaptation."

"He's been very helpful," said Erica. "I have to admit there were times when I wanted to walk away from the whole thing. Just a couple of months ago I got so depressed I wanted to pack my bags and go home." She shook her head. "Professor Cromwell kept me grounded. He gave me encouragement, offered suggestions. It was his idea that I cut out some of the minor characters. The play's more focused now, and I feel really good about it."

"I'm looking forward to reading it," Emma said. "Professor Cromwell says he'll do what he can to help you get it produced."

"I'll probably put it in next year's fringe festival." Erika smiled. "And after that, who knows?" She rose to her feet. "I should be going," she said. "You probably have tons of work to do."

Emma looked at her watch. Lauren would be there any moment now.

"Well, thanks again, Professor Buckle," Erika said.

Emma watched her leave. There was something about Erika that she just couldn't put her finger on. A shame, Erika being such an exceptional student. Were her anxiety and depression rooted in some personal trauma? Emma wondered. *There doesn't always have to be a reason*, she told herself. *Some people are prone to it.* She felt sorry for Erika. She'd been there, and it was hell. She could still recall that dark time in her life as if it was yesterday. She had missed André so much she wanted to die too. She'd started to drink, hiding in her room after she put Dylan down for her naps. Lauren had come by nearly every day urging her to go to the gym. They had been going regularly before Emma had moved to Ottawa. But just the thought of dragging her body out the door had overwhelmed her. All she wanted was to be left alone. But Lauren was relentless: "Just ten minutes on the treadmill," she would coax. "It will make you feel better, I promise." It took a while, but gradually Emma's depression lifted and she started looking forward to her time at the gym. She knew she was lucky to have had Lauren in her life during that difficult time. Erika deserved the same support, and she would do whatever she could to help her.

Lauren arrived a few minutes later. She plopped into the nearest chair, shadows of exhaustion noticeable under her eyes. "You're not going to believe who I saw this morning."

Emma looked up at her with mild interest.

"The platinum lady."

"What?" Emma sat up straighter in her chair. "Where?"

"I went to visit Claire this morning and when I left her apartment, the platinum lady was standing in the yard."

"She was in Claire's yard—the platinum lady?"

"Not a *lady*, exactly."

Emma shot her a puzzled look.

"What I mean is…she's a *he*." Lauren leaned forward. "The platinum lady is none other than Mitch Cromwell."

Emma stared at her. "Are you serious?"

Lauren nodded.

"My God!" Emma said. "And she—*he* was at Claire's house the day Ariel died. You don't suppose…."

"He's certainly a suspect," Lauren said, "but he agreed to go to the police and explain." She fixed Emma with a stare. "You need to be discreet. I'm only telling you this because I got you mixed up in the situation. It's not something Mitch wants getting out."

"No, I don't imagine it is," Emma said, recalling how Mitch had bolted when they spotted him in St. John's. "Does Claire know?"

Lauren tightened her lips. "Oh, *she* knows."

"She should have told us," Emma said.

Lauren agreed. "Mitch could be subpoenaed if the case goes to trial."

"That could be embarrassing," Emma said.

"It was the strangest thing, seeing him this morning."

Emma shook her head as if to clear away her confusion. "Speaking of strange things…I saw Daniel and Bailey at Kiddy Academy this morning." She gave Lauren a sidelong glance. "I never expected him to be so beautiful."

Lauren laughed. "What *did* you expect? A nerd in a clerical collar?"

"Are you a couple again?"

"I don't think we were ever a *couple*. Daniel's married to the church. I've always felt like his mistress. Anyway, he's gone home now."

"That's a shame. He's really good with Bailey. I'm glad you decided to tell him about her."

"Actually, it was Paula who let the cat out of the bag."

At that moment, a knock came at the door and Emma went to answer it. A small, slim woman with reddish dyed hair stood in the hallway. Despite the warm weather, she wore a scarf and a pale yellow ski jacket. Her face was blotchy, her eyes red-rimmed as if she'd been crying.

"Hello, ma'am. Can I help you?" Emma said.

"Dr. Buckle?"

Emma nodded.

"I'm Stella Roberts. My daughter, Jade, was in one of your classes."

Emma held open the door. "Ms. Roberts, please come in."

Stella stepped into the office. "Oh," she said, glancing worriedly at Lauren. "I'm sorry to interrupt."

"It's okay," Emma said. "This is Lauren LaVallee, Jade's criminology instructor."

"You called me about a week ago," Lauren reminded her.

"Oh, yes," Stella said. "I went by your office. They told me you were in class."

"I just finished," Lauren said. "If you need to talk, I have a few minutes."

"Take a seat," Emma said, motioning to a nearby chair. "Can I take your jacket?"

"That's okay," Stella said. "I don't plan to stay long."

"I take it you still haven't heard from Jade," Lauren said, sensing Stella's distress.

"No," Stella said, her voice wobbly. "I drove in from St. John's today to clean out her apartment. She left *everything*. Cara's clothes. All her little dresses and sleepers. Left behind her baby pictures, her birth certificate, all kinds of personal items. And the rent was paid until the end of the month."

Lauren and Emma exchanged looks.

"Something's wrong," Stella said. She pressed a trembling hand to her mouth.

Emma leaned toward her. "When did you last hear from Jade?"

"A week before she disappeared—I lent her money to have her telephone reinstalled. Seems odd now that she'd go to that trouble if she was planning to leave."

"Ms. Roberts, in light of everything that's happened, I think you should contact the police again," Lauren said. "Rebecca Taylor is an RCMP officer in my criminology class. She knows Jade—knows her situation. I can call her if you like."

"That's okay, my love." Stella stood up, calmer now, but Lauren could tell she was still upset. "I plan to go to the police station after I leave here. I'll ask for Officer Taylor."

"Can I give you a ride?" Emma offered.

"No, my love, I have my car. I'll be fine."

Emma saw Stella to the door. "Let us know if you hear from Jade."

"I'll do that."

Emma closed the door and turned to Lauren. "Are you as worried as I am?"

—

"Not the kind of stuff a tenant leaves behind," Constable Rebecca Taylor said as she looked around Jade's apartment. Hours after Stella Roberts left the police station, they'd obtained a warrant to go inside.

"No doubt Jade intended to return," Kyle Harrison, Rebecca's partner, agreed. He opened a tin box filled with cards, photographs, letters, and other personal items.

Rebecca touched a bright butterfly stuck to the patio door. "Interesting," she said.

"Brightens up the place," Kyle said.

Rebecca ducked into the bathroom and pulled open the medicine cabinet. She found a bottle of Tylenol, some rubbing alcohol, and a box of Band-Aids. Under the sink were tampons, Epsom salts, a can of Ajax, and other cleaning supplies. More butterflies were stuck to the bathtub, toilet, and mirror.

When Rebecca returned to the kitchen, Kyle was methodically going through the cupboards. She opened the closet and found several coats and sweaters. More proof that Jade had intended to return.

"What are you looking for?" Kyle asked.

"A red coat—the one Jade wore to school nearly every day. I don't see it anywhere."

They moved to the bedroom, going through bureau drawers. The bed was unmade but the sheets and blankets had not been removed. There were more photographs of Cara on the dresser. A small crib stood in one corner with a box of Pampers beneath. A telephone sat on a night table, its red light blinking.

"Let's see who Jade called last." Rebecca hit the redial button. The phone was picked up almost immediately. "Paddy's Arm Medical Centre," said a curt voice.

"This is Constable Rebecca Taylor," she said. "I'm checking out a number."

"Can I help you?"

"It's okay," Rebecca said. "But thank you." She hung up the phone and turned to Kyle. "Hopefully, they'll have a record of the call."

"We may need to subpoena Ms. Roberts's carrier to access her voice mail."

"Only if it's password protected." Rebecca picked up the receiver again, and dialled *99.

"You have eighteen new messages," said a robotic voice. "To retrieve your messages, press one."

Rebecca did as the machine instructed. The first call was from Jade's mother. "Jade, it's Mom. Give me a call."

Most of the calls were run of the mill: friends wanting to get together, offers from telemarketers, a call from the landlord informing her that the water would be shut off. Erika Jansen had called wanting to "touch base." The last call was from Patrick Shaw: "Jade, where are you? I went by your apartment, but you weren't there. Thought you said to come around seven. Did I get the time wrong?" There was a slight pause. "Anyway, I got the money. I'm going back to my apartment. Call as soon as—" a loud beep signalled the mailbox was full.

Kyle frowned. "Money?"

"Jade borrowed money from all her friends, but I'll have an informal chat with Patrick tomorrow at the preschool," Rebecca said. "He's working the late shift this week. Darren's been picking up Connor, but I'll go get him before I start work."

"Good idea. We'll follow up with the others who left messages as well." Kyle frowned. "You have to wonder, though: why would Jade send emails to friends and professors? Why send an email to her landlord telling him she was moving if she had no intention of doing so?"

"I don't believe she wrote those messages."

Kyle stared at Rebecca, the meaning of her words sinking in. "Someone else sent them?"

"It's possible."

"Now that I think about it," Kyle said thoughtfully, "it's the only thing that makes sense. But that means—"

"It means we're looking at a possible homicide."

CHAPTER

29

Patrick was putting away books and toys when Rebecca arrived at Kiddy Academy. She was surprised to see Lauren's daughter still there; her son, Connor, was usually the last kid to be picked up. Bailey stood by the door tapping her foot impatiently.

"Mommy!" Connor called. "I made you a picture."

"It's wonderful," Rebecca said, taking in the jumble of lines and colours.

"Know what it is?"

"A house?"

Connor looked at his mother as if she'd gone mad. "Nooo!"

"A moose?"

He laughed. "Mommy, you're silly."

"I give up."

"It's *Daddy*."

"Of course," Rebecca said, winking at Patrick. "I should have seen the resemblance."

Bailey came and stood beside them, obviously upset. "Everyone's leaving," she said in a small voice. "Will Momma come get me?"

"Your mom had to meet someone," Patrick explained patiently. "She'll pick you up in a little while."

"Will you still be here?"

"Of course," he reassured her. "I stay until *all* the mommies come."

Bailey looked visibly relieved.

Rebecca smiled. Turning to Patrick, she said, "You must soon be finished your internship."

"I'll be here until about the first week in April to get enough hours to meet my requirement."

"You'll probably be relieved to get it behind you."

"I'll miss the kids." Patrick glanced over to where Bailey and Connor were standing by the fish tank.

Rebecca followed his gaze. "Patrick, do you have a minute to chat?"

Before he could respond, Bailey and Connor came over to stand beside them.

Patrick unlocked a cupboard and took out two wooden puzzles.

"Can we play with them?" Bailey asked.

Patrick nodded. "I was saving them for a special occasion. But if you and Connor can sit quietly while I talk to Connor's mom, I'll let you use them now."

Both children nodded eagerly.

Once he had the kids settled, Patrick turned to Rebecca. "You probably want to discuss Connor's progress report since you couldn't make the parent-teacher meeting."

"I'm very pleased with Connor's report," Rebecca said. "Actually, I wanted to talk about your friend, Jade Roberts."

Patrick stared at her, slightly taken aback. "How can I help? I don't know anything about Jade."

Rebecca got straight to the point. "I know you called Jade shortly before she disappeared."

Patrick put his hands up in mock surrender. "Do I need to call my lawyer or something?"

"Do you *think* you need to call your lawyer?"

Patrick didn't answer.

"This is an informal investigation into Jade's disappearance," Rebecca said. "Her family is very concerned."

"I called her the day before she left," Patrick admitted. "I was supposed to babysit Cara. When I got to her apartment there was no one there."

"On the voice mail, you said you 'had the money.' Were you giving Jade money?"

Patrick swallowed. "Jade was always borrowing money."

"Did you have contact with her after the day she left?"

"No, I…I haven't seen Jade since then."

"Did you notice any changes in her behaviour?"

"Well…" Patrick glanced up at the ceiling. "She was getting impatient with Cara. A couple of days before she took off, Jade asked me to come over. The baby was teething and she couldn't take her crying. I took Cara for a walk in her stroller."

"And that was the last time you saw Jade?"

"I…I guess."

"Did you notice anything unusual, any strange visitors?"

Patrick shook his head. "You think something might have happened to Jade or Cara?" He sounded anxious.

"That's what we're trying to find out."

At that moment Lauren walked in the door.

"Momma!" Bailey got up from the table and ran to her.

"I'm sorry I'm late, darling."

Rebecca handed Patrick her card. "Call me if Jade contacts you, or if you remember anything that might be important."

Nodding, Patrick accepted the card and put it in his shirt pocket.

Rebecca went to retrieve Connor's jacket. *Patrick's keeping something from me*, she thought. *He's not telling the whole truth.*

—

Lauren was on her way out the door when Bailey said, "Momma, I forgot Regis, and I need to go get him."

As Lauren waited for her daughter by the door she could hear Patrick on his cellphone. "I got your message," he said. "You must have deposited the whole amount…I really wasn't expecting *that* much."

Lauren felt her mouth gape open as she strained to listen to the snatches of conversation "I hope to see you…I—"

Bailey came back holding her stuffed animal tightly, but Lauren felt rooted to the spot.

"Momma, can we go now?" Bailey tugged at her sleeve.

Worried Patrick would hear them, Lauren grabbed Bailey's hand and walked straight to the parking lot.

Rebecca and Connor were waiting. "Have you been to see Andrew?" Rebecca asked. "You must know they took him out of the induced coma."

"Yes, Gina told me. I'm planning to go visit him this evening, as a matter of fact. Gina says he's on the mend. They just started allowing visitors other than family." She turned to face Rebecca. "Gina also told me the police placed a security guard on Andrew's door."

"Just as a precautionary measure," Rebecca said. "We're afraid that whoever shot Andrew might come after him if they think he can identify them."

Lauren shivered at the thought. "Do you have any leads?"

"No," Rebecca admitted, "but we're working on it."

"At least Andrew's improving."

"We're all happy about that." Rebecca stared at a grey Lexus parked next to Lauren's car. "Nice set of wheels," she commented.

Lauren had noticed the car when she drove in. "I know! Who drives expensive cars like that around here?"

Rebecca laughed. "None of my colleagues, I'm sure." Turning toward Lauren, she continued in a more serious tone. "Listen, I thought you should know that we've put out a missing person's report on Jade Roberts. We're holding a press conference this evening."

Lauren felt her mouth go dry, but managed a nod. "I'm glad action is finally being taken," she said. "I've had an uncomfortable feeling about Jade's disappearance." She looked around for Bailey. "Come, darling," she called. "It's time to go."

"Lauren," Rebecca began, "you told me Jade called you the day she went missing. Do you remember what time that was?"

"It was just after three."

"Are you certain about the time?"

"Yes, I remember because it was just before I left to pick up Bailey. I took her with me to Claire's house."

"The lady across the hall from Jade said Jade had left the apartment hours earlier and didn't return."

"Could she have been mistaken?"

Rebecca shrugged. "It's possible. But she seems pretty certain. Could Jade have called you from someplace else?"

"I...don't know. I mean, I didn't check the number. I just assumed she called me from home. The number is probably gone by now. They're only saved for a few weeks." Lauren paused for a moment. "Too bad the reception was so poor that day. Who knows, I may have learned something about Jade's whereabouts."

At that moment, Patrick came out of Kiddy Academy and started toward the Lexus.

"Is that your car?" Rebecca asked.

"Yeah," Patrick said proudly.

Lauren and Rebecca exchanged looks as Patrick started the engine with an automatic starter.

"One hundred and fifty horsepower," he added in the bragging tone guys reserved for talking about their cars.

Lauren thought of the telephone conversation she'd overheard. Who was giving Patrick money? And why? For a moment, she considered telling Rebecca what she'd overheard. But she couldn't. Patrick was her client, and that required trust. If she learned anything from *Nelson vs. Little*, it was to always protect the client.

Patrick opened the car door and ran his hands over the material on the seats as if he were stroking a pet. "Front seats are heated and ventilated."

"Nice," Rebecca said.

"Better than that heap of tin I was driving. The muffler's so loud you could hear it for miles. Well, take care, ladies," he said. "Connor and Bailey, I'll see you both in the morning."

"Bye, Patrick," the kids said in unison.

He got in the car and put the key in the ignition.

"Kiddy Academy must pay their interns well," Rebecca said as they watched Patrick drive away.

CHAPTER 30

Lauren picked up the cordless phone in the kitchen, and scrolled down the list of callers to February 12. To her relief, the eight calls that had come in the day Jade disappeared were still saved. Two of them had blocked numbers, one was from an 800 number, and four were from friends and colleagues. A call that had come in at 3:06 P.M. had no name but an unfamiliar number was listed. Lauren hit the talk button, and listened as the phone rang and rang.

She searched online and found the number listed as a pay phone located at Comeau's Cabins on the Lake. It was in Timber Woods, a secluded area about a forty-minute drive from Paddy's Arm. With its campground and various rental accommodations, it had become a popular vacation spot. A lot of people had their summer homes in the area. Could Jade be staying there? Another quick search and Lauren learned that the proprietor of Comeau's Cabins was a Madeleine Comeau.

Bailey was sprawled on the living room floor with a colouring book. "Momma has to go out," Lauren told her. "Christine will come to stay with you." Bailey nodded without looking up from her colouring. Lauren glanced at her watch, and saw it was nearly five-thirty. She had already fed Bailey. If the young girl from down the road didn't mind staying a couple of extra hours, Lauren would go to Comeau's Cabins and be back at the hospital before visiting hours ended.

Forty minutes later, Lauren found herself on a narrow stretch of road heading east when her cellphone rang. Probably the sitter, she thought as she pulled over to the side of the road.

"Lauren. It's Daniel."

"Daniel? Hello." Strangely, she felt happy to hear his voice. "I take it you made it home okay?"

"Safe and sound. How are you, Lauren?"

"I'm doing well."

"And Bailey?"

"She's at home right now—with the sitter."

"I see Paddy's Arm is in the news again," Daniel said. "I read about the young woman who disappeared."

"Jade Roberts. She was in my criminology class." Lauren saw no reason to tell him where she was headed at that moment.

"She has a baby, I understand."

"A little girl. They're searching for both of them."

There was a brief pause.

"Lauren, I got a call this morning. My friend Phillip passed away in his sleep."

"The priest in New Wexford? Daniel, I'm so sorry."

"I'm just glad he didn't suffer," Daniel said. "Anyway, I plan to attend the memorial service. They haven't set a date yet, but I would like to stop in Paddy's Arm while I'm in Newfoundland."

"To see Bailey?" As soon as the words left her lips Lauren felt foolish. Did she think Daniel was coming to visit *her*?

"I'm hoping I can spend time with her. Take her out to supper."

"That's fine, Daniel. Give me a call when you arrive."

"Sure thing. You take care, now."

Lauren stared at the phone a long time before getting back on the road. Glancing at her watch, she saw it was 6:15. She would have to hurry if she wanted to get to the hospital before visiting hours ended.

The dark days of winter had passed and evenings were becoming longer now. As Lauren drove along the deserted highway, she passed a few clapboard houses that stood on the side of the road. Through the skeletal trees she saw summer homes along the jagged coastline. Some had boats and rafts pulled up on the beach.

After a while, she came to a sign with an arrow that said *Comeau's Cabins: Daily and Weekly Rentals*. She hoped her long drive had not been in vain. Since Madeleine Comeau's civic address was the same as the cabins, Lauren assumed she lived on the property.

After driving another mile Lauren arrived at the main house, a ramshackle old building badly in need of paint. The lawn surrounding it needed mowing. A pitchfork and rusty wheelbarrow stood near a shed. She parked the car and walked up to the front door.

A woman answered, opening the main door and peering from behind a worn screen door. She was short and bulky with fingers like sausage, and leaned heavily on a crutch. Her gray hair, cut in a blunt style, made her large head look square. "Cabins won't be ready for another three weeks," she called through the screen.

"Mrs. Comeau? I'm Lauren LaVallee, an attorney with Beck Hayes. I've come to talk to you about Jade Roberts. I know she stayed here a while back."

The woman pulled open the screen door. "Come in, my love," she said. "Watch that step now." She led Lauren into a sitting room with furniture covered in knitted afghans. A long narrow table covered with a white cloth ran along one wall like an altar. On it were various statues, surrounded by dozens of candles. Above the table hung a crucifix and a picture of Pope John Paul II. "Take a seat," Mrs. Comeau said, nodding toward a small sofa. She put aside her crutch and eased herself into an overstuffed chair across from Lauren.

"Mrs. Comeau," Lauren began, "did you rent Jade Roberts a cabin?"

"That's right. Must have been more than a month now."

"I thought you said the cabins wouldn't be ready for another three weeks."

"That's right, my love. My niece is coming from St. John's to help out. Since poor Charlie died, things have been difficult to manage." She looked down at her leg. "Not much I can do with this cast on."

"That would make things difficult," Lauren said. She offered a sympathetic smile before continuing. "How did Jade come to stay here?"

"Poor girl told me she was on the run from an abusive boyfriend. Felt sorry for her, I did. I gave her sheets and blankets. Told her she'd have to fend for herself."

Abusive boyfriend. Lauren thought she'd heard distress in Jade's voice the afternoon she called. "Did she have a baby with her?"

"A baby?" Mrs. Comeau looked stunned. "No, my love, she never mentioned a baby."

"How did she get here?"

"Someone drove her."

"Did you see the car?"

"Yes, it was black...maybe dark blue."

"Did she have other visitors you were aware of?"

"A car came late that evening."

"The same one?"

"It was too dark to see, but the second car sounded like it needed a muffler. The noise was so bad it woke me up."

Lauren sat up straighter in her chair, Patrick's words echoing in her brain. *Better than that heap of tin...the muffler so loud you could hear it for miles.* She had always assumed Patrick and Jade were friends. Could they have been more than that?

Mrs. Comeau stared at Lauren with hooded eyes. "Is the poor girl in some kind of trouble?"

"She's been missing for about five weeks now."

Mrs. Comeau stared at her in disbelief. "Sweet Virgin Mary, mother of the precious baby Jesus, protect her."

"When was the last time you actually saw Jade, Mrs. Comeau?"

"The morning after she moved in. I seen her walking along the beach."

"And when did she check out?"

Mrs. Comeau shook her head. "Can't say for certain. Father Williams was here the next day—he comes every Friday to bring me the Sacrament. I asked him to check on the girl, see if she needed anything. He came back minutes later to tell me she'd checked out."

"Could she have been out walking?"

"The vacancy sign was in the window, and she'd left the key in the mailbox like I asked her to do." Mrs. Comeau shifted in her chair. "She was paid up for the week. I would've given her a refund had she asked."

"Can I take a look at the cabin where she was staying?"

Mrs. Comeau gave her a curious look. "Sure, my love. It's cabin 12." She rose unsteadily to her feet and reached for a key. "You can leave the key in the mailbox when you're finished."

"I'll see myself out," Lauren said as Mrs. Comeau struggled with her crutch.

Cabin 12 was in a little clearing overlooking the lake. Peaceful, Lauren thought, looking around at the trees. There were still patches of snow in the woods. She could hear the cawing of a crow.

Despite a sharp odour of dampness and mildew, everything in the cabin was neat and tidy. The main room was a kitchen and sitting room combined. White cupboards flanked a trailer-size fridge and stove. There was a small wooden table with two chairs, and a bathroom, with enough room for a toilet and a shower. A small bedroom ran along the back.

Lauren opened drawers and looked into cupboards. One was filled with utensils, another with tea towels and dishcloths. Under the sink, she found a small plastic bag filled with garbage. She dumped its contents on a newspaper on the table. There were cigarette packages, candy bar wrappers, crumpled coffee cups. Among the trash, she noticed a blue plastic syringe. Had Jade holed up here to do drugs? Lauren was about to dump everything back in the bag when she noticed the front page of the newspaper underneath; it carried the story of Ariel's death. The paper was from Friday, February 13, the day after the incident.

Lauren stared at the headlines. Coincidence, she wondered, or was there more to it?

She went into the bedroom and began opening drawers. In the night stand, she found two pairs of underwear and a nightgown with the tags still on. *Jade must have left in a hurry*, Lauren thought. *Was she afraid the person she claimed was abusing her might find out where was staying?*

Lauren pulled open the door to a small closet. Except for a blanket and a number of empty hangers, it was empty. She was about to close the door when she noticed a bag beneath the blanket. Through the clear plastic she could see hundred-dollar bills. She opened it up, and quickly counted the money. Close to three thousand dollars.

Lauren scrambled for her cellphone. "I need to speak to Constable Rebecca Taylor."

CHAPTER

31

There were only a few patients in the waiting room when Rebecca arrived at the clinic. They had questioned the girl at the switchboard, but there was no record of the call Jade had made the day she disappeared. The clinic housed a variety of specialists, including dentists, dermatologists, physiotherapists, pediatricians, and psychologists. Jade could have been calling any one of them.

"Dr. Kaminsky is waiting for you," the receptionist told Rebecca. She gestured toward the hallway. "Second door on your left."

The office door was slightly ajar, and as Rebecca approached she heard a male voice: "You're not making things easier for me, Anya."

"I've tried to be patient," Anya replied. "Just what do you expect of me?"

The door opened and Bram Warren looked out. "Hello there, Constable," he said, looking sheepish. "Can I help you?"

"I have an appointment with Dr. Kaminsky. Police business."

"Come in, Rebecca," Anya called. She was sitting behind her desk, a stethoscope draped casually around her neck.

"Sorry to interrupt your meeting," Rebecca said.

"I'm finished here," Bram said, stepping past her.

Rebecca closed the office door behind her.

"Please forgive Dr. Warren," Anya said. "He can be difficult at times." She shook her head. "We try to ignore his outbursts. He's lost his only child."

"Yes, I can only imagine."

Anya folded her hands on her desk and smiled. "How can I help you, Constable Taylor?"

"I understand Jade Roberts was one of your patients."

Anya frowned. "*Was?*"

"We don't know where she is. She disappeared weeks ago and no one's heard from her."

"I see...but how can *I* help?"

"Apparently, she called the clinic on February 12, the day she disappeared. We can't establish which doctor she called, but I'm assuming it was you."

"February 12...that's the day Ariel died."

Rebecca nodded.

"I don't recall a phone call from Jade, but as you know, things were really chaotic that day." Anya leaned back in her chair. "Jade could have called while I was out, but she didn't leave a message. I always get back to my patients."

"Had you noticed anything unusual about Jade's behaviour?"

"I was concerned about Jade *and* Cara," Anya admitted. She spoke carefully, as if weighing her words. "I worried Jade might be neglectful, abusive even. However, I could not see any direct evidence. I gave her my cell number in case she needed to get in touch with me."

"You go well beyond the call of duty, Dr. K."

The doctor carried a dedicated cellphone so her patients could get in touch with her directly if they were in distress and the clinic was closed. Rebecca had used it once when Connor had a very high fever and she wasn't sure what to do.

"Did Jade happen to send you an email before she disappeared?" Rebecca asked.

"An email?" The doctor looked puzzled.

"She sent emails to some of her friends and professors," Rebecca explained.

Anya shook her head. "No, I have never received an email from Jade Roberts."

—

It was nearly eight by the time Lauren got to the hospital. During the drive back from the lake, she couldn't keep her mind off the bag of money she'd found. Was this more proof that Jade had sold her baby? If so, why would she leave the money behind? Was she planning to return for it? If that was the case, why would she leave the key in the mailbox when she was paid up for a week? It didn't make sense. Lauren was almost certain that Patrick was involved. She thought of the phone call at the preschool that afternoon. Who had deposited money in his account?

The guard outside Andrew's room asked to see ID before Lauren could enter. *They're really taking his safety seriously*, she thought. Andrew was lying in bed, sheets pulled up to his chin, eyes closed. Sitting around his bed were Anya and Gina, who was looking though a photo album. She looked up when Lauren came into the room. "Hi," she said. "Thank you for coming."

Anya nodded and smiled. In her pink hoodie and blue jeans, she could pass for a teenager.

"How is he?" Lauren whispered, walking to the foot of the hospital bed. Andrew was deathly still, his face pale.

"He's going to pull through, thank God," Gina said, her voice wobbling.

"He will be going home soon," Anya said.

Lauren took a seat next to Gina. "Does he remember anything?"

"The police questioned him," Gina said. "I don't think he remembers anything, but that's not to say his memory won't return."

"Sometimes it takes months—even years," said Anya.

Gina closed the album and handed it to Lauren. "Pictures of Andrew when he was growing up," she said. "My sister Vonnie put it together. She sent it from Brampton for his birthday last week."

Lauren opened the cover. On the first page was a picture of a bald, red-faced baby, the kind photographers take in hospitals. *Our Andrew at twelve hours old*, the caption read. Smiling, Lauren turned the page. There were pictures of baby Andrew with his parents, with various siblings holding him. Turning the pages, she watched a chubby toddler morph into a tall slim boy on his first day of school. "He was adorable," she said. She turned another page to a photograph of Andrew and three of his siblings. They were sitting on a sofa holding baby rabbits. "Were the rabbits pets?" Lauren asked.

Gina glanced at the album. "We found a nest of them down by Long Pond," she said. She pointed to a chubby little girl with a moon face. "That's me with the weird haircut." She laughed. "It looks like mom just put a bowl on my head and cut around it."

Lauren studied the picture. Although Gina's hair was now neatly coifed and she had lost most of her chubbiness, she still had the moon face. "Did you keep them?"

Gina shook her head. "Dad made us take them back." She chuckled. "Poor Andrew was so upset. I still remember how he cried. He's always loved animals. Dad used to call him St. Francis of the Arm."

"He's especially fond of birds," said Anya. "Every morning he gets up early and feeds them on his way to work."

"That's something he's been doing since he was very little," said Gina. "He's particularly fond of crows. Mom often managed to get a bag of stale bread for him. But I remember one morning he took the loaf she intended to use for breakfast." Gina laughed. "She was fit to be tied. With so many mouths to feed, we couldn't afford to give good food to the birds."

Lauren continued to turn pages in the album. There were pictures of Andrew in his Boy Scout uniform; Andrew opening gifts on Christmas morning. In one photograph, he was sitting at a long table with other children playing cards.

"Andrew liked to gamble," said Gina.

"Gamble?" Lauren laughed.

Gina nodded. "When we were kids, we played poker for marbles—for jellybeans if we had them. But Andrew wanted to play for money. He would gamble away his allowance, the money he got for selling pop bottles or running chores for people." Gina smiled, remembering. "One day Reverend Owen, the minister, came to visit and Andrew challenged him to a game. He took twenty pennies from his pocket and placed them on the table. The reverend was outraged. He called gambling the work of the devil. Mom burned the playing cards after that."

"Does he still like to gamble?" Lauren asked.

"Oh, yes," Gina said. "He often buys lottery tickets."

"He's joined a poker group," said Anya. "They call themselves the Gang of Six. Dr. Warren is a member too."

Gina looked amused. "Well, I should be going," she said, rising from her chair. "I promised my family I'd be home early."

I should be going too, Lauren thought. She glanced at Andrew, who had barely stirred since she, and turned to the last page in the album. There were pictures of Andrew graduating from high school. In one, he was with a girl in a cap and gown. He had his arm around her waist and they were smiling into the camera. "Is that Emma?" Lauren asked.

Gina nodded. "They used to be a couple back in the day. We all thought they would marry." She reached for her bag just as Bram appeared in the doorway. He was wearing scrubs, a mask dangling from his neck. A stethoscope was tucked in his pocket. "Hello, ladies." He looked around the room. "Where is everyone?"

"The family was here all afternoon," Gina said. "They've gone home to eat. Some of them will be taking a flight out tonight."

"How's the patient?" Bram asked, approaching Andrew's bed. He turned to look at Gina. "Has he been sleeping all afternoon?"

"I've been here since one," said Gina. "He was awake for maybe fifteen minutes during that time."

As if on cue, Andrew opened his eyes.

"How are you, pal?" Bram asked.

Andrew closed his eyes again.

"Andrew is lucky to have such a concerned family," Anya said.

"Yes, it's always good to have people around who care about you," said Bram.

"One of the bonuses of having a large family," said Gina.

"Yes," Bram agreed, a cloud passing over his face.

Lauren wondered what was going through his mind. As close as she was to Claire, Lauren had never really gotten to know Bram. She wondered if he regretted that he had not grown up surrounded by people who cared for him. He had been so alone after his parents died.

Gina glanced at her watch. "I really do have to go."

"I think Lauren and Anya should leave too," Bram said.

Lauren was taken aback. Was he ordering them out of the room? She glanced at Anya, who had her lips set in a thin line. She gave Bram a look that could only be described as a glare.

Lauren stood up. "Well, you're the doctor," she said. "I'm sure you know what's best for the patient." But despite her light tone, she felt a flush of embarrassment at Bram's rudeness.

—

"Why would Jade leave all that money behind?" Rebecca said, as much to herself as to Kyle. They had left Comeau's Cabins after receiving a frantic call from Lauren LaVallee and were on their way back to the station.

Kyle shook his head. "There's something really strange going on here."

Rebecca recalled Patrick driving off in his expensive car that afternoon. "First a preschool teacher, an intern no less, buys a Lexus, and now this." The bigger mystery was where Jade and Patrick got that kind of money. Rebecca knew Jade had struggled with financial problems even before her partner, Willy, left her. She wouldn't be surprised if Willy had something to do with Jade's disappearance. She recalled all the times the police had been called to their apartment. Jade was a textbook case of battered-woman syndrome. She lacked confidence and was forever second-guessing herself. Her self-worth was so low she couldn't see the assets she had to offer.

"We need to rule out who sent those emails," Kyle said.

Rebecca nodded absently. They had established that the emails had been sent from an internet café. Anyone could have sent them; users were not required to show ID. If Jade hadn't sent the emails, it was obvious someone had gone to a lot of trouble to make it look like she had. If family and friends thought she had moved away, they wouldn't be as alarmed by her disappearance.

Rebecca's cellphone rang. She took it from her purse and glanced at the number. Seeing it was her husband, Darren, she put the phone away.

Kyle cast a curious look.

"I'll get it later," Rebecca said. She didn't feel like talking to Darren right now. Ever since her mother-in-law's visit, things had been tense between them. Maggie often rubbed Rebecca the wrong way, but this visit had been worse than any other. She had harped on about all the time Rebecca was spending away from home. She questioned why she needed to take courses. Her uncle was a police officer, Maggie kept reminding her, and he got all his training on the job. Rebecca had tried to explain that the courses would not only benefit her career, but also be good for the whole family. Rebecca sighed, causing Kyle to give her another look.

"Something on your mind, partner?"

"It's Maggie, my mother-in-law. She can't understand why I'm spending so much time away from home."

"Did you explain how important it is to get a degree?"

"I tried to but she just doesn't understand. It's stressful working full-time and going to school, but with Darren off work, it's a great opportunity for me to pick up some credits."

"Makes sense," Kyle said.

Rebecca's phone rang again—her brother, Ivan, this time. Probably wanting to hit her up for another loan. She ignored it, and turned her attention back to Kyle. "How did you get along with your in-laws?" she asked, silencing her phone. She knew Kyle's divorce had just become final.

"Fine," he said. "In fact, they still call me from time to time." He turned to look at her. "I take it that's not the case with you."

"Maybe I'm overreacting, but Maggie gets under my skin." Rebecca tightened her lips. "She's upset because Darren quit his job to move here."

"How does Darren feel about it?"

"He was fine with it until recently. Now he's complaining that he's bored. One of my classes is two nights a week. And as you know, I do a lot of night shifts."

"It's difficult being married to a police officer," Kyle said. "All the moving around and late nights." He tapped his fingers on the steering wheel. "I remember how upset my wife was when I had to go out west for training. She was young and didn't want to be away from her family. I don't want to trivialize things but if Darren's bored, maybe he should get a hobby."

"I've urged him to take some courses at the college. He's always been interested in pottery."

"It could lead him into a whole new career."

Rebecca smiled. "I doubt that will happen." Still, she wished Darren would do *something*. She had suggested he apply at some of the garages in town. He didn't see the sense when Rebecca was going to be transferred to Halifax in a few months.

"Are you worried about your marriage?" Kyle asked bluntly.

"Things are kind of stressful right now," Rebecca admitted.

"It's a difficult balance," Kyle said. "Our spouses don't always have an easy time."

Rebecca nodded. But as much as she worried about her marriage, she was determined not to end up like her mother, who had given up a nursing career she loved to raise four children. Their father walked out on the family when Rebecca was twelve. Because her mother had let her nursing license expire, the only job she could find was as a nurse's aide at a nursing home. The job barely paid minimum wage. She remembered her mother coming home stressed and worn out. *That will never happen to me*, Rebecca vowed. Her phone vibrated in her pocket, and this time she saw it was Lauren LaVallee. She picked up.

"I'm just wondering if you found out anything new about Jade and Cara," Lauren said.

Rebecca felt a wave of annoyance. "Lauren, I know you're concerned," she said, her voice sharper than she intended, "but this is a police matter. You need to stay out of it."

CHAPTER

32

Madeleine Comeau watched from the window of her living room as divers in orange suits plunged into the water. Less than an hour after the RCMP's visit, they'd arrived. After securing the area they'd spent a sleepless night waiting for daylight. They were now dragging the lake.

Officers walked along the shore. Through the open window, Madeleine could hear the static of their two-way radios. There were rescue boats on the lake, and from time to time a helicopter flew over the water, circling low. They had been searching for nearly nine hours now. Madeleine shuddered to think that poor girl might be lying beneath the cold water. She had stayed awake all night, offering up prayers to the Virgin Mary for Jade and her little one. She knew the police suspected foul play from the questions they asked. One of the officers made a point of telling her she should keep her door locked at night. Precious Jesus. Did they believe she was in danger?

She folded her arms across her chest as if hugging herself. Never had she been so happy to see Father Williams's car pull up in front of the house. It was not his usual visiting day, but when she'd called him that morning, he suggested taking her out for a change of scenery, as he put it.

Just as Madeleine opened the door, the priest turned toward the lake. Following his gaze, she saw two divers haul something into a boat.

"Looks like they found what they were looking for," Father Williams said.

"Police are seeking the public's help in solving the drowning death of a Paddy's Arm student." The newscaster's voice was solemn as she read the report. "Twenty-three-year-old Jade Roberts's body was pulled from a small lake less than an hour's drive from Paddy's Arm." Lauren sucked in her breath as a picture of Jade, holding Cara in her arms, flashed on the screen. "Police have ruled the death a homicide," the newscaster continued. "Roberts was last seen on February 13 at Comeau's Cabins on the Lake." There was a quick cut to a view of the lake. "Still missing is Roberts's nine-month-old baby girl, Cara." Again the picture of Jade and Cara flashed on the screen. This time the camera zoomed in for a close-up of Cara. "The infant was last seen on February 12. Anyone with information about the victim or her child's whereabouts is asked to call the RCMP."

Claire picked up the remote and turned off the television. "I pray that whoever has Cara is taking good care of her," she said.

Both Lauren and Emma nodded. The trio was having tea in Claire's living room.

"They're dragging the lake for Cara," Emma said.

Lauren shuddered. "Let's hope they don't find her there."

"I suppose they need to rule out that the baby died with her mother," Claire said.

"I feel guilty for not taking Jade's disappearance seriously," Emma said. "God knows I had enough students voicing concerns. I should have gone to the police."

"You mustn't blame yourself," Lauren said. "There was no way to prevent what happened. The outcome would have been the same no matter what you did. After receiving those emails we all thought Jade had found a job and left."

"Why were the emails sent?" Claire asked.

"Rebecca Taylor thinks they were sent by the killer," Lauren said. "Someone who wanted us to believe Jade was still alive."

"The police must have suspected foul play before the body was recovered," Claire said.

"I'm sure they considered that possibility," Lauren agreed.

Emma turned to Lauren. "Have you had a chance to visit Annabelle and Frances?"

Lauren shook her head. "I don't know if you heard, but Annabelle's father passed away. I didn't want to bother her at such a difficult time. I'm planning to visit her this week."

A silence fell between the three women. There was no need to put into words what Lauren knew they were all thinking: It was one thing to buy a baby, but murder was a whole different equation. No, she thought. Surely Frances and Annabelle could not be part of that. Still, Lauren needed to find out why there was so much secrecy around the baby they'd adopted. She had decided not tell Emma or Claire that Patrick had been at Jade's cabin just before Jade died. She owed him that, as his lawyer. Only the police had that information.

Just then a knock came at the apartment door, startling them. Claire got up to answer it. All three women were surprised when Bram stumbled into the room.

"Bram?" Claire folded her arms over her chest.

"Good afternoon, Claire." Bram crossed the room, his gait unsteady. He plunked himself down on the sofa as easily as if he was in his own home.

He'd been drinking, Lauren realized, taking in his flushed face and unfocused eyes. His clothes were rumpled, his hair mussed. She'd never seen him so dishevelled.

Bram looked from Emma to Lauren. "Good afternoon, friends of Claire." He made no apology for showing up unannounced.

Frowning, Claire looked out the window.

Lauren followed her gaze to the Jeep Cherokee parked in the driveway.

"Goddammit, Bram! How could you drive in your condition?" Claire asked. "You could have killed someone. At the very least, you could have been arrested for impaired driving."

"You look lovely, Claire," Bram said, ignoring her reproach. "What have you done to your hair?"

Claire glared at him.

"Carry on with whatever you were doing," Bram told them.

Claire's lips tightened, but she said nothing.

"Whew!" Bram said. "It's hot in here." He stood to remove his jacket. He was about to hang it on the coat tree when a package fell from the pocket. Photographs skidded across the hardwood floor. "Damn," he muttered, bending to pick them up.

Lauren stooped down to help him. She gathered up some of the photos and placed them on the nearby coffee table. They were pictures of Ariel, she realized with a pang. In a number of them, she was wearing a pink ruffled dress with red hearts. It had white lace on the collar and sleeves. "I found some film that hadn't been processed," Bram explained.

Claire picked up one of the photos and studied it. "I don't remember taking this," she said, clearly puzzled.

"I shot them," Bram said.

Lauren leaned forward to get a better look. "I remember that little dress."

Claire put down the photograph and picked up another.

"We have a beautiful baby, Claire," Bram said proudly.

Claire's eyes filled with tears.

Lauren shot Bram a look of contempt. How could he be so insensitive?

Emma took Bram's arm and pulled him to his feet. "Bram, my son, let's go to the kitchen for coffee," she said diplomatically.

Claire's eyes were riveted to one of the photographs. She turned to Lauren, her expression troubled. "I don't remember that dress," she said. "What kind of a mother was I? Was I so out of touch, so detached from my daughter that I can't even remember the clothes she wore?"

"Claire, if Ariel's like—was like—" Lauren quickly amended, "Bailey, her closet would've been full of dresses. Chances are, if someone took pictures of Bailey and showed them to me months later, I wouldn't remember the dress either."

"You remembered Ariel's dress."

"I seldom saw Ariel. She was probably wearing that dress the last time I did. That's why I remember."

Although Claire seemed to accept this, she was still clearly troubled.

Lauren was searching for words to make Claire feel better when her cellphone rang. "Excuse me," she said, stepping to one side of the room. The caller ID told her it was Patrick Shaw; even before she answered, she knew the police had taken him in.

As Lauren drove to the police station, she felt a sense of unease. Bram had always been responsible and reliable, certainly not someone who'd get behind the wheel of a car drunk. Was it grief that had made him so reckless? And now this business with Patrick. Lauren frowned. She had always believed in Patrick's innocence. Now she was beginning to have doubts. *Your job is not to speculate*, she reminded herself. *Your job is to give the best possible counsel.*

Patrick was waiting for her in a small room at the station. No charges had been laid, but he was no doubt a person of interest. Lauren found him slouched in a chair, his eyes bloodshot, his blond hair tousled. She had requested a few minutes alone with him before he was interrogated by the police. "Why did you lie to Constable Taylor?" she asked. "Why did you say you'd had no contact with Jade? Why couldn't you tell the truth?"

"I just couldn't," Patrick replied.

"You're going to have to do better than that, Patrick. You could be facing some very serious charges. Tell me why you lied to the police."

"Jade wanted drugs," Patrick said. "Not something I could admit to Constable Taylor."

Lauren frowned. "Patrick, are you dealing drugs?"

"Hell no."

Lauren was tempted to ask him where he'd found the money to buy the Lexus. "How long did your visit with Jade last?" she asked instead.

"Thirty…maybe forty minutes. We smoked a couple of joints."

Lauren uncapped her pen and wrote in his file. "Do you know why Jade was at Comeau's Cabins?"

Patrick shook his head. "I asked her why she left her apartment, but she didn't want to talk about it. I had the feeling she was in some kind of trouble."

"Was Cara with her?"

"No, she was alone. Whenever I mentioned Cara, Jade got all teary. Cara was with a friend, she told me. She said she was safe." Patrick pushed his long bangs away from his eyes. "Jade was scared…like really paranoid."

Pot will do that.

"She promised to call me the next day," Patrick continued. "When I didn't hear from her, I went back to the cabin. She'd already checked out."

"Patrick, the police are going to ask if you had anything to do with Jade's death. They're going to ask if you had anything to do with Cara's disappearance."

"I absolutely did not," he replied.

Lauren closed his file. "Are you ready to face the detectives? This could be gruelling."

Nodding, Patrick got to his feet.

Because Jade's death had been ruled a homicide, the case was out of the hands of the local police. The officers in charge were Detectives Earl Sampson and Susan Dwyer, who had travelled from St. John's. Both detectives were wearing street clothes. Dwyer, who looked to be in her late thirties, had on khaki pants and a white turtleneck. Her red hair was pulled back in a sloppy ponytail. Sampson, who Lauren took to be in his late fifties, was short and so stout he looked like he might burst the seams of his grey tailored suit.

Detective Dwyer was blunt. "Patrick Shaw: did you kill Jade Roberts?"

"Absolutely not," Patrick answered.

She eyed him skeptically. "More than three thousand dollars was found in Jade's cabin. Do you know where the money came from?"

Patrick shook his head. "No."

"Why did you lie to the police, Mr. Shaw?" Detective Dwyer continued. "In your statement you said that you had no contact with Ms. Roberts after she left."

Patrick looked away. "I brought her some pot," he said. "I didn't want to tell that to the police."

Lauren put a hand on his arm. "You don't have to reveal that," she said. "The onus is on the police to prove your guilt."

Frowning, the detective gave Patrick a hard glare. "Do you know where Cara Roberts is?"

Patrick shook his head. "Absolutely not."

"When did you last see Cara Roberts?"

"February 11, the day before Jade disappeared."

Detective Sampson, who up until this time was silently taking notes, spoke up. "I believe Jade's death was an accident," he said. "I don't think you meant to kill her."

Lauren knew a trap when she saw one. "Patrick already said he had nothing to do with Jade's death," she cut in. Turning to Patrick, she said, "You don't have to say anything."

"It's okay." Patrick looked the detective straight in the eye. "No, sir," he said, "I did not kill my friend Jade Roberts. She was alive when I left the cabin that evening."

"Ms. Roberts told Mrs. Comeau that she was on the run from an abusive boyfriend," Detective Sampson said. "Do you know who Ms. Roberts was running from, Mr. Shaw?"

"No, sir, I don't."

The questions went on relentlessly with the detectives trying to bait Patrick—who, to his credit, answered every question without hesitation.

After two hours, Lauren and Patrick left the station together. The police didn't have enough evidence to charge him. "You have no idea at all who Jade was running from?" Lauren asked him in the parking lot. "Was she seeing someone?"

Patrick shook his head. "As far as I know, Jade hasn't dated since she broke up with Cara's father."

"Could she be back with him?"

"I doubt it," Patrick said. "Last I heard, Willy had another girlfriend."

Lauren frowned. "Why would Jade say she was being abused? Why would she make up a story like that?"

Patrick shrugged. "I don't know." He looked as though he was about to say something, but at that moment his phone rang. "Excuse me," he said, walking away from Lauren. "Annabelle?" he said into the phone. "Things went really well, actually." He glanced toward Lauren. "Look, I'm with someone right now. This evening...sure... what time should I come by?"

Lauren raised an eyebrow. Annabelle Chandler. They were getting really cozy, those two. Again, she recalled the conversation she'd overheard at Kiddy Academy. Someone was giving Patrick money. A thought struck her: Had *Patrick* kidnapped Cara? Is that how he got the money for his fancy car—from Annabelle and Frances? And did the couple have anything to do with Jade's death? Lauren felt disloyal thinking such thoughts. Annabelle was sweet and gentle, Frances an ex-RCMP officer who'd always been on the right side of the law. Still, there were things about Dinah Marie's adoption that didn't add up. She would go to Deep River tomorrow, she decided. She couldn't put it off any longer.

CHAPTER

33

As Lauren took the exit to Deep River, she felt a twinge of guilt for deceiving Annabelle and Frances. She should've been more direct, asked outright if they had Jade's baby. She hoped her excuse about just happening to be in the area wouldn't seem too transparent. *Jade was murdered,* she reminded herself. *Jade is dead, and Cara is missing.*

She found the address easily enough. It was nearly two when she pulled into the driveway. The house was made of logs and surrounded by tall evergreens. She parked the car, walked up to the front door, and rang the bell. Annabelle had been the one to take maternity leave, so Lauren hoped she'd be home with the baby while Frances was teaching.

Annabelle answered, looking lovely in a yellow blouse, her blond hair spilling around her shoulders. "Lauren?" she said, obviously taken aback. "I…I didn't expect you."

"I meant to call when I got into town, but I misplaced your number. Hope I'm not getting you at a bad time."

"No," Annabelle said, but she sounded uncertain.

"I picked up a few things for the baby," Lauren said, holding out the package.

Annabelle accepting it. "Thanks," she said, holding open the door. "Come in. It's good to see you. We don't get many visitors out this way."

Lauren removed her shoes in the foyer. Annabelle took her coat and led her into a living area where exposed beams supported a high ceiling. An enormous stone fireplace dominated one wall at the far end of the room. The floor was dark hardwood with woven rugs scattered about.

"Nice place you have here," Lauren said, looking around.

"Thank you." Annabelle put the gift on a coffee table. "Make yourself comfortable," she said. "I'll make us some tea." She disappeared into the kitchen.

Lauren took in her surroundings. Elegant sofas and chairs were upholstered in matching shades of gold and brown. A number of paintings by Newfoundland artists hung on the wall, including *Just Between Friends* by Carla Crawford. It was one of Lauren's favourites; the little girl holding the teddy bear always made her smile. It looked out of place among the framed diplomas and certificates. There were photographs of Annabelle and Frances: Annabelle receiving her degree, Frances being presented with an award. Oddly, there were no pictures of their baby.

Annabelle returned with the tea and a plate of store-bought cookies.

"I'm so sorry to hear about your father," Lauren said. "Was it unexpected?"

"Dad was not well for some time, but yes, his death was sudden. I'm in the process now of taking care of his estate and other affairs." Annabelle picked up the gift, and looked at Lauren. "Shall I?"

"Of course."

Annabelle tore off the paper and ribbon, exclaiming over the gifts. "Dinah Marie will love this," she said, holding up the book. "I read to her all the time, and I swear she understands every word."

"Babies are smarter than we give them credit for."

"Dinah Marie sure is."

Lauren took a sip of tea. "You look good, Annabelle."

"Thanks." Annabelle flashed a smile. "I love being home with Dinah Marie, but I miss work at times."

"I know the feeling."

Annabelle bit into a cookie. "Things were starting to get kind of crazy around the department."

Lauren looked up at her. "Oh?"

"Mitch and his drinking." Annabelle shook her head. "He's a loose cannon."

"It's a difficult situation," Lauren said.

Annabelle nodded. "He had us all walking on eggshells, faculty *and* students. Sadly, a number of talented students dropped out of the program because of him."

"You must have known Jade Roberts?" Lauren carefully watched Annabelle's face for a reaction as she broached the subject.

"I met Jade when Frances and I lived in Paddy's Arm. Frances had her class come to the house for a potluck at the end of term." She shook her head. "I could cry whenever I think of what happened to the poor girl."

"Her baby is still missing." Again Lauren watched Annabelle carefully.

"I hope she's okay," Annabelle said, averting her eyes.

For a moment they sat in silence, sipping their tea, and then Annabelle spoke: "A lot of bad things have been happening. Look at poor Dr. Collins." She turned to Lauren. "How is he, by the way?"

"Better than expected. He's out of his coma, and they expect to have him home soon. I went to visit him a few days ago. He slept for most of it. Still, I'm pleased that he's doing so well. I am hoping to go see him again soon."

"That's great news," Annabelle said. "I know that his family was quite concerned. They worried that he might have suffered permanent brain damage. Thank God it didn't turn into a tragedy like poor Ariel Warren."

"That was so tragic."

"I feel so sorry for Claire and Dr. Warren. He just adored that baby. Every time I went to his office he had a recent picture of her on his desk. He always had a story to tell about some new skill she'd learned." Annabel frowned. "He must be devastated."

"They both are," said Lauren, feeling defensive. "It's a double whammy for Claire, being charged with Ariel's murder."

A small whimper penetrated the air from a room down the hallway.

"Oh good, Dinah Marie is awake," Lauren said. "I was afraid I wouldn't get to see her before I left."

Annabelle looked at her watch. "Her naps are usually much longer," she said, making no attempt to go to the crying infant.

"This may be the only chance I'll get to see her before you and Frances move away."

Annabelle had the look of someone who'd walked into quicksand.

The baby's cries picked up in volume.

"Lauren, there's something you need to know about Dinah Marie."

Dear God, was Annabelle going to tell her she was hiding Jade's baby?

"I feel I should prepare you."

"Prepare me?" A shaky laugh escaped Lauren's lips. "What for?"

By now, the baby's cries had turned into piercing howls. They were not the cries of a baby used to being ignored.

Annabelle scurried down the hallway.

She seems nervous, Lauren thought. *Something is not right.*

Minutes later, Annabelle returned to the living room carrying a pink bundle.

Lauren stood up. "So I finally get to meet Miss Dinah Marie."

Annabelle clutched the baby protectively, the pink blanket shrouding her head. "We haven't let many people see her."

"Why not?"

Annabelle pulled back the blanket.

Lauren drew in a startled breath. For a second, she was too shocked to say anything. Then she gathered herself and moved swiftly to Annabelle's side. "Hello, little one," she whispered, taking the baby's hand in her own. *Poor baby*, she thought. *Life is not going to be easy for you.*

"She has neurofibromatosis," Annabelle explained softly. "It's a rare genetic birth defect."

Like the Elephant Man, Lauren thought, taking in the enormous disfiguring tumours on both sides of the baby's face. Her forehead bubbled grotesquely, and folds of loose skin hung from her neck. Where her nose should have been was just a small slit. Her eyes, however, were alert and intelligent as she held Lauren in her gaze.

Annabelle held the baby close. "We love her," she said, "and we can't bear to have people recoil at the sight of her."

Lauren nodded, too choked up to speak.

"She'll need a lot of surgery," Annabelle continued. "That's what clinched our decision to move to Arizona. They have better facilities to deal with her condition. With a lot of work, we can have her looking almost normal."

"She's a lucky girl to have you and Frances adopt her," Lauren said. "A very lucky girl."

CHAPTER

34

That weekend, the annual end-of-term fair was in full swing when Lauren and Bailey arrived on campus. Newfoundland jigs and reels blared from loudspeakers. They walked past tables laden with everything from used books to fresh fruits and vegetables. Like most people connected with the university, Lauren had donated stuff—books, CDs, toys, furniture. The proceeds would be used to buy sports equipment, musical instruments, computers, and other items for under-funded departments.

Lauren spotted Claire near the Student Union Building. She was sitting on a wooden bench drinking coffee from a paper cup. "Hi, Claire." She waved, pleased to see her out of the house, especially on a busy Saturday.

"Hi, Auntie Claire," Bailey called.

Claire waved. "Hi, darling. Are you enjoying the fair?"

"Yup." Bailey nodded enthusiastically.

"We just got here," Lauren said. "How are you?"

"I have good days and bad days," Claire said. "This is one of my better days."

"Well, I'm happy to see you." Lauren looked around at the various booths displaying flowers, crafts, preservatives, knitted mittens, socks, and sweaters. Children with painted faces walked beside their parents, clutching balloons, teddy bears, and cotton candy. "Quite the event this has become."

"I know," Claire said. "Apparently people have come all the way from St. John's this year." She drained her cup and got up from the bench to join them.

They strolled around the campus, stopping at display tables. A booth set up by the Anglican Ladies' Auxiliary was draped with embroidered pillow cases, lace doilies, and homemade quilts. "This would be a perfect gift for my grandparents' sixtieth anniversary," Lauren said, running her hand over the elaborate pattern on a quilt. "Such fine craftsmanship."

"That herringbone pattern is nice," the woman behind the table said. "So is this one." She held up a multicoloured quilt. "Joseph's Coat of Many Colours."

"Wow," Lauren said. "So many hours of labour must have gone into that."

"Momma, look!" Bailey shouted.

Lauren turned to see Rebecca and Connor approaching. Connor had a helium balloon tied to his wrist and a bumblebee painted on his cheek.

"Well, hello," Lauren said, not quite meeting Rebecca's eyes. She recalled their last encounter and wondered if Rebecca felt the same discomfort she did. Lauren turned to Claire. "You've met Rebecca Taylor?"

Claire nodded. "I believe the last time we met, you put me in handcuffs," she said wryly.

Lauren sucked in her breath. *As if things weren't awkward enough*, she thought. She glanced at Rebecca, who had her arms crossed over her chest, clearly embarrassed. Lauren tried to think of something to say to ease the tension. Thankfully, just then Elena Petrov strolled up to them, her newborn resting against her chest in a carrier.

"Elena!" Claire exclaimed. "I heard you had your baby. I've been meaning to call you."

The women crowded around Elena, eager to get peek at the newborn.

"Boy?" Lauren asked, noticing the baby's blue hat.

Rebecca laughed. "The only way you can tell at that age is by their clothing."

"He's beautiful," Lauren said, taking in the baby's tiny perfect features. He yawned, clenching fists as small as cherry tomatoes. "I remember when Bailey was that age."

"What did you name him?" Rebecca asked.

"Alexander Nicholas," Elena said proudly. "Named for his papa."

"Nicholas must be over the moon," Lauren said.

"Yes, Nicholas very happy."

Lauren was about to say something but stopped when she saw that Claire's eyes had filled with tears. She touched her shoulder. "Are you okay?" she whispered.

"Yes," Claire said, dabbing at her eyes, "I'll be fine."

Elena looked toward the Student Union Building where a cab had turned in. "My taxi arrive. I must go. Glad I see you all again."

Claire waved as Elena boarded the cab. After watching it drive off, she turned her attention to Connor. "Enjoying the fair?" she asked, forcing lightness in her voice.

"We're going to the fish pond to fish for prizes," Connor said, his eyes wide. "Can Bailey come?" he asked his mother.

Bailey looked eagerly at Lauren. "Can I, Momma?"

Lauren and Rebecca turned toward each other, but neither quite met the other's gaze.

Lauren shook her head. "I...don't...."

"We'd love to have Bailey come with us," Rebecca said.

"Are you sure?"

"Yes, of course," Rebecca assured her. "She can keep Connor company."

"Can I, Momma?" Bailey pleaded.

"Well...I suppose...as long as you behave." Lauren reached into her jacket pocket, took out a strip of tickets, and handed them to Rebecca. "You'll need these," she said.

"Thanks." Rebecca put the tickets in her shirt pocket and turned to Claire. "It's been nice seeing you again, Professor Ste Denis," she said formally.

"You too, Constable Taylor. Take care."

"Have fun at the pond," Lauren called as Rebecca walked away, a child on each hand.

Claire stared after them. "A nice lady," she said.

"Yes," Lauren agreed. "One of my best students." She gazed at Claire. "Are you sure you're going to be okay?"

"I'm fine, really. Sometimes I see a baby, and I'm reminded of Ariel. My emotions get the better of me. I hate going to the doctor's office and seeing all the mothers with their new babies." Shrugging, Claire picked up the multicoloured quilt and held it out to Lauren. "If I were you, I'd take this one."

"A good choice, my love," said the woman behind the table.

Lauren smiled. "You've convinced me."

Clutching her purchase and with Claire at her side, Lauren walked from one end of campus to the other. She bought books, mittens, preserves, and a stuffed toy for Bailey. After a while, they came to a booth that sold educational games and puzzles. Patrick Shaw was talking to one of the salesmen, a pile of items in front of him.

"Hello, Patrick," Lauren said. "On a buying spree for Kiddy Academy, I see. I didn't realize that was part of your job description."

"I don't have a job description," Patrick said. "In fact, I don't have a job, since it's an internship. These are for *my* preschool. I just purchased a building in St. John's. I'll be ready to open by the end of summer."

Lauren stared at him. "You're opening your own school?" She was dying to ask him how he could afford it.

"Your own school so soon after graduation," Claire said. "Amazing. It takes most people years before they're in a position to do that."

"I've hired a director," Patrick said. "She's going to stay a year, teach me about finances and everything else about running the business."

"Well, good luck with your endeavour," Claire said.

"I wish you all the best," said Lauren. "If you need me, just call." More than a week had passed since Patrick had been interrogated by the police and he had still not been charged with anything. Lauren knew he was still a person of interest, but unless new information came to light, the police could not indict him.

"Thanks, both of you." Patrick moved away from the booth, his arms piled high.

Lauren and Claire continued their walk around the campus, stopping at tables and booths, and looking at displays. At a table set up by the drama department, Lauren stopped to look at used books. "Literature is my second love," she told Claire. After carefully perusing the stack of titles, she settled on *Such a Long Journey* by Rohinton Mistry. "He's one of my favourite authors. When I was doing my English minor I took a course in world lit and couldn't read enough Asian literature."

"All books cost a loonie," said the girl tending the table.

"Hi, Angie," Claire said.

"Professor Ste Denis! I didn't notice you standing there."

Lauren was reaching for her change-purse when something on the table caught her eye. "Oh, God!" she exclaimed. "Look at that."

"What is it?" Claire asked.

Lauren pointed to an infant carrier with a shiny purple butterfly stuck to its side. Leaning toward Claire, she lowered her voice. "I'm pretty sure I saw that carrier in Jade Roberts's apartment back in February."

"How do you know it's the same one?"

"I remember the butterfly," Lauren said. She saw Angie looking at her and realized she was waiting to be paid for the book. "How much do you want for the baby carrier?"

"We're asking ten dollars."

"I'll take it." Lauren handed her a twenty. "Do you happen to know who donated it?"

"No, but Tara might." Angie put the money in a tin can and fished out change. "David and Tara picked up the donations. She's coming to relieve me—"she looked at her watch"—in about an hour. I can ask her then, if you like."

"Thanks," Lauren said, picking up the carrier.

"Here," Claire said, taking the quilt as Lauren struggled with her purchases, "let me help."

Lauren thanked Claire and grabbed the carrier.

"What do you plan to do with it?" Claire asked as they were walking away.

"Lab tests can determine if Cara's DNA is on the seat. It might be important to the investigation."

"How do you suppose it ended up here?"

Lauren shrugged. "Jade could have donated it after she sold her car. But I doubt it. The carrier can be used for a variety of purposes. I remember when Bailey"—Lauren stopped talking when she saw Claire's look of sadness.

"It's okay, Lauren," Claire said. "Finish your thought."

"I was going to say the seat is useful in and out of the car."

Claire nodded. "Yes, I had one myself. Still do, I guess."

They walked in silence for a few minutes.

"Jade may have taken money for Cara," Lauren said after a while.

"You think she sold her baby?" Claire sounded horrified.

"It's a possibility. Jade's mother told me someone from the drama department offered Jade money. At first, I thought it was Frances and Annabelle, but I've seen their baby and she's…certainly not Cara."

"I can't imagine any of our staff doing that," Claire said.

"Neither can I," Lauren said. The department's faculty was made up of either young parents or parents of grown children. There was no reason any of them would want to buy a child.

"A student perhaps," Claire said.

Lauren stopped walking. She hadn't considered that possibility.

"Would it help if I asked Mitch to fax you a list of the students in the program?"

A student, Lauren wondered. Why hadn't she thought of that? "Thanks, Claire. It would be a place to start."

She knew Rebecca didn't want her involved in the case, and felt a tinge of guilt going behind her back. *I'm only going to check out the students,* she told herself. If she came across anything that might be relevant to Cara's case, she would call Rebecca straight away.

CHAPTER

35

It was late Sunday evening before Mitch faxed Lauren the list of students. Beside each name was an address and phone number. Lauren shook her head, amused. Wasn't Mitch aware of the Privacy Act? Didn't he realize the trouble he could get into for giving out this information?

She took the list to her computer. In less than fifteen minutes she'd learned that one of her students had been charged with drunk driving, another with shoplifting, and yet another for disturbing the peace. *Not much is secret anymore*, she thought. But what was she looking for? She hardly expected to find information on Cara's disappearance. Still, she continued to google the names on the list.

Many of the students' names came up in connection with reviews of plays they'd been involved in. When she typed in Erika Jansen's, she got over thirty hits. A number of other reviewers praised Erika's talent as an actress. JANSEN SHINES IN STUDENT PRODUCTION OF MACBETH, one critic wrote. RISING STAR read another headline. Both the *Daily News* and the university paper had done profiles on her. Scrolling down the list, Lauren found an article published in the local newspaper of a small town in northern Ontario: TRAGEDY STRIKES YOUNG COUPLE. Lauren clicked on the link. The story was accompanied by a photograph of a much younger Erika. Eagerly, she scanned it. *Tragedy struck the small town of Dundalk, Ontario, when a transport truck crashed into an oncoming vehicle. Dead are Paul Jansen, 24, and his daughter Sadie, 9 months. Jansen's wife, Erika, 20, escaped the accident with minor cuts and bruises. Police who arrived on the scene arrested the truck driver, Gary Wade, 40.*

Lauren sat for a long time staring at the screen, stunned by her revelation. Poor Erika. It was remarkable how well she hid her pain. Then she recalled how upset Erika had been the day following Ariel's death. Had it brought up memories of her own baby girl?

There were at least a dozen other articles connected with the accident, but the story that caught Lauren's interest was in the *Dundalk Daily News*: MOTHER SETTLES FOR 1.5 MILLION IN WRONGFUL DEATH OF HUSBAND AND INFANT DAUGHTER. As she read the account, Lauren was struck with another thought: Had Erika tried to buy Cara? With her settlement money, she could easily have paid Jade thousands of dollars. Unless she'd spent it all, she would most likely be the only student in the department who had that kind of money.

Lauren thought she'd learned everything there was to know about Erika Jansen when another article caught her eye: MOTHER WHO SETTLED WRONGFUL DEATH SUIT NOW ON PROBATION. The article had been written more than a year ago: *Erika Jansen, who settled a wrongful death suit after her husband and infant daughter were killed, was placed on probation after stealing makeup from a local Walmart. Jansen's lawyer, Mike Graham, argues his client was under tremendous stress following the death of her family when the incident occurred. "My client could easily afford the items she lifted," Graham told the court at Jansen's trial. "It was depression brought on by overwhelming grief that caused her to act out."*

Picking up the phone, Lauren dialled the number next to Erika's name on Mitch's list. Almost immediately, a recorded message cut in: "The number you have dialled is not in service. Please check the number and call again."

Lauren's mind raced. As far as a suspect in the disappearance of Cara Roberts was concerned, Erika Jansen fit the bill. But if that was the case, where had Erika been keeping her? Cara had been missing for more than seven weeks now.

—

In bed that night, Lauren tossed fitfully, her mind sifting through the information she'd learned. She fell asleep around two o'clock but awoke an hour later. Not able to go back to sleep, she put on her housecoat and went downstairs to make hot chocolate. Bailey would be awake in another three hours. Daniel was coming around nine to spend the day with her. *Tomorrow I'm going to be a mess,* she told herself.

She was startled by the sound of the doorbell. When she went to answer it, she found Rebecca Taylor standing outside with Connor in a baby carrier. He was wearing a pink dress with lace ruffles. Rebecca walked past Lauren into the living room without a word of greeting.

"Why is Connor wearing a dress?"

Rebecca didn't answer. She put the carrier on the table and began taking pictures with her cellphone.

"Why did you put your son in a girl's dress?" Lauren demanded.

Rebecca laughed harshly. "They all look alike at that age. The only way you can tell them apart is by their clothing."

"But Connor is a boy."

Rebecca laughed. "They all look alike when they're dead."

"He's *not* dead," Lauren said, her voice rising.

The doorbell rang again.

"Let it ring," Rebecca said.

Lauren continued down the hallway.

"I said let it ring." Rebecca grabbed her arms and tried to handcuff her.

CHAPTER

36

"*Take your hands off me!*" Lauren shouted.

"Lauren? Wake up. You're having a bad dream."

Daniel was leaning over her, holding her wrists, a concerned look on his face. He was so close, she breathed in his aftershave—a mixture of spices and old leather.

"Daniel?" At first glance, she thought she was dreaming. He was dressed in denim jeans and a pullover. He looked so handsome that Lauren felt the pang of her loss all over again.

"Bailey let me in." He released her wrists.

Lauren sat up and rubbed her eyes. "She knows she shouldn't open the door to anyone."

"I've already lectured her about that."

"You should have called," Lauren said.

"I tried, but you didn't answer the phone." Daniel frowned. "Is everything okay?"

Lauren nodded, the dream still tugging at her memory. "I'm sorry, Daniel. I keep the ring volume on low while I'm sleeping. I woke up at three and didn't go back to sleep until a couple of hours ago."

Daniel continued to stare at her, concern clearly etched on his face. "You sure everything's okay?"

"I had trouble falling asleep. I learned last night that a student in the drama department lost her husband and child. It happened some time ago but she never mentioned it."

Daniel sat on the sofa beside her. "We never know the burdens another person might be carrying."

"True," Lauren agreed. "A couple I know adopted a baby girl. I got the shock of my life about a week ago...I dropped by their house unannounced, and found out the baby has neurofibromatosis."

"Neuro...?"

"Neurofibromatosis, the same disease as the Elephant Man."

"Lord help her," Daniel said.

"Her deformities aren't as severe, but they're similar."

"Weren't you aware of the baby's condition before the visit?"

Lauren pulled her housecoat around her, and reached for her slippers. "Apparently they were keeping it a secret," she said.

"Did they think they could hide it forever?"

"Well, they're moving to Arizona soon. The medical services for her are better there." Lauren got up from the sofa. "Where's Bailey?"

"She went to her room to get dressed."

"I better go check on her." Lauren gestured toward the kitchen. "Help yourself to coffee or tea."

"I'm fine." Daniel glanced at his watch. "I'm taking Bailey to McDonald's. You're welcome to join us."

"Thanks, Daniel, but I'm not up to it."

At that moment, Bailey came downstairs wearing a frilly dress, her corkscrew curls sticking out in all directions.

"You look pretty," Daniel told her.

"Let me comb your hair," Lauren said.

"You always take too long," Bailey complained, but she allowed Lauren to brush her unruly curls into a ponytail.

After Bailey and Daniel left, Lauren made a cup of tea and sat at the kitchen table. She stared out at the dark ocean, trying to recall the dream that had unsettled her. Siggy, her psychologist father, called dreams coded messages from the unconscious. He was forever quoting Freud and Jung. *Is my unconscious mind trying to tell me something? Could such a jumble of nonsense have meaning?* Lauren stared out the window at the dark ocean. *It's only my confused state of mind,* she told herself.

The phone rang. "Lauren? It's Mitch returning your call."

"Mitch. Thanks for getting back to me, and for faxing that list of students."

"Glad I could help."

"I tried calling Erika Jansen, but her phone's disconnected."

"Erika called me yesterday, as a matter of fact. She's in the process of moving back to Ontario."

"Erika's moving away? Why?"

"She said it was because of a family crisis," Mitch said.

"Doesn't she have an exam coming up soon?"

"I excused her from taking the exam. I'm going to average out her final grade. She's a good student. She always showed up for her classes, always had her assignments in on time. I'm not going to penalize her for this one time. She'll graduate with the rest of her class."

"I hope everything is okay with Erika and her family," Lauren said.

"She's doing really well," Mitch said. "In fact, she got an offer for a part in the television series *Candlewood Lane*."

"I'm happy for her," Lauren said. "With her talent, she'll go far. I just wish I could have reached her."

"I can give you her cell number if you need to contact her," Mitch said. "I don't think she's moved yet."

"That would be helpful." Lauren picked up a pen as Mitch rattled off the number.

After she hung up, Lauren studied the number scrawled on the back of her telephone bill. She would go see Erika, she decided. Her address was on the list Mitch had faxed her: Pitcher Plant Road, less than two kilometres away. She could jog there in no time.

Lauren emailed Rebecca, informing her as to what she had learned about Erika Jansen. She worded the message carefully, knowing Rebecca was not going to be pleased; she had made it clear that she didn't want Lauren involved in the investigation.

By the time Lauren left the house the sky was overcast, threatening rain. Fog had rolled in over the ocean. The moist salt air felt wonderful, and she inhaled deeply as she ran. She was out of breath by the time she reached Pitcher Plant Road.

A moving van was parked on the street outside Erika's house. Men in overalls were carrying furniture, crates, and boxes. The door was open and Erika stood in the foyer wearing faded blue jeans and a white shirt rolled up at the sleeves. "Professor LaVallee?" she said, stepping aside to let one of the movers pass.

"I know this is probably not the best time to visit," Lauren said, "but I was hoping to have a word with you."

"Come in. I should warn you, though, the place is upside down." Erika led Lauren down a short hallway to the dining room. The only furniture was a stool and a couple of collapsible lawn chairs. "Have a seat," she said, indicating the stool. She unfolded one of the chairs for herself.

"Mitch told me you got a part on *Candlewood Lane*," Lauren said once they were seated. "Congratulations."

"Thank you. I was thrilled and *very* surprised." She smiled at Lauren. "But I'm sure you didn't come over here to discuss my success. I'm not being sued, am I?"

"I'm a criminal defense attorney," Lauren said, playing along. "We don't sue."

"Do I need to be defended?"

Lauren smiled. "As a matter of fact, I came to talk about your friend Jade Roberts."

Erika eyed her warily. "The police already interviewed me about Jade and Cara. Constable Taylor asked about a message I left on Jade's voice mail." She lowered her eyes. "I was devastated when I learned what happened."

Lauren nodded. "We all were."

"I mean…who would do such a terrible thing?"

"The police are still investigating."

A brief silence passed between them.

"When was the last time you heard from Jade?" Lauren asked.

"The day before she disappeared. I told the police that already."

"Erika," Lauren said, cutting to the chase. "I know you offered Jade money…money for Cara." It wasn't exactly the truth, but it got the reaction she wanted.

Erika's face went pale, her lower lip trembled. "How…? Who told you that?"

"It must have been difficult losing your own baby and husband," Lauren continued, evading the question.

Tears glistened in Erika's eyes. She looked down at her hands.

Lauren felt a pang of guilt for upsetting her, but she needed to know the truth.

Erika quickly composed herself. "I don't know where Cara is," she said. "I certainly don't have her, if that's what you're implying." She got up from her chair and went to stand by the patio doors. "Yes, I offered Jade money. It was foolish, I realize that now. At the time, I didn't think of it as *buying* a baby. Jade needed money. *I* desperately wanted a baby. What I *wanted* was Sadie back," she amended. "I was so confused I didn't realize I was trying to replace her."

"Did you give Jade money?"

"I lent her a couple hundred."

"A couple hundred?" Lauren thought about the three thousand she'd found in the cabin.

Erika glared at Lauren. "Jade was my friend. I saw no harm in helping her out. Now, if you'll excuse me, I'm very busy."

Well, at least I know who offered Jade money, Lauren thought as she walked away. But was Erika telling the whole truth? Her story was plausible enough and she sounded convincing, but she was one hell of a good actress.

By the time Lauren reached Main Street, it had started to rain. She jogged past Tim Hortons, wishing she'd remembered to bring money; she could use a bagel and some coffee. Except for a cup of tea this morning, she hadn't eaten anything. Hansel and Gretel's was across the street, a good place to hole up until the rain stopped.

The shop's interior was spacious and bright. Reproductions of Anne Geddes's photographs added to the cheerful atmosphere. A handful of customers were browsing the racks and display tables. Lauren picked up a couple of play outfits and a pair of denim overalls for Bailey. She would ask the clerk to hold them until she could return. She then headed to the dress section. Dylan's birthday was in a couple of weeks, and Bailey could use a new dress for the party.

Lauren was looking through a rack of dresses when Patrick Shaw came out of the toy section, his arms loaded with puzzles, books, and other toys.

"Still picking up things for your preschool, Patrick?"

"Oh. Hi, Lauren," Patrick said. "I didn't notice you standing there."

"Looks like your school is going to be well-equipped."

"I still have more things to buy. The place needs a sandbox, easels, tables and chairs. I'm going to have to buy bicycles and other riding toys." He shook his head. "It never ends."

As Patrick was walking away, Daisy Flynn, the salesclerk, approached Lauren; she had met Daisy on numerous occasions. "Patrick is opening his own school," Lauren said.

"Yes, I heard," Daisy said. "A good investment of his inheritance, I'd say. Most young people would just waste the money on booze and God knows what."

"Inheritance?"

Daisy nodded. "Patrick's father left him a large sum of money."

Lauren stared at her in disbelief. "Wayne Shaw?"

"Oh, no, my dear. Not Wayne."

Lauren squinted in confusion.

"Patrick's father was Tom Chandler. Patrick only found that out recently."

Annabelle's father?

"We were all shocked." Daisy lowered her voice. "They say Josephine was pregnant with Patrick when she married Wayne." She paused. "Imagine now, letting the youngster grow up not knowing who his father was."

Lauren was too stunned to say anything.

"Patrick only learned the truth after poor Tom got sick," Daisy continued. "I imagine he wanted to acknowledge his son before he passed on. God rest his soul. In the end he did right by the boy. Left him half his estate."

"Oh, my," Lauren managed.

"Must've got a pretty penny when he sold his house and business," said Daisy.

"I can only imagine," Lauren said. Tom Chandler had owned Mops and Brooms, a large hardware store on Main Street.

"They say the daughter was right pleased to find out she had a brother," Daisy continued.

Just then, a customer came into the store and Daisy excused herself to go greet her.

Mystery solved, Lauren thought as she continued to look through the rack of dresses. After some time she came across a pink dress with red hearts. Puzzled, she lifted it from the rack. It was identical to the dress Ariel had been wearing in the photographs that had fallen out of Bram's pocket at Claire's apartment. For the longest time, Lauren stood staring at it, the hearts standing out with stark clarity.

Understanding suddenly shot through her. How could she have missed this? Her knees went weak and she felt the need to sit down. There was a bench nearby and she lowered herself onto it. Pieces were falling into place now, making a disturbing kind of sense. She felt a chill run up her back. "Oh, dear God!"

"You okay, my love?" Daisy asked, giving her a curious look.

Lauren barely heard. She got up from the bench, placed the clothes on the counter, and bolted out the door. She raced down the street, heedless of the pouring rain.

CHAPTER

37

Lauren stood in the kitchen, dripping wet. Her heart was hammering as she picked up the phone and called Claire. A recorded voice cut in almost immediately, prompting her to leave a message.

"Claire," she said, her words rushing out, "I know what happened to Ariel and Cara. I'll call back later when I know more."

She hung up the phone and went upstairs to change. Numbly, she pulled on a pair of jeans and a baggy sweater, all the while shivering so hard her teeth chattered. She stood for a moment, debating her next move. She was putting herself at risk, but she had no choice. She called Rebecca and took a deep breath as the phone rang. No luck. Rebecca was in a meeting, she was told, and couldn't be reached. "Please have her call Lauren LaVallee as soon as she gets out," Lauren said. "Tell her I was mistaken about Erika Jansen, but I now have new information regarding the case." She left her cellphone number.

Lauren didn't know how long Rebecca would be, and she couldn't wait. After scribbling a note for Daniel, she grabbed her car keys.

She turned the heater on high, hoping the hot air would help stop her shivering. Raindrops exploded against the windshield. Thunder rumbled, and from time to time lightning streaked the dark sky. She drove steadily, her attention fixed on the road ahead. Even with the wipers at full speed, she could barely make out the road. She passed large open fields and drove through tiny outports where fishing boats, tied to their moorings, tossed and pitched.

After some time, Lauren came to a sign that said *Duffy's Mountain* with an arrow pointing to the left. The car shook as it climbed a twisting, narrow road. She drove past summer homes and cottages perched on cliffs that dropped steeply toward the ocean. After a few minutes, the pavement gave way to a narrow dirt road that wound through thick woods. She'd only been in this area once before—a New Year's Eve party a couple of years ago—and she had been struck by the isolation. Following the road for some time, she came to a clearing that offered a view of the ocean. She could see a house in the distance, built of cedar and set among tall maples. A sun porch ran the length of the house with a wall of windows facing the ocean. A sleek blue sports car was parked in the driveway.

Lauren parked a fair distance from the house. She took her phone from her purse and checked for any missed calls. Rebecca was taking a long time getting back to her. Lauren decided to check in with Daniel. Before she even dialled his number, she realized there was no signal. Rebecca would not be able to reach her. *I should have emailed her*, she thought. Too late now. Lauren got out of the car and, with a stir of apprehension, walked toward the house. The rain had let up, but the sky was a tumult of black clouds.

The woman who answered the door looked to be in her late sixties, tall with short grey hair. She gave Lauren a curious look.

"I'm a friend of Anya's," Lauren said.

"Anya," the woman repeated, and then said something in Russian.

"May I come in?" Lauren asked, gesturing with her hands.

The woman stepped aside to let her enter.

The sun porch was filled with comfortable sofas, armchairs, and rockers. Tables were set up with a chess set and various board games. A squeal of delight came from somewhere in the house. "Beibi," the woman said, and hurried down a wide hallway. Lauren followed after her until they came to a bright family room. A baby dressed in a pink sleeper was bouncing wildly in a Jolly Jumper.

Lauren's heart leapt to her throat. In one quick stride, she crossed the room and picked the baby up. "Ariel," she said, hugging her close. The baby smiled, showing two tiny bottom teeth. All the while, the old woman hovered protectively. "Oh, Ariel, your momma is going to be so happy to know you're alive and safe."

The baby gurgled happily.

"I'm going to take you home," Lauren whispered against Ariel's silken hair. She felt a rush of happiness. *How in the world did Bram and Anya pull this off?* she wondered.

"What the hell do you think you are doing?"

Lauren stepped back, startled. Anya stood in the doorway, her face twisted in anger.

Lauren tightened her grip on the infant. "I'm taking Ariel home to her mother."

Anya's eyes hardened. "Like hell."

"She belongs with Claire. She—"

"Shut up!" Anya held out her hand, and Lauren saw the glint of metal. Ariel trembled in her arms.

Anya shouted something in Russian before turning to look at Lauren, her eyes filled with hatred. "Give the baby to Olga."

The older woman's eyes grew wide with alarm as she reached for Ariel.

Lauren clutched the baby tighter.

Anya pointed the gun at Lauren. "Give the baby to Olga," she repeated, her voice harsh. The crazed look in her eyes made Lauren tremble.

Reluctantly, Lauren handed the baby to a terrified Olga, her heart racing. Forcing herself to keep calm, she looked for a way out. There was a side door, but she knew if she tried to escape Anya would shoot her. *I am trapped with a crazy person*, she realized.

"Why did you come here?" Anya asked.

"I knew you had Ariel," Lauren said. "I figured it out this morning."

"Anya, put the gun away." The voice came from the doorway. Lauren turned to see Bram. He had entered the room so quietly she hadn't noticed.

Olga held the baby against her chest, her face pale.

"Put the gun down," Bram repeated. "Enough people are dead and injured. This has gone on long enough."

Anya fixed him with a hostile stare. It was the same look she had given him at the hospital when Bram suggested that Lauren and

Anya leave. Had he been scared then that Anya might do something to harm Andrew?

Anya turned her attention back to Lauren. "So, you figured it all out," she said.

Lauren nodded. "The photographs Bram brought to Claire's apartment gave it away."

Anya shifted her gaze from Lauren to Bram.

"The day I saw you at Hansel and Gretel's, you were looking at baby dresses," Lauren reminded her. "You told me it was a gift for Elena. I thought nothing of it at the time—but Elena had a boy. And if you recall, the store manager said the dress was part of an exclusive line that had arrived that week. Hansel and Gretel's was one of only a few stores to carry it. Ariel was wearing the same dress in the photographs Bram brought to Claire's apartment. I didn't realize it at the time, but this morning when I saw the dress on the rack in the store I remembered." She met Anya's dark eyes. "Ariel could only have worn that dress if she was alive after I saw you at Hansel and Gretel's."

Anya glared at Bram. "Fool," she spat. "Why would you do such a foolish thing?"

Siggy would say it was because Bram felt guilty—because he *wanted* to get caught, Lauren mused. However, she kept that thought to herself. She looked from Anya to Bram. "It was Jade's baby who was taken in the ambulance on February 12, *not* Ariel." Lauren glanced defiantly at Anya. "Claire doesn't remember calling the clinic because you gave her drugs that interfered with her memory."

"You must think I'm cold-hearted," Bram said, "to put Claire through so much emotional trauma." Lauren heard sadness in his voice, but it was difficult to muster up any sympathy for him.

She shook her head in bewilderment. "I don't know how the two of you cooked up this scheme or how you managed to pull it off."

"Too bad you will never find out," Anya said, pointing the gun at her.

She really is going to kill me, Lauren thought. She would never see Bailey again. Why had she acted so rash? She should have waited for Rebecca to call her. "Don't do this, Anya," she pleaded.

"You know too much," Anya said. "You should have kept your nose out of this."

Before Lauren could say anything else, a deafening explosion filled her ears. She closed her eyes.

—

Claire was no sooner in the door than the phone rang. "Hello?" she said, holding the receiver while shrugging off her coat.

"Professor Ste Denis?"

"Yes, this is she."

"It's Tara Regan. I spoke with Angie Hayes. Sorry it took me so long to get back to you. You said you wanted to know where the baby carrier came from."

"Actually, it was Lauren LaVallee who wanted to know, but I can pass along the information."

"Tell her it was among the things dropped off at the fire station."

"I see," Claire said. There had been a number of places designated for dropping off items for the fair. The fire station was in the Shore Road area. Anyone could have dropped it off.

"Thanks, Tara. I'll give Lauren the message."

It wasn't until Claire hung up that that she noticed the blinking red light. She dialled her voice mail; there were two new messages. The first was from Mitch inviting her to supper. The second was from Lauren; she sounded out of breath. "I know what happened to Ariel and Cara," she said. "I'll call later when I know more."

Claire went still. What was Lauren talking about? Had she come across new information? Claire had not heard anything from the police. Lauren's message was from nearly three hours ago.

She sounds distressed, Claire thought. *Something is not right.*

—

Lauren sat up, dazed, and looked around. The acrid odour of gunpowder filled the room. The blast had startled her, knocking her backward. Ariel was crying. Olga was shouting in Russian. Bram was holding his arm, blood turning his white shirt red. It took a moment for Lauren to realize what had happened. Anya had pointed the gun at her. Bram had jumped in and tried to wrest it from her hands. The gun must have gone off in the struggle.

The gun, Lauren thought, *where is the gun?* Looking around, she spotted it on the floor, half hidden under the rocker. For a moment, she was too paralyzed to act. It was only after she saw Anya reach for it that Lauren sprang into action. Ariel's Jolly Jumper was between them. She gave the frame a kick and it went crashing into Anya, knocking her sideways. Anya swore as she scrambled for the gun.

In one movement, Lauren was on her feet. Grabbing the baby from a stunned Olga, she rushed for the side door. Once outside, she ran around the house to the front where her car was parked. She ran swiftly, knowing every second counted. Anya was behind her, muttering in Russian, her shoes swooshing in the wet grass. Lauren tried not to imagine a bullet in her back.

Please, Lauren thought, offering up a silent prayer. *Please don't let her harm me. Help me get Ariel home safe.*

After what seemed like forever, Lauren reached the car and wrenched open the door. She put the baby on the seat beside her and with trembling hands started the engine. It sputtered once and died. She tried again. The car jerked forward. From the rear-view mirror, she saw Anya aim the gun. "No!" she cried, ducking her head.

A shot rang out. The car jerked to a halt, rocking forward. Ariel nearly rolled off the seat beside her. Anya, Lauren realized, had shot out one of her back tires. Another shot quickly followed, and a second tire blew out. *I'm trapped,* she told herself. *There's no way out.*

CHAPTER

38

"I hope this trip isn't a waste of time," Rebecca told Kyle Harrison as the police cruiser veered down a winding, rutted road.

"We have to check out every lead."

"Lauren needs to understand that this investigation is best left to the police," Rebecca said. "She's become much too involved." That morning Lauren had sent an email implying that Erika Jansen may have had something to do with Cara Roberts's disappearance. Rebecca and Kyle had gone to Erika's house, only to learn that Lauren had been by earlier to question her. An hour later she had left another message, saying she was mistaken about Erika but had some new information. She'd left her number, but Rebecca had not been able to reach her.

"I understand her interest in the case," Kyle said. "Claire is Lauren's friend as well as her client."

"Still, she needs to back off." Rebecca frowned. She didn't like this at all. Shortly after they'd come back from Erika Jansen's house, they'd received a call from Claire Ste Denis. She'd told them about another strange call from Lauren. Claire also informed them that a baby carrier donated to the fair—one that Lauren thought belonged to the Roberts baby—had come from donations dropped off at the fire department. When Rebecca couldn't reach Lauren's cell, she tried her home number. The man who answered the phone said Lauren had gone to Duffy's Mountain. Rebecca had no idea who Lauren had gone to see, but there were no more than a dozen cottages in the area. Wherever Lauren was, her car wouldn't be difficult to spot.

They came to an unexpected bend in the road, and Kyle braked suddenly, causing them to lurch forward. Tree branches clawed against the windshield.

"Must be hell in the winter," Rebecca said.

Kyle shook his head. "I can't imagine living in a place this isolated."

The road stretched on for another two miles before widening into a clearing. Up ahead Rebecca could see a parked car. A person—no, two people—were standing near the vehicle.

"Looks like Lauren and Dr. Kaminsky," Kyle said as they neared them.

Rebecca stared out the window in stunned disbelief. "God in heaven!" she gasped, taking in the scene before her. "What's going on?"

"Call for backup." Kyle stopped the car, his hand automatically going for his gun. He opened the door and practically flew from the cruiser.

Reeling from shock, Rebecca continued to stare at the drama outside the window. It was like a scene from a movie. Was Dr. Kaminsky really holding a gun on Lauren? Lauren looked stricken with fear, her face white. At the unexpected arrival of the police, Anya froze, panic on her face.

"Drop the weapon!" Kyle shouted.

Anya looked down at the gun in her hand, then back at Kyle. "Drop it!" Kyle ordered, moving toward her.

Rebecca held her breath. Slowly, Anya lowered her hands and let the gun fall to the ground.

Rebecca's heart raced as she picked up the mic to her radio. By the time she got out of the car, Kyle had Dr. Kaminsky in handcuffs. Lauren was standing near her car looking pale and shaken. "Are you okay?" Rebecca asked, approaching her.

Lauren nodded, her eyes fixed on Officer Harrison, who was leading Anya to the cruiser. Only after he had put her in the back seat and closed the door did Lauren turn to Rebecca. "Bram's been shot," she said. "He's inside. You better call an ambulance."

"Bram Warren?" Rebecca stared at her. *Why would Dr. Warren be involved?* But she knew there'd be time for questions later. "Call an ambulance, Kyle," she shouted. "Dr. Warren's been shot."

Kyle started toward the house. "Keep Dr. Kaminsky covered," he told Rebecca.

Nodding, Rebecca turned her attention back to Lauren. "Anyone else inside the house?"

"An elderly Russian woman."

At that moment, a thin wail came from the partially opened car window. Rebecca wasn't sure if it was human or animal.

"The baby!" Lauren hurried to the car. "I forgot about the baby." She threw open the door, peeled off her jacket, and wrapped it around the crying infant.

"Jade's baby?" Rebecca asked.

Cradling the baby against her chest, Lauren walked toward Rebecca. "Jade's baby is dead, Rebecca. This is Ariel Warren."

Rebecca shot her a pitying look. Victims of trauma often said bizarre things. She put a comforting hand on Lauren's arm. "It's Ariel who died, Lauren, not Cara."

Lauren gently rubbed the baby's back. "No, Rebecca," she said, "Bram and Anya switched babies."

Rebecca stared at her blankly.

Lauren removed the coat from around the baby's face. "It's Ariel. See?"

Rebecca had never seen the Warren baby, but from the pictures on display at the service, she'd been struck by how much Ariel looked like Claire. This baby had the same large dark eyes. But no, it couldn't be. She shook her head. She had attended the Warren baby's funeral, for heaven's sake. Why would Anya and Bram switch babies?

"I imagine they were planning to take Ariel to Alaska," Lauren said, answering Rebecca's unasked question.

Rebecca's mind reeled. This case was becoming more and more bizarre.

For the second time that day, Lauren recounted the incident at Hansel and Gretel's. She told Rebecca about Bram bringing photographs to Claire's apartment. "When I saw the same dress on the rack this morning, it all came together."

"It's the little things criminals do that give them away," Rebecca said, talking as much to herself as to Lauren. But no, she decided.

It wasn't possible. Bram and Anya couldn't have pulled off something like that. How could they?

Lauren hugged the baby close. "I'm just happy Ariel's safe," she said. "I'm sure all the details will come to light in time."

—

Less than an hour later they were at the police station, where Lauren gave a signed statement. Ariel was on her way to the hospital to be examined. "She seems healthy and happy, but we're following procedure," Rebecca explained.

Lauren nodded, impressed by the officers' efficiency. A caseworker from child protection services had been called, and DNA tests were underway. Although there was little doubt the baby was Ariel, the department wanted absolute proof. They had taken DNA samples from Bram before he was transferred to the hospital in St. John's.

"When will you contact Claire?" Lauren could barely resist the urge to pick up the phone. She was dying to tell Claire that Ariel was alive and well.

"We need to wait for the DNA tests to come back," Rebecca told her. "It shouldn't take more than twenty-four hours. As soon as we get the results, we'll contact Claire."

"She's going to get the shock of her life."

CHAPTER

39

Claire was sitting at the kitchen table having tea with Mitch when she got the phone call.

"Hello?"

"Is this Claire Ste Denis?"

"Yes, speaking."

"It's Constable Rebecca Taylor from the RCMP. We need you to come to the station."

"Do you have information about Ariel?" Claire recalled the strange message Lauren had left on her voice mail yesterday. She had tried to get in touch with Lauren but got no answer.

"Yes," the constable replied, "but I'll explain when you get here."

"What about Bram? Should I call him, let him know?"

"Well...we've already spoken with your husband."

"Okay," Claire said. "I'll be along shortly." With trembling hands, she replaced the receiver.

Mitch came to stand beside her, a questioning look on his face.

"They want me at the police station." Claire bit her lip. "They must have new information about Ariel's death."

Mitch laid a hand on her arm. "Well, that's good news."

Claire nodded. "If it sheds light on her death, it might eliminate me as a suspect." She had waited for this moment, wished and prayed for it. But now she felt her stomach tighten. Was she ready to face whatever had happened to her baby?

Mitch squeezed her shoulder. "Would you like me to accompany you to the police station?"

"Thanks, but that won't be necessary." Claire forced a smile. "I'll call you as soon as I know anything."

At the station, Claire was ushered into a room with comfortable chairs and sofas. Cinder-block walls, painted bright purple, had posters and notices taped to them. It reminded her of her dorm during her undergraduate days at McGill.

Lauren and Rebecca rose simultaneously from an overstuffed couch when Claire came into the room.

"Hello, Claire," Rebecca said. "Have a seat."

"What's going on?" she asked, her eyes fixed on Lauren. "I got your message, and I returned your call. Daniel said you went to Duffy's Mountain. You said you knew what happened to Cara and Ariel."

Lauren and Rebecca exchanged glances.

"Did they find the Roberts baby?" Claire asked.

Rebecca shook her head. "No," she said, her voice sad. "But we have a good idea what happened to her." She glanced quickly at Lauren.

"Claire," Lauren began, "do you remember the photographs Bram brought to your apartment the day after they found Jade's body?"

"Well…yes." Why was Lauren bringing that up now? And where was Bram? Officer Taylor said they'd contacted him.

"Ariel was wearing a dress you didn't recognize," Lauren continued.

"What's that got to do with anything?" Claire said, an edge of impatience creeping into her voice.

"That dress was bought *after* Ariel died," Lauren continued. "Well…not *after*…." She looked at Rebecca. "I'm not doing a very good job articulating this."

"Just tell her," Rebecca urged.

Lauren took a deep breath. "Claire…Ariel is alive."

Claire looked at them, bewildered.

"It was Cara, Jade's baby, who died. *Not* Ariel. Anya and Bram switched the two babies."

Claire stared past them, trying to fathom what she was hearing.

"They were keeping Ariel at Duffy's Mountain," Lauren hurried on. "Rebecca and I brought her back yesterday. She's here at the station. A caseworker from child protection services is with her right now."

Claire continued to stare. What were they saying?

"We've made a positive identification through DNA," Rebecca said.

"Positive identification," Claire echoed dumbly.

"Dr. Ste Denis," Rebecca said, putting a hand on Claire's arm, "we know how bizarre this must seem, but your child is alive."

"Claire—" Lauren began.

From a partially open door down the hallway, a baby's wail pierced the air.

"Ariel!" Claire shot from the chair, looking wildly around. She knew that cry. Even in the hospital nursery with dozens of other babies, she had known Ariel's cry.

Rebecca stood up. "Follow me," she said.

On rubbery legs, Claire followed Lauren and Rebecca down the hallway. She could barely breathe.

"In here," Rebecca said, leading her into a room where a caseworker was watching the baby. Ariel was in a carrier on top of a desk.

In one swift movement, Claire had her baby in her arms. "Ariel," she kept repeating over and over, cradling her child against her breast. How many times had she fantasized about this moment? She would have given anything just to hold her baby for five minutes, to feel the softness of her tiny body. This was beyond her wildest dreams. *Was* she dreaming? Would she wake up to find that Ariel had disappeared again? Claire looked from Rebecca to Lauren. Both of them had tears in their eyes. "But...how...?"

"We're still putting together the details," Rebecca said. "There will be a hearing. Bram and Anya will be tried. You will need to prepare a statement for the media. When the time is right, I can put you in touch with our public relations department." She shook her head. "The press is going to have a time with this."

CHAPTER

40

THREE WEEKS LATER

Lauren sat on the hard wooden bench between Claire and Mitch. The courthouse was packed, and people were standing outside the door. Cameras were not permitted inside, but dozens of journalists were jotting down notes. "All rise," the bailiff said as the judge entered the courtroom, his robes flowing like black sails.

Spectators waited in anticipation as the Crown prosecutor called Andrew Collins to the stand. They hadn't expected Andrew to be well enough to be here today, but he was eager to testify. It was the first time Lauren had seen him since her visit to the hospital over a month ago. His movements were slow and jerky as he made his way to the witness stand. He was still pale, and had lost so much weight his dark blue suit hung from his gaunt frame.

"Dr. Collins," the prosecutor began after Andrew had been sworn in, "when did you suspect that Dr. Anya Kaminsky was giving her patient, Claire Ste Denis, large doses of major tranquilizers?"

"It was while Professor Ste Denis was in remand," Andrew stated. "I was filling in for Dr. Kaminsky, who was out of town." Andrew paused before continuing. "I noticed the patient was experiencing involuntary movements of the mouth and face, symptoms consistent with Phenothiazine use. I ordered blood work, and my suspicions were confirmed."

"And what did you do then?"

"I approached Dr. Kaminsky to inquire why a patient diagnosed with postpartum depression was given an anti-psychotic drug."

"What was the doctor's explanation?"

"She basically told me to mind my own business." Andrew glanced at Anya sitting in the front row with her lawyers. "I decided to speak with Dr. Bram Warren, Claire's husband. He has an office in our clinic. Before I had a chance to speak with him, I witnessed something unusual…I was working late one evening when I saw Dr. Warren and Dr. Kaminsky embrace. At first I thought nothing of it; Bram was her friend and colleague, and he'd just suffered a terrible loss. But then I saw him kiss her." Another pause. "It was not the kind of kiss one gives a friend."

Lauren was aware of a disapproving hum around her.

"Did either one of them see you?"

"I don't think so," Andrew answered. "However, I became suspicious after that. I began to wonder if Anya and Bram were giving Claire drugs that interfered with her memory in order to keep her in a stupor. I think Dr. Kaminsky suspected I knew what was going on."

"Did you tell anyone about this?"

"I arranged a meeting with Claire's lawyer, Lauren LaVallee." Andrew glanced to the back of the courtroom. "Before I had a chance to meet with her, I was shot."

After a few more questions, the Crown excused Andrew. "Thank you, Dr. Collins, you may step down."

"Your Honour," the Crown said, "at this time I would like to call Dr. Bram Warren to the stand."

All eyes followed Bram as he made his way to the witness stand. He looked almost as thin as Andrew, Lauren thought. His clothes were shabby, his face shadowed by a two-day stubble. He'd been freed on bail, but faced charges of kidnapping, obstructing justice, and accessory to murder.

"When did your affair with Dr. Kaminsky begin?" the prosecutor asked after Bram was sworn in.

"It was a couple of months before Ariel's birth. At first, it was nothing more than a fling, but I grew to love Anya. She was moving to Alaska and I wanted to be with her." Bram swallowed nervously. "I knew custody would be an issue. Claire would never let me take Ariel so far away. I couldn't imagine only seeing my daughter once or twice a year." Bram paused. "Following Ariel's birth, Claire suffered from depression. Anya prescribed drugs. Later, she prescribed more powerful tranquilizers. The intent was to make Claire unstable, make her an unfit parent in the eyes of the court. That way, I'd be granted full custody of Ariel." Bram looked down at his knuckles. "Later, we made plans to kidnap her. It would have been easy. My wife was usually drugged. Our plan was for Anya to go ahead to Alaska, and I would follow a few months later. Anya's Aunt Olga would care for Ariel until I could get her out of the country. Olga doesn't speak English, doesn't listen to radio or television. We had arranged the kidnapping for early April, but…" Bram looked nervously around the courtroom before continuing. "A dead baby became available, and we decided to make a switch."

Although everyone in the courtroom knew the story, there was a collective gasp.

The Crown nodded, urging Bram to continue.

"Jade Roberts had left her baby alone in her apartment. She said she returned to find the baby wasn't breathing. She called Anya in a panic." Bram rubbed his chin. "Jade said nothing about shaking her baby, or abusing her in any way. Anya warned her that she could go to jail for a very long time for child endangerment. She gave Jade money, urged her to move away." He shook his head grimly. "But Jade became a problem. Anya was afraid she would talk."

"Dr. Warren, take me through that day when you and Dr. Kaminsky switched babies."

"Anya called to tell me a baby had died of SIDS. She tried to convince me that switching babies would be better than kidnapping Ariel." Bram looked down at his hands. "If everyone believed Ariel was dead, there'd be no reason to search for her. No faces on milk cartons or age-enhanced photographs. There would be closure for Claire."

"And you agreed?"

"Initially, I had doubts," Bram admitted. "But we discussed it. Anya pointed out that no one at the hospital was going to question the baby's identity. The more we talked, the more convinced I became that it would work."

"What about your wife, Dr. Warren? Weren't you afraid she would demand to see her child's body?"

"The drugs Anya prescribed for Claire had the effect of a frontal lobotomy," Bram explained. "She became very docile, and couldn't remember anything from one day to the next."

Lauren felt Claire stiffen beside her.

"Bastard," Mitch muttered.

"When Anya brought the Roberts baby's body to our house, Claire was out like a light," Bram continued. "Anya dressed the dead baby in Ariel's clothes before laying her in the crib. She drove Ariel to Duffy's Mountain to stay with Olga. I went back to the hospital where I had surgery scheduled. We had decided that I would come home, find the baby, and call 911." Bram looked around the courtroom before continuing. "We didn't realize Claire would wake up before I had a chance to carry out my plan." Bram took a sip of water before continuing. "Anya called, said she had no choice but to call the emergency team. I urged her to get to the house as soon as possible. I thought she could arrive before the ambulance. I told her to give Claire Rohypnol. With the combination of other drugs she was taking, she wouldn't remember anything."

Lauren shook her head. Rohypnol, the "date rape drug," was a powerful sedative. On two occasions women had come to her believing they had been given it. They had no memory of the events leading up to it. It was little wonder Claire couldn't remember anything from that day.

"Anya arrived just minutes after the ambulance," Bram said. "During all the confusion, she was able to get Claire upstairs and sedate her."

The Crown frowned as Bram went on.

"The most difficult decision," Bram said, unprompted, "was to let Claire's parents view the body. I was afraid they'd suspect it wasn't their grandchild. But as Anya pointed out, they hadn't seen Ariel in months. Besides, Ariel and the dead baby were the same size and had the same colouring."

"What baffles me, Dr. Warren, is how Dr. Kaminsky could misdiagnose the cause of death." The prosecutor paused. "I'm certainly no expert in the field of medicine, but I know abusive head trauma is much different than sudden infant death syndrome. Wouldn't there be bleeding in the eyes, bruises on the neck—"

Lauren winced at the thought of Jade taking out her frustrations on her innocent child.

"I didn't examine the body," Bram said, "but Anya was convinced it was SIDS." His lips tightened. "Or so she said. I now wonder if Anya deliberately misdiagnosed the baby's death. She was jealous of Claire, and I think she might have wanted her to be arrested. She knew there'd be an autopsy since the child died under questionable circumstances."

The prosecutor moved closer to the witness stand. "Dr. Warren, even after your wife was arrested, you did not come forward," he said, with a strong note of reproach.

"No," Bram said. "But I made sure my wife had a good lawyer. I wanted to make sure she didn't go to jail. Claire didn't deserve that. And besides...I would always be the doctor whose wife murdered her baby."

Arrogant son of a bitch, Lauren thought.

Bram looked around the packed courtroom. "I swear I had nothing to do with the murder of Jade Roberts or the attempted murder of my colleague, Dr. Collins. When I learned Anya was involved, I was horrified. It was not something I condoned."

"Dr. Warren, this is only the preliminary hearing," the Crown reminded him. "You are not on trial here."

Your turn will come, Lauren thought, bitterly. *And when it does, I hope they throw the book at you.*

After the hearing, Lauren accompanied Claire to a downstairs room where a former student was watching Ariel. Lauren was surprised Claire had left her baby even for a short time. Since Ariel's return, she hovered over her as if she were a soap bubble that would disappear at any moment.

The sitter was crouched on the floor encouraging Ariel to walk to her. At nine months, the baby had already taken her first step. When Claire and Lauren came into the room, Ariel took two steps toward Claire before falling on her bottom. Claire gathered her up in her arms. "Thanks for watching her, Haley," she said.

"No problem, Dr. Ste Denis. She was an angel."

After Haley left, Claire sat down at a small wooden table, Lauren across from her.

"I didn't think it was possible to be this happy and this sad at the same time," Claire said. Tears filled her eyes as she looked down at Ariel. "How am I going to explain about her father? What he did to our family was monstrous."

"You must feel betrayed," Lauren sympathized.

Claire's lips tightened. "I don't know if I can ever forgive Bram."

"It's going to be difficult," said Lauren. "And you don't have to forgive him, but you do need to move on."

Claire smoothed back Ariel's dark hair. "I will do that for her sake."

"Have you given any thought to going back to work?"

"Next year…maybe. Right now, I'm enjoying every moment with Ariel." Claire tightened her hold on the baby. "I've been emotionally absent for most of her short life. Now, I have a chance to be a real mother." She shook her head. "If it wasn't for you, Lauren, Ariel might be in Alaska now."

"I doubt that," Lauren said. "Bram and Anya's relationship had soured. Bram did a terrible thing, but he's not a cold-blooded murderer. After he learned that Anya had murdered Jade, he realized he had painted himself into a corner."

Ariel began making little cooing sounds that made them both smile.

"So, what's happening with you and Daniel?" Claire asked.

"He's coming to visit Bailey in a couple of months. I'm actually glad that he's in her life, though I'm not sure if he'll ever be in mine." Lauren shrugged. "But I can live with that." Taking the conversation in another direction, she asked, "Did you see the interview Erika Jansen did with the CBC?"

"I did," Claire said. "Mitch says he expects *Candlewood Lane* to be a hit. I've never been more proud of Erika."

"She always was a shining star."

"Yes," Claire agreed. "My heart aches for her, though. I know the pain she must be feeling. After all her loss, I hope she can find some happiness in her career."

"She deserves to be happy," Lauren said. "A lot of our students are doing well. Did I tell you that Bailey and I dropped by Patrick's preschool while we were in St. John's last week? It won't be open until the end of summer, but he's there getting things ready."

"Good for him. I've always liked Patrick. He was great with Ariel."

Lauren looked at her watch. "I should probably be going," she said. "I have a client at eleven."

Nodding, Claire gathered up stuffed toys, a sippy cup, sweater, and other things that belonged to Ariel. She kissed Ariel on the head before snugly pulling on her hat and placing her in her stroller. "I was told that we should leave by the side door to avoid the press," she said. "It's this way."

The door opened into a narrow alley. "The coast is clear," Lauren said, looking around.

No sooner had the words left her mouth than a small wiry man came to stand beside her. His horn-rimmed glasses gave him a scholarly look. "I'm Stephen Coleman," he said. "I wonder if you're up to doing an interview."

Both Claire and Lauren stared at him. The Hawk? Somehow, Lauren had expected him to be much larger.

"How do you feel about your husband's testimony?" he asked.

"I'm moving on with my life," Claire said curtly. "That's all I have to say." She gripped the handles of Ariel's stroller and began to hurry out of the alley.

"Do you hate your husband for what he did?" Coleman called, going after her.

Claire quickened her pace, pushing the stroller purposefully ahead of her. She was walking so fast, Lauren could barely keep up.

"Have you spoken to Dr. Warren since he's been charged?" Coleman called.

"I have no comment," Claire said. She kept walking, not looking back once.

ALICE WALSH writes fiction and non-fiction for children and adults. She studied early childhood education, has an MA in English, and has worked as a preschool teacher and creative writing instructor. Her juvenile novel, *Pomiuk: Prince of the North* (Beach Holme), won the Ann Connor Brimer Award. Her recent picture book, *A Change of Heart* (Nimbus), was shortlisted for the 2017–18 Hackmatack Award for Non-fiction. Alice grew up in Newfoundland and currently lives in Nova Scotia.